Books by Sonja S. Key

The Huguenot Romance Trilogy
Love Under Siege (book 1)
Love in the Abbey (book 2)
Love and Betrayal (book 3)

LOVE IN THE ABBEY

The Huguenot Romance Trilogy

SONJA S. KEY

WestBow Press books may be ordered through booksellers or by contacting:

WestBow Press
A Division of Thomas Nelson & Zondervan
1663 Liberty Drive
Bloomington, IN 47403
www.westbowpress.com
1 (866) 928-1240

ISBN: 978-1-5127-8194-6 (sc)
ISBN: 978-1-5127-8195-3 (hc)
ISBN: 978-1-5127-8193-9 (e)

Library of Congress Control Number: 2017904978

Print information available on the last page.

WestBow Press rev. date: 05/08/2017

Scripture

"For if you forgive people their trespasses [their reckless and willful sins, leaving them, letting them go, and giving up resentment], your heavenly Father will also forgive you." –Matthew 6:14 (amp)

Dedication

Love in the Abbey is dedicated to my loving husband Jim,
Who has supported and encouraged me throughout the process of writing this book

Preface

It all started with a phone call. My cousin Stanley Chastain called to invite me to a Chastain Family Reunion. My grandmother was Susan Elmira Chastain Smith. I wasn't interested in the reunion, but my interest was sparked when he told me his sister Ruth had done a family tree of the Chastain family. She discovered that all members of the Chastain family in America were descended from a certain Pierre Chastain, a Huguenot, who had fled to America in 1700 to escape the persecution of the Huguenots in France.

What is a Huguenot? I didn't know, but I knew I had to write about it.

The Protestants in France were called Huguenots. The origin of the name was derived from the German *Eldgenosen* which meant (confederates bound together by oath). They followed the teaching of John Calvin.

Religion had ruled the society of Europe for over a millennium. Most all European monarchies were tied to the Catholic Church and the Papacy.

Things changed with the invention of the printing press in 1455, and the publication of the Gutenberg Bible was made available to the people. It provided unrestricted circulation of information to the masses, and threatened the power of political and religious authorities, and shattered the monopoly on education and learning.

The Bible gained precedence over the doctrines of the Papacy and the Catholic Church traditions. They learned that salvation was by grace alone, not by works, but by faith.

A cry for change echoed throughout the European countries, and that change came in the form of the Huguenot Reformation, often known as the Protestant Reformation.

Chapter One

London, England - March 9, 1566

"Is he dead?"

James Stuart, 1st Earl of Moray of Scotland, stood up when Lethington entered the room.

"Yes, David Rizzio is dead," Lethington said.

"And Mary, Queen of Scots?"

"She is alive, but her husband, Lord Darnley, has placed her under house arrest."

"And the baby?"

"The baby lives. Kerr, the ruthless pirate, held a pistol to Mary's pregnant belly, but was too squeamish to pull the trigger."

"Ah, the Queen's beauty and charming manner no doubt swayed the young Kerr from killing her. She has always had that effect on men. My half-sister's beauty is legendary and she has brought several lovers to their death. We must not underestimate her feminine wiles."

The room suddenly turned dark. Thunder crashed outside and the rain splashed through the open window and onto the floor.

Moray quickly relit the torches from the fireplace and then rushed to close the window. He slowly adjusted the curtains and fetched a towel to dry the floor, keeping his back toward Lethington to hide his rage because Mary and the child still lived.

His face flushed and he clenched his fists. Why had life handed him such a cruel position? Born an illegitimate son of King James V and his mistress Margaret Erskine, his illegitimacy disqualified him as a successor to the Scottish throne. Mary, Queen of Scots was the rightful successor and the present queen of Scotland. Her only weakness was she was a female. Moray grunted. There were many ways of usurping authority from a woman. Moray planned to use them all.

Lethington cleared his voice, gaining Moray's attention. "You are right about Mary's influence over men. Lord Morton scolded Darnley scaring him into obedience to the Protestant lord's plans to kill Rizzio. He was terrified by seeing the actual murder of Rizzio and ran to Mary begging for mercy. She has pretended to be supportive of him, and he is falling for it. He cannot be trusted to remain loyal to our cause."

Lethington waited for Moray's answer. Was Moray hurt by the fact that Lethington had become Mary's chief advisor, literally taking Moray's positon? He had Rizzio killed because he wielded too much influence over Mary. Even though Lethington was part of Mary's Privy Council, he had joined the Protestant lord's agenda to promote Protestantism as the main religion of Scotland, and run the Catholics out of the land. He wanted nothing more than to see Scotland and England united under Queen Elizabeth the First as their sovereign.

"It's true, Lord Darnley cannot be trusted. But I compliment you on how you have handled the situation."

"Thank you, my lord. I dropped a word to Lord Darnley that Queen Mary was having an affair with Secretary Rizzio, and Lord Darnley lost all perspective. And with the other lord's help, they made fun of him, calling him a cuckold, making jokes, and humiliating him until he agreed to participate in murdering Rizzio. We promised him the crown matrimonial if he would obey our instructions."

Moray grimaced. "The only consequence of that tactic is that Lord Darnley might think that the child Mary is carrying is Rizzio's instead of his. And if he denies being the father of her child, then the child would be considered illegitimate and unfit for the throne. Mary cannot antagonize him until he publicly declares the child as his."

"We can't touch Darnley until after the baby's christening?" Lethington asked.

"Correct," Moray said.

"Darnley is holding Mary captive and has taken over the government. He has sided with the Catholic faction, promising them if they will support him as king, he will establish Catholicism as the main religion of Scotland. Since we have outlawed Catholicism and the mass, Protestantism has flourished, and we must not let Queen

Mary or Darnley establish Catholicism again or change our way of life," Lethington said.

"Do not worry. Murdering that Italian dog Rizzio was only the first step to putting the government into the hands of the Protestant lords," Moray said.

"And making you regent over Scotland," Lethington added.

"Yes. And making me regent over Scotland." Moray smiled. "If she turns to Darnley, we will dispose of him as we did Rizzio. After the baby's christening, we will take action against Darnley. Mary won't be able to tolerate Darnley and his deviate behavior for too long, especially now that she knows he consented to the attack on Secretary Rizzio. I'm sure she realized that she was meant to be killed too, along with her child."

"The bill of attainder issued by Rizzio against us is due to be presented in parliament in two days. You must return to Scotland. You have been in exile for too long. Mary has promised to pardon all the exiled Protestant lords who took part in the attack. And she will restore their property holdings as well," Lethington said.

"Darnley also promised a pardon," Moray said.

"The queen is scared that Darnley may make another attempt on her life. She needs your protection. She sent me to bring you home."

"Tell the queen, I will be at my home in Fife if she needs me," Moray said.

After Lethington departed, Moray sat at his desk and wrote a letter to Cecil, Moray's co-conspirator to Rizzio's demise and Queen Elizabeth's senior advisor. Cecil must know that their joint plan to get rid of Rizzio was successful. He placed a wax seal on the letter and placed it into his doublet. Cecil and Queen Elizabeth will be pleased.

Moray considered the call to Scotland. If Rizzio hadn't issued a bill of attainder against him, Rizzio might still be alive. No one defied the Earl of Moray if they valued their life.

Even though his methods were cold, calculating, and treacherous, he saw himself as the champion of the Scottish people and a man of principle who guarded Scotland's best interest.

Moray laughed to himself. His time of power was near. He vowed never to be exiled from Scotland again. He would never again bow to the rule of a female. Scotland was his kingdom, not Mary's.

Chapter Two

Eilean Donan Castle, the Western Highlands
of Scotland - March 9, 1566

Lady Violette MacKenzie and her four-year-old son, Camden, sat on the northeast lawn of the castle. Camden amused himself throwing sticks for the family dog, Scotty. Running and giggling, they could play for hours on end.

The rain had passed, and now a pair of majestic rainbows appeared, arcing down from the Cuillin Mountain peaks through fluffy white clouds, and into the waters of Lochalsh that surrounded the castle. The crystal blue waters reflected the double rainbow colors of red, orange, yellow, green, blue, indigo, and violet, which created a great shimmering, pearl-like sparkle across the waters.

Violette sighed. The Western Highlands' radiant beauty never failed to stir her heart. Soaking in the magnificent view caused her to reflect on God's glory and the blessings He had bestowed upon her. As if in reply, chimes rang out from the Dornie Village church on the mainland.

Her husband, Ty MacKenzie, was Laird of the Clan MacKenzie, who for generations had lived at Eilean Donan Castle along with their allies, the MacRaes. The magnificent stone castle consisted of two large living structures, a spacious courtyard, a heptagonal bastian, and a stone footbridge that connected with a causeway over the marsh to the town of Dornie. Sometimes at dusk, the setting sun transformed the brown castle into a vision of golden delight that danced in the evening silky waters.

Suddenly, a scream pierced her reverie. Camden fell, trying to catch Scotty. And now Camden was rolling down the slope toward the water.

Violette ran as fast as she could, her mouth open with terror and her heart beating loud as thunder. She lost sight of Camden as he passed through a copse of trees near the water's edge. Her heart cried, "Run faster. Run faster." Her legs ached from exertion. They grew weak. She had to stop to catch her breath. She bent over with hands on her knees, gulping for air and sweat dripping from her face. That's when she spotted Camden.

He was lying on the grass near the water's edge. Scotty stood between him and the water holding Camden in place.

When she got to Camden, she knelt to find him smiling as Scotty licked his face. His luminous brandy eyes glowed as he fought off Scotty's kisses. Violette didn't know which one to hug first, Scotty or Camden. She picked Camden up and set him in her lap. Then she hugged Scotty and gave him a good tummy rub.

"You're the best dog ever." Violette stood and headed back to the castle with Scotty running ahead looking for a treat.

Estelle, Camden's nanny, met her at the door with a distraught look on her face. She took Camden from Violette's arms and hugged him. For a short time, she whispered in his ear to reassure him everything would be all right. Then she put him down for a nap in the anteroom off the great Banqueting Room.

Violette smiled. Estelle loved Camden almost as much as she did. She wondered why Estelle had never married. She was a lovely young woman with wavy cinnamon hair twisted up into a chignon. Her figure was slender and curvy. In times of stress, she was unscrupulous and often snooty. Often she challenged Violette's instructions when it came to taking care of Camden. Estelle's only saving grace was her love for Camden. Yet Violette was going to speak to Ty about replacing her when he got home from Edinburgh tomorrow.

When Estelle returned, she handed Violette the mail.

Violette laid the letters on a nearby table and invited Estelle to sit and talk to her for a while. Violette asked her, "Ty says you have been seeing a young man from Huntly. Is that true?"

Estelle straightened. "Yes, milady. His name is Fergus Gordon. He manages the Earl of Huntley's estate in Aberdeen. Huntly is his uncle."

"Has he asked you to marry him?" Violette asked.

"No. But we have talked the matter over. I'm not sure if I want to marry yet. I love taking care of Camden. I wouldn't want to leave him."

Scotty barked.

"Excuse me, milady. I need to feed the dog. He deserves a special treat for saving Camden," Estelle said and headed toward the kitchen, her footsteps fading as she climbed the stairs.

A rich and warm silence filled the room. An uneasy feeling swept over Violette. She always had difficulty talking to Estelle. She leaned her head back against the upholstered chair. This room soothed her senses. She soon forgot about Estelle and enjoyed some hot cinnamon tea as she viewed the room.

The Banqueting Room was a place for celebrations. The long rectangular space boasted polished oak floors covered with a MacRae tartan plaid rug of blue, red, green, and gray. A chandelier of candles mounted on a three-tiered circular iron frame hung above a long cherry wood table and matching chairs. Giant wood beams, and stonewalls surrounded the space. A huge fireplace that reached from floor to ceiling warmed the room. A grandfather clock, bookcases, and the MacKenzie and MacRae Crests completed the room.

Large portraits of the MacKenzies and the MacRaes filled the walls. There was even one painting which told the story of how Duncan MacRae killed Donald Gorm MacDonald with his last arrow when MacDonald attacked Eilean Donan Castle.

Violette picked up the mail from the side table. There was a letter from her friend in Lombardy, Celine. She was Thomas Montmorency's sister.

Violette's heart fluttered. She had once been engaged to marry Thomas. Then on a trip to Vassy to order her wedding gown, he ran into a burning building and was hit on the head by a fiery beam. As a result, Thomas lost his memory. Had he regained it? Was that why Celine was writing to her? She ripped open the letter.

The letter was sweet and congenial. No, Thomas hasn't regained his memory, but the vineyard is doing well, and they were shipping out their first harvest of wine this week. She closed with, "Just a word to let you know you are still loved and missed."

Violette thought of Thomas and how he must feel that he couldn't remember most of his life. She ached for him and for herself. She had loved him deeply and oftentimes longed to see his face, hear his voice, and kiss his lips ...

Tears welled up in her eyes. She had felt so abandoned when Thomas had lost his memory. She was hurt and alone. He was such a rogue. Every time he looked at other women, her jealousy flared, but now he didn't even know her. That was the hardest thing to bear to look into his eyes and see no recognition of who she was or feel the love they had once shared.

She couldn't just sit and wait for Thomas to remember who she was. She had a life to live, and what if his memory never returned? She would be older and alone still.

So when she met Ty, she eagerly accepted his proposal of marriage. He was loving, and his eyes never wandered to other women when they were together. He wanted a home and loved children. He was everything she wanted in a husband, but her heart had its own desires.

She wondered how she would have reacted if Thomas had regained his memory. What if he was here now? How would she react?

She jumped up. She shouldn't be thinking these thoughts!

Aloud, she said, "Ty please hurry home. Hurry home."

Chapter Three

March 10, 1566

Someone was kissing her cheek. Half asleep, Violette turned towards the caress. She opened her eyes; it was Ty. She lifted her arms to pull him closer. A long, ardent kiss made her heart hum with delight.

"Wake up, my love. We need to talk." Ty plumped some pillows and placed them behind her back, propping her upright against the headboard.

Violette touched his face and smiled. "It is good to have you home. I missed you so."

"I missed you too." Ty kissed her forehead.

Laird Tyson MacKenzie was handsome with eyes the color of brandy, soft, warm, and inviting. His voice was strong and full of confidence, his grip firm and sure. In times of trouble, he was like a rock in the midst of a raging sea. He was her husband and protector. How could she have been thinking about Thomas yesterday? Ty was all she needed.

"What's wrong?" Violette asked.

"Something strange is going on at Holyrood Palace."

Violette sat up straight. "Is Queen Mary all right?"

"I don't know. When I visited the castle to tell Queen Mary about coming home, they refused to let me inside."

"But you are part of her Privy Council. How could they deny you entrance into the queen's presence?"

"Well, they did. There were guards posted at all entrances. No one was allowed to enter except for Mary's ladies." Ty stood up and began to pace.

"What are you thinking?"

Ty stopped pacing for a moment. "All the guards were Morton's men."

"Oh, Ty, Morton is ruthless and a Huguenot sympathizer. He tried to have Mary's mother, Marie de Guise, deposed when she was regent of Scotland. He is against any type of Catholic rule. Do you think he has killed Queen Mary? She is Catholic like her mother."

"I don't know, but we will find out. Get dressed. We are going to Holyrood Palace. Since you are one of Mary's ladies, they may let you see her." Ty hurried downstairs.

Violette threw back the bed covers and started to dress. She laid out her riding outfit, which consisted of a brown leather bodice, skirt, and boots. They would travel by horseback; a carriage was too slow.

As Violette thought about Mary, tears filled her eyes. Mary was not only the queen of Scots, but she was also her friend. When Catherine de Medici had imprisoned Violette, Mary was the one who rescued her from Catherine's clutches. If it had not been for Mary, Violette could be rotting in prison. If Mary was in trouble, Violette was bound to help her, even if it meant facing death or imprisonment.

Violette dressed quickly. She braided her long black tresses and wound them into a chignon. She covered them with a snood. She placed a small headdress of gold lacework on her head. She smoothed violet eye makeup on her lids to match her eyes. She looked in the mirror. Just a touch of vanity always lightened her mood.

When she entered the Banqueting Room downstairs, Ty was sitting at the table holding Camden in his lap. Violette kissed Ty and placed a kiss on Camden's forehead. She sat next to Ty and watched the loving exchange between father and son as Ty teased Camden with an apple slice. Camden giggled.

Estelle entered and stood beside Violette.

Violette gave her instructions concerning Camden. After she listed the usual things, like letting him play outside, seeing he actually ate his food, and making sure he took at least one nap a day, she looked at Ty.

"Estelle, if something sinister should happen to us while we are in Edinburgh, we want you to take Camden to Violette's mother, Jeanne, who lives in the Netherlands. She will take care of you and Camden. Her address is in my desk, along with enough money to pay your transport to the Netherlands."

"You do not have to worry about Camden, my lord. I will guard him with my life." Estelle took Camden and left the room.

The atmosphere turned dark. Was death awaiting them in Edinburgh? Violette's spirit shrank. She turned to Ty. "What do you think is happening at Holyrood Palace?"

"I don't have any facts, but I heard a rumor among the Protestant lords that Lord Darnley believed that Mary was being unfaithful to him," Ty said.

Violette gulped. "I don't believe it. He is her husband. She loves Darnley regardless of his occasional bouts of drunkenness at the taverns. She wouldn't betray him. Who are they naming as her lover?"

"They accuse her secretary, David Rizzio."

Violette laughed. "Impossible." She noted the serious look on Ty's face. "I know he is a competent secretary and she values his advice, but he is ugly with his hunched back and dark skin. And he is Italian. Yes, he is born of Italian nobility, but he is not the type of man a queen would choose as a lover. Who would believe such an accusation?"

Ty grimaced.

"You are serious." Violette thought for a moment, remembering the times she had seen Mary and Rizzio together. She remembered the long nights they spent together playing cards until dawn, the many favors Mary bestowed on him like promoting him as her chief advisor and debasing her half-brother, Moray. But Mary's ladies were present with her at all times, weren't they? Violette wasn't sure of what took place after she came home to Ty. In her mind, doubt lurked like a hungry vulture waiting to feast on the fallen dead. Violette shook her head to dispel its hold.

Ty placed his hand over hers. "You understand the implications of the accusations against her." Violette nodded. "Hopefully, when you talk to Mary, we will know what happened and how to help her."

"What about the baby she is carrying. Could it belong to Rizzio instead of Lord Darnley?" Violette's heart sank when Ty shook his head. He didn't know.

Too distraught to eat, Violette pushed her plate away. She refused to pass judgment on Mary until she had more facts.

She and Ty moved outside to the horses that had been packed. Jules, Violette's ebony Andalusion stallion, pawed the ground. He was ready to run. She didn't ride anywhere without him. His speed was faster than a hawk swooping onto its prey. She said a silent prayer thanking God for Bishop Bernard's gift, even though she had disappointed him by siding with the Huguenots.

Ty led the way across the footbridge and along the causeway to the mainland of Dornie. From there, they settled into a steady gallop that would take them out of the Highlands down to Edinburgh.

Violette thought about Mary. What reason could they have for shutting down the palace? It could a number of things, such as a troop of English soldiers besieging the castle or something as simple as a man who was in love with Mary trying to force himself on her. She remembered one instance when a young man of twenty-two had come to Mary's court. Mary loved music and dancing. His name was Pierre de Bocosel, Sieur de Chastelard from France. He glided across the dance floor like a swan. Intrigued by his expertise, Mary proclaimed him her favorite dance partner. Mary was gracious and loved to bestow gifts on the people whose company she enjoyed. She gave Pierre a sorrel gelding.

Pierre fell under Mary's charming spell and deserted his wife. He had fallen in love with Mary. One night, he was found in Mary's bedchamber hiding under the bed.

Moray rousted him out and warned him of the impropriety of his actions. Yet Pierre didn't listen. The second time he burst into Mary's bedchamber unannounced, Mary was preparing for bed and was only wearing her nightdress. The guards had to remove him from her room.

This time, Moray was not so lenient. He handed Pierre over to parliament. There was a trial. Pierre was found guilty of treason and was beheaded at the Mercat Cross. As Pierre laid his head on the chopping block, his last thoughts were of Mary. Pierre called goodbye to Mary, saying, "Adieu to the most beautiful and most cruel princess of the world."

Things like that happened to Mary again and again.

Elegant and alluring, Mary was tall, almost six feet. She was slender and graceful with auburn hair and dark eyes. Her skin was as smooth as marble. Her charming manner captured the hearts of people everywhere she went. Men fought over her attentions. Many men professed their love to her.

Of course, Moray advised her that she had bestowed too many favors on Pierre to the point that it offended the Scottish nobility. She should be more cautious. But Mary had a generous heart, and Moray's advice was like telling a mother not to spoil her child.

Violette chose to think it would be something of that nature behind the lockdown of The Abbey, as the palace was often called by Scottish natives.

Chapter Four

Town of Coccaglio in Lombardy, Italy – March 10, 1566

Thomas Montmorency was lonely. He held a glass of Franciacorta sparkling rosé in one hand, freshly poured from the half-empty bottle on the table next to his chair. The bubbles failed to lighten his mood. Instead, the wine left a bitter taste of disappointment in his mouth. The light of day had oozed away, leaving a salmon-pink sky on the horizon. He sat hypnotized by the patter of raindrops on the veranda.

His sister, Celine, and her husband, Fabrice, were spending the night in Lombardy after going to the opera house for a night of great Italian music. And his friends, Niccolo, Giovanni, and Lorenzo, had all married and built homes in Rome.

Four years had passed since his memory loss. He had no warm memories to comfort him, only a dark gloom and sense of oppression surrounding him. He often thought of the dark-haired beauty Violette, who filled his dreams as she rode through his mind on an ebony stallion. He should have never let her go free. Somehow, he felt life would be better if she were present with him. But now life seemed to have drifted over the icy gray Apennine Mountains, leaving him alone and depressed.

Violette's touch was on everything. For a time, he had enjoyed being home. He had labored to revive the fruitless vineyard and succeeded in establishing a thriving winery. But he wouldn't have had the vineyard if Violette hadn't risked her life to recover the key and deed, which Catherine de Medici had confiscated for the French crown, to help pay their debts.

Life had been good, but he had no one with whom to share his success—no wife, no children, no family, no friends.

He should have married Violette even if he had no memory of their being together. At least he would have someone with whom to share his success. Every time he looked at the vineyard, he thought of Violette.

He gulped down the wine in his glass and poured another drink. A man without memories is like a corpse—dead, cold, and empty. He rose and headed to his bedchamber. He would go to the tavern in town where other lonely men like him gathered on rainy nights. He found a tan doublet and nether hose, which Celine had laid out for him. He dressed quickly. He looked around for his pocket watch but couldn't find it. Then he felt a hard object in the doublet pocket.

He pulled the object out, thinking it was his watch, but instead it was the golden locket Violette had given him at Touraine when he last saw her.

He had felt awkward at their last meeting. Everyone was expecting him to suddenly regain his memory when he saw Violette. They expected him to fall at Violette's feet and beg for her hand in marriage, but that did not happen.

At the time, he felt the coldness of their expectations dampen the atmosphere, and he had become impatient. He decided to be honest, but honesty is like a dose of sour medicine; it may be good for you, but the taste makes it hard to swallow.

He had told Violette the truth and he saw the love light disappear from her violet eyes. He knew then it was a terrible mistake. She had sweetly given him the golden locket. He had stuffed it in his doublet pocket and forgotten it until now.

Out of curiosity, he opened the locket. He gazed upon the portrait of Jeanne de la Marne, Violette's mother.

Suddenly, a flash of light blinded him. He covered his eyes, but the light penetrated his head with pounding fury. The pain so severe, he fell to his knees, holding his head. He screamed and moaned as he swayed back and forth on the floor. The pain, like a thunder storm, raged for a time and moved on, leaving in its wake an anguished and tormented man.

Thomas gasped for breath. What had just happened? He hadn't

experienced any memory flashes in the past four years, and he never would again, for now he remembered everything.

For the next two hours, he rejoiced in recalling bits of his past. He remembered his blond wavy hair blowing in his face as he parried swords with his father and as his mother, Elena, flinched at every blow. He remembered walking along the streets of Antwerp on his way to school. The girls surrounded him, vying for his attention. He remembered fighting alongside Coligny for the Huguenot cause in France, but most of all he remembered loving Violette.

"Oh," he moaned. Remembering was more painful than he expected.

Thomas pushed down the pain and instead danced around the room. The memories were breaking upon him like ocean waves during a harsh rain storm, filling his head with things he hadn't been able to recall since his childhood. The clarity of the memories brought back the good and bad things he regretted.

One of his most painful memories was the first time he had hurt his mother. The Huguenot uprising in the Netherlands had taken his father's life. And when Thomas joined with Gaspard Coligny to fight for the Huguenot cause, his mother had cried all night, thinking when he left he would never return to her. And he hadn't for she died soon after he had left.

Other memories where he had wronged the people in his life kept flashing across his consciousness. As they came to mind, he stopped and asked God for forgiveness for each one. How would he ever gain Violette's forgiveness?

"What a fool I have been."

Chapter Five

Holyrood Palace, Edinburgh, Scotland
March 10, 1566

Violette and Ty arrived at the entrance to Holyrood Palace. Violette requested to see Mary and the guard left to confer with his leader.

As she waited for the guard to return, Violette thought about Holyrood Palace or Holyrood house. The structure was over five hundred years old, and it sat alongside the Holyrood Abbey, which gave it its name—house of the holy cross. It was the favorite residence of the kings and queens of Scotland. Queen Mary resided here in the northwest tower ever since she had returned from France.

The guard returned and escorted Violette inside the palace.

Ty yelled to her, "I'll wait here for you."

Violette nodded and followed the guard through the Great Gallery to Mary's audience chamber. There were two guards posted at the door, but they opened the door, letting her into the chamber.

Immediately upon entering the audience chamber, Violette froze. Something sinister had taken place here. The furniture had been pushed against the walls and red stains covered the floor. Fear gripped her heart, and her knees weakened. Someone had tried to wipe away the stains, but found it was impossible to remove them.

Violette turned to run, but Lady Fleming, who was standing in the bedchamber door, called to her. Lady Fleming waved Violette forward towards Mary's bedchamber.

Her stomach churning, Violette lifted her skirts and tiptoed carefully through the audience room until she reached the bedchamber door.

Lady Fleming caught her arm and pulled her into the bedchamber. Inside, the bedchamber was quite large with polished oak floors and high ceilings. Wooden squares set on a diagonal divided the ceiling into boxes filled with floral designs in various colors. The upper walls were covered in a silver tapestry that reflected silver and white when the light struck it. The lower half of the walls were of oak panels.

A large recessed window filtered light into the room as it washed over a long walnut trestle table.

On the opposite wall was a four-poster bed draped in a floral pattern of yellow and blue bed curtains. A canary yellow counterpane covered the bed. Beside the bed, a large fireplace warmed the room.

Mary was seated on the window seat, staring out the window that overlooked the Abbey. She stood and smiled at Violette. Lady Fleming left them alone.

After bowing before Mary, Violette rose and wrapped her friend in a warm hug.

Mary led her to the window seat where they could talk in private.

"Oh, Violette, I've felt so alone. It warms my heart that you have come to me," Mary said, tears glistening in her eyes.

Violette grasped Mary's hands in hers and whispered, "What has happened? Are you all right? Is the baby all right?"

"It's all too tragic. It is beyond belief what has happened," Mary said in a raspy tone while she struggled to restrain the tears. "So far, the baby and I are managing but not very well. If I don't calm myself, I fear a miscarriage. I believe Darnley hoped I would miscarry."

Violette spoke softly. "Maybe it would help to talk about it no matter how horrid it may be."

Mary nodded and took a deep breath. "Night before last, Lady Fleming, Lady Beaton, David Rizzio, and I were playing cards. We had just finished supper and started our fourth round of cards when Lord Darnley burst into the room and grabbed and held me so I couldn't move. Then Morton and his men rushed in. I demanded that Morton leave the room or be charged with treason. Instead of leaving, he said, 'I've come to defend your honor against this insolent dog, Rizzio.' Morton pulled out his dagger and walked toward Rizzio. Rizzio ran and hid behind me for protection, but one of the men reached across my shoulder and stabbed Rizzo. The blow came so close to my head, I could feel the swish of the blade. Then that pirate, Kerr, pulled a gun and held it to my pregnant belly. He would have killed me and my baby, but he couldn't do it. I'm alive only because Kerr was too squeamish to pull the trigger." Mary stopped to catch another breath and wipe the tears streaming down her cheeks.

Mesmerized, Violette sat rigidly, her heart thumping wildly.

Mary continued, "My knees grew weak, and I almost fainted, but Darnley held me up, making sure I saw everything that happened. The men began stabbing Rizzo. They pulled him out of the room onto the stairs. I could hear his screams ... echoing ... up the stairwell as they ... stabbed ... him ... to death."

"Why would your husband betray you?" Violette asked in a soothing tone.

"He was jealous over Rizzio's influence over me. I don't know why ... for Darnley spent most of his time in the taverns drinking and lying with other women, even young boys. Rizzio was kind to spend time with me. I enjoyed his company," Mary said. Then she leaned forward. "But, Violette, I was never unfaithful to Darnley. Rizzio and I enjoyed each other's company. We shared the same interests in music, singing, and dancing. He was a competent secretary, but we were never lovers. Never! The Protestant lords inflamed him against me because they wanted to control the government. They keep stating their fear that I would establish a Catholic rule, but I never had that intention. I have told them again and again that they can keep to Protestantism if I am allowed to follow my faith as well."

"Who do you think was behind the attack?" Violette asked.

Tears flooded down Mary's face. "The Protestant lords made sure I knew that Darnley had consented to the attack. It was Darnley's dagger used to execute Rizzio. He is guilty of plotting my death and the death of our child." Mary broke into sobs.

Trembling, Violette put an arm around Mary's shoulders and comforted her.

Through sobs, Mary murmured, "I am certain that my half-brother, Moray, was also involved. He wants me dead. He has yearned to be king of Scotland all his life, but his illegitimacy disqualified him from the line of succession. We no longer talk as we once did. His jealousy has grown into hatred." Mary relaxed and continued her story. "The next day after the murder, Darnley knelt before me and asked my forgiveness. He was scared ... even trembling. The Protestant lords warned him if he accused them of this murder and failed to pardon them, they would not let him rule Scotland. If he remained loyal to the Protestant lords, they would give him the crown matrimonial and make him king of Scotland ... but only if he followed their instructions."

Mary paused. "He knew he had written his death warrant. He wanted me to save him. He begged me to reconcile with him. He proposed that we escape, so together we planned our escape."

"What do you intend to do? I know you don't want to go with him," Violette said.

"You are right. I abhor him now for what he has done. But I saw a chance for escape and I agreed that we would leave together." Mary wiped her eyes and sat up.

"I need to get in touch with Bothwell. He is the only one who can deliver me from Darnley's clutches," Mary said.

"How can you escape with guards everywhere?" Violette asked.

"There is a small tunnel that my father, King James, designed as an escape route from the palace. Only I know about it. Darnley and I will use it."

"What can we do?"

"I have written a note to Bothwell with instructions to free me. I can't give it to you now because Morton's guards are searching everyone who visits me." Mary paused. Where could she hide the note?

Mary finally decided. "I'll leave it in my stool room. Just open the outside panel and take the note from the stool room. Get the note to Bothwell so he can intercept me and Darnley at Seton Castle. Darnley is guilty of treason and I no longer desire to be his wife."

"Of course, milady. As soon as I leave, I will move to the back of the palace and take the note from the stool room. I'll have Ty carry the note to Bothwell."

Mary wiped her eyes. "Thank you, Violette. You and Ty have been great supporters."

Violette squeezed Mary's hands. "Don't worry. You'll be freed tomorrow. Now get some rest. In your condition, you will need strength for the ride to Seton Castle."

Mary rose. "I will sleep well tonight."

Violette left, making her way out of the audience chamber and through the palace entrance out to where Ty was waiting for her.

Together they rode through the palace gate and out of sight of the palace guards.

They found a shady spot to rest the horses and give Mary enough time to place the note in the stool room. As they waited, Violette told Ty all that Mary had revealed to her.

Ty jammed his fist into his hand. "I'll see that Darnley pays for how he has treated Mary. All he has done since their marriage is beg for power to rule Scotland."

"But Mary was wise enough not to grant him the crown matrimonial. After this, she will never allow him to rule by her side," Violette said.

Violette and Ty rode to the back of the palace. Violette watched as Ty opened the panel to the stool room and retrieved the letter. The letter was sealed with the queen's royal seal. Ty placed it in his doublet.

Violette rode with Ty to their apartment on the royal mile. After they kissed goodbye, Violette watched Ty ride away on his dangerous mission—to take the queen's instructions to Bothwell.

Violette would ride with Queen Mary tomorrow during the escape from the palace.

Poor Darnley thought that he and Mary had reconciled and were escaping together. Mary was escaping not only from the palace but also from Darnley.

After Violette left, Mary looked out the window onto the courtyard below. People still crowded the courtyard. They had lit bonfires around the courtyard in protest of her imprisonment.

She thanked God that she still had a good number of supportive citizens, but they were not enough to snatch her away from Lord Darnley, who controlled the government. She missed her ladies. Instead, she had to sit locked up in her rooms alone—or so she thought.

Just then, Lord Darnley burst into her bedchamber.

Mary turned to face him. "What are you doing here? I told you we would escape in the morning. Please don't debase me any further."

Lord Darnley came toward her, and then he dropped to his knees. "Please, my love, let me stay the night."

"I can't. I am tired and need to sleep. The baby is restless within me. It will calm down if I lie down. I must be ready for our ride tomorrow." Mary hesitated. "Why are you afraid? Aren't the lords protecting you?"

"I am afraid the Protestant lords may pounce upon me in the night and kill me," Lord Darnley said.

"Then let me escape alone. They will never know I'm gone unless you tell them."

"They would still kill me. I betrayed them by breaking the bond I signed agreeing to let Morton kill you and our child. They want to kill me now for fear you might have them punished. Please let me stay."

"I agree to let you stay on one condition. You must sleep on a cot in the audience room, not in my bedchamber," Mary said.

"But I thought you forgave me." Lord Darnley rose to his feet.

"I have forgiven you for foolishly siding with the Protestant lords against me and our child, but I am not ready to resume our relationship as husband and wife. I need more time, for your treachery is still upsetting."

"Very well, I will sleep on the cot in the audience room, but it is just for tonight," Lord Darnley said. He turned and left the room.

After he was gone, Mary pulled a chest in front of the door.

Pain ripped through her back, and she made her way to the bed to rest.

Chapter Six

Holyrood Palace – March 11, 1566

Violette rode out into the waning light of a full moon. A faint breeze skimmed her neck, and the wind teased the trees with a rustling murmur. The hoot of a night owl imposed a portentous foreboding into the twilight. Was it an omen? Was this venture destined to end in tragedy?

Violette shivered and prayed. "Lord, let this day end quickly."

She gave Jules a gentle kick in the side, pushing him forward onto the street, where splotches of shadows cast by the trees lay across her path. Bravely, she rode forward, increasing the speed from a trot to a canter.

Two horses were tied to the back of her saddle, one for Lord Darnley and one for Queen Mary that was fitted with a sidesaddle. Mary's pregnancy didn't allow her to ride astride the horse as she usually did. The sidesaddle would make the five-hour trip easier for her and her unborn child, the heir to the Scottish throne.

Danger abounded for those who risked riding at nighttime, but the full moon helped. The land held many holes, bogs, and steep dips along the treacherous road to Dunbar Castle, which was their destination. Dunbar Castle was an impenetrable fortress that guarded the east coast of Scotland from the English and other foreign invaders.

If Mary succeeded in reaching Dunbar Castle, she could defend any attack from the Protestant lords, and she would have ample time to plan her victory march back to Edinburgh to roust the Protestant lords from power and retake her throne.

Violette was near Holyrood now. She approached the palace from the back under cover of clumps of trees and positioned the horses in the shadow of the Abbey's walls.

A horse neighed behind her; someone was approaching the palace.

At first, Violette could see no one, then a faint shadow appeared and then the rider. It was a woman. As the rider came closer, she saw the rider's face; it was Lady Fleming.

Violette sighed with relief. Lady Fleming pulled up beside Violette and eased to the ground. She took an iron bar from the saddle bag. She went to a niche in the palace wall and pried open a hidden door. She walked inside. A few minutes later, she reappeared, and following her were Queen Mary and Lord Darnley.

Violette dismounted and released the two horses that had been tied to her saddle.

Lord Darnley snatched the bridle from Violette and mounted one of the horses. He kicked the horse in the side and raced ahead across the flat site until he disappeared into the trees.

Lady Fleming shook her head in disgust and came to help Violette boost Queen Mary into the saddle.

"The insolent, uncaring coward!" Mary spat out the words.

Violette and Lady Fleming remounted, and together with Queen Mary, they trotted across the palace grounds and into the trees onto the road to Dunbar Castle.

Violette didn't know what to expect. She knew only that Ty and Bothwell would meet them somewhere along the road. She settled into the saddle for a strenuous ride.

Queen Mary rode out in front setting the pace, just as she had done on the night she rescued Violette from the Guise Manor Tower in France. Tonight the pace was gentler than the one in France.

Queen Mary knew the road well. She knew the location of all the twists and turns and peat bogs. She rode with confidence.

They were an hour into the ride, when a large shadow bolted out of the trees with a bull whip in one hand. It was Lord Darnley! He fell in behind Queen Mary. He increased his speed until he was close enough to strike her horse with the whip. He cracked Mary's horse with the whip. It sounded like lightning striking the ground but without the flashes.

Queen Mary's horse whinnied and took off running. If she or the horse fell, Queen Mary could be killed or suffer a miscarriage. Violette groaned; she had to stop Lord Darnley. She pulled Jules from behind Lord Darnley and pushed him into a heated run.

Jules came alive as if he knew what must be done. He snorted, and the breaths from his nostrils shown like silver smoke in the twilight. He passed Lord Darnley and moved in front of him, coming between Lord Darnley and Queen Mary so Lord Darnley could no longer whip Queen Mary's horse.

Queen Mary, like the skilled horsewoman she was, pulled her horse to a halt. In five minutes her horse was under full control. Just then a huge stampede of dark riders appeared ahead of them. It was Bothwell and Ty with over two thousand highlanders moving like ghosts through the night. They came straight toward Queen Mary.

Lord Darnley, fearing the revenge of the Protestant lords for disobeying their instructions, jerked his horse around and headed in the opposite direction.

Bothwell rode up beside Queen Mary. "Your Majesty, are you all right?" Bothwell placed his hand over hers. His tender touch brought tears to her eyes.

Queen Mary placed her hand over his and smiled while tears streaked her face. The tears turned into sobs. Bothwell dismounted and lifted the queen from her horse and carried her off into the shadows. Her sobs resounded across the night air.

Meanwhile, Ty came rushing from amid the troops and caught Violette in a warm embrace. Ty led her to a large rock where they could rest. "Are you all right?"

"Yes, I am fine, but a little shaken up," Violette said.

Lady Fleming joined them.

"What a wild ride," Lady Fleming said, holding one hand to her forehead.

"What wild ride?" Ty asked.

"Darling, Lord Darnley attacked Queen Mary's horse with a bullwhip and sent the horse plunging through the dark. I think he wanted her to fall, forcing her to have a miscarriage, or even kill her. He is vicious," Violette said.

"Where did he go?" Ty asked.

"He rode off towards Seton Castle." Violette pointed toward a junction in the road that led to Seton Castle.

Ty left Violette and Lady Fleming and sent a couple of men after Darnley.

Violette turned to Lady Fleming. "Don't you think that Bothwell was presumptuous in his handling of the queen?"

Lady Fleming sighed. "He is a bold and authoritative man. That is one of the things Queen Mary likes about him. He is bold, strong, and trustworthy. He is the type of man every woman desires."

"How did they meet?" Violette asked.

"Bothwell served under Mary's mother, Marie de Guise, who appointed him Lord High Admiral of Scotland. That position required several trips to France, and that is where he met Mary. Mary was married to Francis II. After Francis died, Bothwell organized Mary's return to Scotland. That was when he caught Mary's attention," Lady Fleming said.

"But he is a married man. How can he be so impudent?" Violette's eyes widened in disbelief.

"That is the kind of man he is. He doesn't ask for permission. He takes whatever he desires," Lady Fleming said quietly.

"I knew a man like that once," Violette said as a picture of Thomas flashed through her mind as she remembered his passionate kisses. She shook her head as if to clear her mind. That man no longer existed.

Ty returned, "We are ready to ride. Dunbar Castle is just an hour's ride from here."

As Ty walked her to Jules, she saw Bothwell and Mary exiting the woods. Mary had a warm smile on her face. Bothwell was holding her hand. He hoisted her into the saddle and never left her side until they safely reached the castle.

Chapter Seven

Dunbar Castle – March 12, 1566

It was midnight when the escapees reached Dunbar Castle. The full moon cast a warm yellow glow on the red brick castle walls, making it appear tangerine in hue. Dark clouds were gathering over the harbor, and the wind pelted the rocks with foamy waves. The rain was close.

Mary sighed, weary from the journey. The weight of the child within her pulled her over into a hunched position. She thanked God that she was an expert horsewoman, or she might have been laying on the ground suffering from a miscarriage.

Darnley's attack with the whip caught her off guard, but Violette had stopped his assault long enough for Mary to gain control of the horse.

She broke out in tears when Bothwell arrived. She didn't have to be strong anymore, for she knew he would take care of her. His presence strengthened her. Ahead, she saw the octagonal walls of the castle. Just a few more minutes and she would be safe. Dunbar Castle was a safe haven, and that was what Mary needed most at this moment.

Finally, they reached the castle gate, and Bothwell was at her side extending his arms to help her off the horse. She let go and slid into his arms. Her knees gave way, but he caught her as if she were a baby.

For a moment, she let him wrap her in his arms until she regained the will to push him away.

Violette and Lady Fleming rushed ahead to prepare Mary's bedchamber in the northwest quarter.

Mary looked behind her, and Bothwell took her arm. "Don't worry about Darnley. I'm sure my men have caught him by now. I instructed them to take him to his father's house until you decide what to do with him."

"Thank you—"

Bothwell put a finger on her lips. "Put Darnley out of your mind," he said as they moved inside the castle entrance and along the corridor to the northwest apartment. When they reached the stairs, Bothwell whisked her off her feet and carried her up the stairs to her bedchamber.

Lady Fleming and Violette were waiting beside the bed. After Bothwell set her on the bed, the ladies took over. Lady Fleming began undressing Mary, as Violette heated water over the fire. They bathed her and dressed her in a warm night gown, and by the time Violette pulled the bed covers over her, Mary was already asleep.

As Mary slept, she dreamed that she and Bothwell were married, and as king and queen of Scotland, they attacked England to take the throne. She exiled Elizabeth and dissolved the Protestant government and brought back Catholic rule. The Pope pronounced her queen of England and placed the golden crown upon her head.

A crash of thunder and a flash of lightening bolted Mary awake, and she screamed. Suddenly, Bothwell was by her side, and she relaxed and lay back on the pillows. She slept holding Bothwell's hand.

In the morning when she opened her eyes, Bothwell was gone. Mary walked to the window and looked out over the harbor. The rain had stopped, and the calm sea glistened in the dawn. Mary watched as a dozen boats left the safety of the harbor. The fishermen were headed out to sea.

Her life was shattered, and it felt as if she had been shipwrecked. Her marriage was in shambles like a ship dashed upon the rocks. What must she do about Darnley? She couldn't tolerate his presence any longer. She shivered at the thought of letting him into her bed. Then she thought of her child, and she gently rubbed her stomach. She couldn't let her child be labeled illegitimate and lose the right to the Scottish throne. She had to find a way to pacify Darnley until he publicly acknowledged the child as his.

Only God could provide her the strength to succeed in appeasing Darnley until the child's christening. She knelt and began to pray.

Within the hour, Lady Fleming entered the bedchamber to help Mary dress. The clothing had been washed and dried and smelled fresh and clean. Then Lady Fleming brushed Mary's long auburn hair and pinned it into a chignon with ringlets around her face.

"You look beautiful, milady," Lady Fleming said.

"Thank you, Fleming. I feel rested and ready to face the day," Mary said.

"Breakfast is ready, milady. Shall I bring it up to you?" Lady Fleming asked.

"No, I will come down and eat with the others," Mary said.

As Mary and Lady Fleming entered the downstairs corridor, Mary noticed some of the castle walls were crumbling and the floor was wet where the rain had fell.

Mary turned to Lady Fleming and said, "Remind me to issue an order for repairs to the castle when we get back to Edinburgh." They walked into the dining room where the men were being fed.

Bothwell stood to his feet, and the others followed his lead. Mary headed in his direction. She sat at the head of the table with Bothwell to her right and Ty and Violette on her left. The men stood until she sat down. During breakfast, no one mentioned the escape; instead, they laughed and told silly tales.

After breakfast ended, the men left, and only Bothwell, Ty, and Violette remained.

Mary looked at Bothwell. "What do we do now?"

"I've sent men to the Highlands to pick up more of your supporters. We wait here until they come, and then we will ride back to Edinburgh and take Edinburgh Castle from Morton and his rebel Protestant lords."

Mary looked at Ty and Violette. She thanked them for their help. "Bothwell seems to have everything in hand, so you two can return home. We will let the highlanders do the fighting. I'll commission six men to escort you home."

Ty and Violette left and headed home to Eilean Donan.

Bothwell extended his hand. "Let's stroll around the castle grounds. It will relax you."

Mary took his hand, and they walked along the entrance road down to the harbor and sat by the seaside watching the ships come and go.

"Sometimes I wish I was just an ordinary person without thoughts of politics or the good of the people. I wish I could jump on one of those ships and sail around the world and visit all the mysterious places it holds."

"Would I be with you?" Bothwell teased.

"Certainly! You have come to mean so much to me. I can hardly live one day without seeing you. I get depressed when you are not around. My heart aches every time you are called away to dispel a border dispute or force out intruding English forces."

"That is my job—protecting you and Scotland."

"I must give you a new job title to keep you close to home."

"What kind of title?"

"Making love to the queen."

Bothwell caught her by the shoulders, but Mary pulled away.

"How is Jean?" Mary asked.

"How can I talk about my wife when we are here together?" Bothwell groaned.

Mary blushed. "Do you still care for her?"

"She is my wife and I care for her. But you are the love of my life, and my desire is for you." Bothwell forced her back to the ground and showered her with kisses.

That night Bothwell slept on the floor in Mary's room. He wanted to make love to Mary, but it was too soon. So far, he had been able to disguise his feelings for her, but when she expressed her feelings for him, he should have told her that he desired her love as much as she did his, but he couldn't. Not yet anyway.

He had always had feelings for Mary from the first time he had met her in France. He hadn't made any advances to her at the time, for he was a wanted man. He had just deserted his first wife, Anna Throndsen, and he was considered an outlaw in Denmark-Norway where they had lived.

Sometimes, he couldn't control his feelings or his actions. He wasn't a fearful man and usually just took whatever he desired, but with Mary, he must be careful. She was too young to really know her own heart. Besides, she was a married woman and the queen of Scots.

Chapter Eight

Eilean Donan – March 13, 1566

Violette could hardly wait to get home. When she and Ty arrived, Estelle was playing with Camden on the lawn outside the castle. They were having a great time tossing a ball back and forth. When Camden missed the catch, Scotty chased after the ball and retrieved it and laid it at Camden's feet.

When she and Ty appeared on the lawn, Scotty barked and headed in their direction. Camden dropped the ball and ran straight into Violette's arms. She bent down and caught Camden in her arms and squeezed him tightly.

Ty took Camden from her arms and wrestled him onto the ground.

Violette looked up when Estelle joined them. She had a sour look on her face. "Back so soon?" Estelle smirked and, in a huff, walked off toward the castle door.

Ty asked, "What was that all about?"

As they walked toward the stables, Violette told him about Estelle's behavior. "I was planning to tell you about Estelle's behavior, but I forgot when you came home and we rushed off to Holyrood Palace to find out about Mary."

"Estelle seemed overly rude to you," Ty said.

"Yes. At first, I thought she felt badly, but it has gotten worse. She challenges me every time I ask her to change Camden's routine or add new foods to his diet. She thinks she knows what is best for him."

"She seems overly possessive of him," Ty said.

"That is what worries me. Her love for Camden has intensified to the point of worship. I want to replace her."

"Do what you think is best." Ty kissed her cheek.

Violette linked her arm in his, and together they entered the stables. She felt relieved that Ty hadn't challenged her. She would look for a replacement for Estelle, and she knew whom to ask.

Violette watched Ty set Camden on a hay bale so he could watch as Ty groomed the horses. "I am going into Dornie and talk to Fenella at the tavern. She will know if someone is looking for a position as a nanny. Do you mind?" Violette asked Ty.

"No, I'll watch Camden until you return. He loves playing with the horses." Violette mounted her horse, and soon she was tying Jules to the hitching post in front of Fenella's Tavern.

Fenella's Tavern served traditional Scottish food. Violette could hardly wait to see what Fenella had cooked for today's meal.

When Violette entered the tavern, Fenella called out, "Look everyone, our French femme fatale Lady Violette MacKenzie." Everyone yelled hello, and Violette waved back. She took a seat near a window. It wasn't long before Fenella came over to talk.

"Good morning, Lady Violette. It is good to see you. You haven't been around lately," Fenella said.

Before Violette could respond, Fenella slapped one hand on the table. "You are just in time to taste a Scottish treat called 'Haggis pudding.' It is made from fresh sheep parts ground into mincemeat and boiled to perfection inside the sheep's stomach sac. It comes with mashed potatoes and bread. I'll get you an order." Fenella ran back to the kitchen before Violette could refuse.

Violette had not experienced too many traditional Scottish dishes. She mostly cooked French meals at home, but if she didn't like haggis, she would take it home to Ty. He loved everything Scottish.

Fenella brought the haggis, mashed potatoes, and hot tea, remembering that hot tea was Violette's favorite drink. She sat opposite Violette as she tasted the pudding.

"Mmm, this is good, Fenella. I am surprised, but you have always been an exceptional cook," Violette said as she continued to eat while Fenella told her about today's news.

"Queen Mary is back at Edinburgh Castle this morning," Fenella said.

"Oh, I hadn't heard," Violette said.

"She brought over two thousand highlanders led by Bothwell. She rousted the Protestant lords from the castle and announced that she had taken back the reins of the government. I'm glad she is back. Those Protestant lords have done nothing but harass her since she returned from France." Fenella paused. "Were you and Ty part of her escape?"

Violette confessed that they were and told her everything that had happened over the past week.

"So they lied to Lord Darnley about the queen having an affair with Rizzio. Poor thing, she is just a lass. Those Protestant lords are power hungry. They won't stop with this one attack. They will seek every opportunity to shame her and discredit her in the eyes of the people. In fact, it has already stirred up vicious rumors," Fenella said.

"We know and we will do everything in our power to restore the queen's good name, but it is a hard thing to do." Violette finished the food. "What I wanted to ask you, Fenella, is if you knew anyone who is looking for a position as nanny? I need someone trustworthy to take care of Camden," Violette asked.

"It's about time you rid yourself of that arrogant Estelle," Fenella said.

"You don't like her either?" Violette said.

"No, and neither do the locals. She is haughty. When she brings Camden here with her, she acts like he is her child, not yours. She calls him Lord Camden Robillard de Maubeuge." Fenella waved her hand in the air.

Violette sat astonished. Estelle's fascination with Camden was worse than she expected. She was fantasizing about Camden as her child.

"She dresses him like a nobleman's child in green velvet nether hose and doublet and a green velvet hat adorned with a white feather. She orders the most expensive lamb chops and potatoes for the lad. She slowly cuts the meat into small chunks and makes a big show about how he likes his food," Fenella said, shaking her head.

Suddenly, a simple situation had turned dangerous.

"I appreciate your candor, Fenella. Do you know of someone who would make a good replacement?" Violette asked.

Fenella stood. "Yes, I do." She took a pad of paper and a pen from her apron and wrote down a name and handed it to Violette. "Doralee MacRae is an excellent nanny. The MacRaes are allies of the MacKenzies. Doralee's mother works in the kitchens for the clan

Huntly. She would be perfect for you and little Camden. Shall I send her over tomorrow?"

Violette got up to leave. "Yes, Fenella, tomorrow evening would be fine. Thanks for your help."

As Violette rode home, she wondered how Estelle knew about Camden being a fourth-generation baby and an heir to French nobility. The French name Robillard de Maubeuge sounded familiar, but Violette couldn't recall where she had heard it before. The name struck fear in her heart.

Why was she fearful?

As she rode, in her mind, she reviewed her past and everyone who had hated her or tried to hurt her. Catherine de Medici was the first person that came to mind, but why would she be looking for her now? What had happened between them was well into the past, and she couldn't know where Violette was, could she?

Then there was the old conflict between her mother, Jeanne, and her twin sister, Anne. Anne had tried to hurt Jeanne by getting Violette arrested, but she was not nobility and had no real title.

Then she remembered. When she and Anne were arrested and taken before Queen Catherine, Anne had only one thing to say in her own defense. She had kept telling Queen Catherine that she couldn't arrest her, for she was Baroness Ramona Anne Robillard de Maubeuge, and she demanded to be released.

Violette stopped Jules and rested beneath the shade of an Elm tree.

Why had Anne made such an outrageous claim? How was Anne connected to Estelle? She remembered that Thomas had visited Anne's aunt, Adela, in Meaux. She was the only person who could tell him where Anne was at the time.

Thomas was the only person who could tell her how Estelle and Anne were related. Her heart ached for losing him. Sadly, Thomas had no memory.

She kicked Jules in the side and rode home.

The sooner she got rid of Estelle, the better.

Chapter Nine

Town of Coccaglio in Lombardy, Italy – March 14, 1566

For the last four days, Thomas enjoyed reflecting on his memories. They were like hidden treasures that he cherished. Every time one arose, he lingered on it for several hours, squeezing out every nuance of meaning from it whether good or bad, laughing, sometimes crying.

The memories of Violette were the hardest to linger upon, but he forced himself to examine every look she had given him, every word she had spoken, looking for a clue on how he might see her again without shattering her life with Ty.

He needed to see her. He couldn't move forward with his life until the issues between them were settled. She may refuse to see him, but seeing her and talking with her would give closure to him. Then he could move ahead.

He could find another love with whom to share his life. He groaned at the thought. He berated himself. What good would it do to see her? It could only cause her heartache and arouse suspicions between her and Ty.

His other option was to forget about Violette and concentrate on his new life. It would be a grand life, throwing wine tasting parties and arranging tours for the tourists. He could build a new villa that reflected his new status as a successful sommelier in the area, but somehow everything seemed lackluster without Violette.

He remembered how brave she had been, breaking into Queen Catherine's secret room and retrieving the property deed to his vineyard after the queen had confiscated it for her own purposes.

Even after he had lost his memory, she made sure he had the deed, as if she knew how hard life was going to be for him without his memories.

Thomas shook his head. He had been a true rogue in the way he had treated her. Yet she still loved him. He could return to being a rogue, but that lifestyle didn't appeal to him any longer.

His sister, Celine, kept reminding him that Violette was happily married and had a child. Besides, he needed to be here for the upcoming grape harvest in august. He couldn't run off to Scotland to find a woman from his past. There were many beautiful Italian women fighting for his attentions. Marry. Raise a family. Be happy. Enjoy his new life. Let the past remain in the past.

He wanted to follow her advice, but he couldn't. He wanted Violette by his side.

The dinner bell rang, invading Thomas's thoughts. He was hungry for the first time today. His memories had kept him occupied all day. He hurried to the house, and Celine met him at the door.

"Go wash. You have a guest waiting for you in the kitchen." Celine waved him upstairs to clean up.

When Thomas had washed and changed into fresh clothes, he made his way to the kitchen.

A young woman dressed in a burgundy dress and low-cut bodice that exposed her shoulders, like the popular Spanish fashion, swished around when she heard him enter. It was Lunetta.

Thomas bowed and kissed her hand as she curtsied, her coal black eyes flashing with delight.

"You remember me. Celine said you had regained your memory. I had to see you for myself," Lunetta said.

"Yes, Lunetta, I remember you. I am happy you have come to visit. Celine has prepared a wonderful meal for us. Shall we go to the dining room?" Thomas said, taking in her dark erotic beauty.

Lunetta blushed with pleasure and let him lead her to sit beside him.

Thomas knew Celine was trying to get his mind off of Violette, and he had to admit, inviting Lunetta to dinner was working well. The quick, hard pulse in his throat reminded him of their last encounter. They had met in Tuscany at the Picardy Vineyards. She had come to stomp the grapes from the harvest. They had drunk wine and sang until dawn. She was a delightful woman, and Thomas enjoyed spending time with her.

At dinner, they laughed together, remembering those nights in Tuscany.

"Why didn't you return to Tuscany? I waited for you a long time," Lunetta asked.

Thomas explained that he was being held captive there and wanted only to get back to France. "I'm sorry if I disappointed you."

The food arrived, and their thoughts turned to eating. Celine had prepared a wonderful meal of roasted quail, salad greens, mashed potatoes, and a chocolate frangipane tart for dessert.

After dinner, Thomas grabbed a bottle of white wine and two wineglasses and took Lunetta on a walk through the vineyard where sunshine lingered and bees hummed as they found a bench. Thomas poured the wine, and for a few moments, they enjoyed the lingering sunset.

Lunetta broke the silence. "You've changed. I've been here for over two hours, and you haven't tried to kiss me once. I was hoping ..."

Thomas took her hand. "Don't hope, Lunetta. It is too soon for me to make any serious decisions about my life. Let's just enjoy the evening."

Lunetta nodded. "My father is giving a masque ball next week. I'd like for you to come. It might help you forget the past."

"I'm not sure if I can come, but I will consider it." Thomas hedged.

"I must leave now," Lunetta said and stood.

Thomas walked with her back to the house. In a few minutes, her carriage arrived.

Lunetta kissed him goodbye and he waved as the carriage disappeared into the twilight.

That night as Thomas lay in bed, he thought about Lunetta. She would be a good wife if he decided to marry her, but he had no feeling for her. They had met when he was at the Picardy Vineyard in Tuscany. Flynn Picardy had graciously taken him in until Thomas could regain his memory.

Lunetta had arrived during the harvest to help press the grapes. Her beauty had captured his attention the first time he saw her, but his dreams of Violette made him unsure of himself, and he had let Lunetta go.

He didn't even know if he could ever love again. He had been numb for so long. Now his memory had returned, and his next move would be crucial. He wanted to be sure it was the right one.

Finally, Thomas closed his eyes and slept. In his dreams, an ebony stallion reared on its hind legs, his mane tossed by the humid night winds. Violette walked up to Jules and caught him by the reins. "Come home, Thomas," She called to him, her arms outstretched before him.

The next morning, he awoke with tears on his cheeks.

Chapter Ten

Edinburgh Castle – June 3, 1566

The royal apartments at Edinburgh Castle consisted of a great hall with wood beamed ceilings, an audience chamber, a bedchamber, and a tiny cabinet or closet. All the rooms boasted grand views of the southern gardens. The rooms were furnished with Turkish carpets, oak furniture, and white damask curtains.

Mary, Queen of Scots was preparing for her lying-in period. The birthing room was a small area in the southwest corner of the Crown Square in the heart of the castle complex. To ensure absolute privacy, one had to pass through two other rooms and along a short corridor to reach it.

Because so many women died from complications of giving birth, it was a common custom for royal mothers to make out their will beforehand and read it before the Scottish lords, both Catholic and Protestant.

She had all four of her ladies—Mary Livingston, Mary Beaton, Mary Seton, and Mary Fleming—taking inventory of her possessions.

Her wardrobe held 181 items fit for a queen. At present, Mary had sixty gowns of gold cloth; dresses of red and yellow taffeta; bonnets of black silk; furs to trim her clothes; shoes of white, purple, black, and red; and gloves of deerskin.

Also, listed in Mary's wardrobe are thirty-four *vasquines,* or corsets, and a farthingale, which was a series of hoops that held the skirt out to an increased size. She also had a number of petticoats, silk doublets, black and white silk brassieres, and hose made of gold and silver silk.

The dressing process began with the undergarments listed above, a skirt, a stomacher, and then the sleeves, which were attached separately to the outfit and often were slashed to show a contrasting color underneath.

Then Mary Seton dressed her hair. Queen Mary often wore a wig and an ornamental headdress made of gold tissue adorned with pearls.

Mary yearned to wear the beautiful clothes, but she was too large with child to fit into them at the moment. She missed her favorite pastimes of falcon hunting and horseback riding. For the last three months, she had entertained herself with billiards, backgammon, and music, but her interest had waned, and all she could do was wish for relief of the heavy weight she carried.

She managed to play the lute, the viols, and listen to the choir, but the choir had no bass singer, no Rizzio with his booming bass voice to add depth to the ensemble. The singing only reminded her of Rizzio and his tragic demise.

His death was brought about because of jealousy. Mary was kindhearted and generous with her favors toward Rizzio. She chose to follow his council instead of the advice of her half-brother, Moray, who had been her chief advisor until Rizzio had gained her favor. Moray refused to serve her any longer and went into exile in England.

Lethington was angered when she placed some of his duties under Rizzio's care. She did so because Lethington had sided with the Protestant lords against her on important issues. She couldn't trust him, but she let him remain on her Privy Council.

She turned her thoughts back to the inventory. She possessed 186 pieces of furniture, more than a hundred tapestries, and thirty-six Turkish carpets. Ten cloths of state decorated her thrones, which carried the arms of Scotland and Lorraine. Twelve embroidered bedcovers worked with gold and silver thread and twenty-four table covers, of which two were fourteen feet long.

She had a litter covered in blue velvet and fringed in golden silk. There was one coach which she hardly ever used in Scotland because the terrain was too rough. Besides, she preferred to ride on horseback.

The inventory of Jewelry was 180 pieces including a cross of gold set with diamonds and rubies. Also, a fine collection of Scottish black pearls, some of the best in the world. One set was a gift from Pope Clement VII to his niece, Catherine de Medici, when she married Henry

II of France. Catherine passed them to Mary after her marriage to the dauphin, Francis, Catherine's son. The set consisted of six strings of large pearls and twenty-five larger pearls set on a shorter chain.

Also among the royal jewelry was a gold signet ring, which contained a crystal engraved with the arms of Mary, Queen of Scots. Plus, there was also a matching gold pendant with a medallion encircled by a gold band of gemstones.

As the ladies inventoried her possessions, Mary wrote her will in triplicate. One copy was for her, the second copy for her French Guise family in Joinville, and the third was for her successor if she should die during childbirth.

In the will, Mary leaves all of her possessions to her child. If she and the child should both die, she listed beside each item the name of each recipient. To Darnley, she gave a number of jeweled buttons, a diamond watch, and her betrothal ring. It was made of gold and was inscribed with the entwined letters H and M tied together with two lover's knots. On the inside was an inscription which read, 'Henry L. Darnley 1565.' Below it was an emblem of a crowned shield and a lion rampant rearing on its left hind leg with its forelegs elevated and its head in profile.

Most of her ladies received jewelry and embroidered linens. Her ladies were witnesses of the validity of the will, and each one of them signed their names to the document.

After the will was finished, the Scottish lords entered the room and listened as Lady Mary Fleming read the will. They received one copy which would be used to distribute her goods if she should die.

Afterward, the lords left, leaving only Bothwell behind to talk to Mary about Darnley.

Bothwell said, "The lords have reached an agreement concerning Lord Darnley. If you will pardon Morton, Ruthven, and Lindsay for the murder of Rizzio, we will find a way to get you a legal divorce from Darnley. They suggest a divorce on the basis of consanguinity since both you and Darnley share the same ancestry as first cousins. You won't be bothered with the details. All you must do is trust me."

Mary winced. "If you do this, it must not deter my child's succession to the throne. Nor can your actions bring dishonor to my good name. And you must wait until after Lord Darnley publicly acknowledges the child as his."

Bothwell said, "We agree with those terms."

"I don't think you can use consanguinity as a basis for our divorce because we married before we received the actual consent papers from the Pope, which arrived later. If you insist on using this tactic, the Pope could declare our marriage invalid, and my child would be labeled a bastard and disqualified to be ruler of Scotland. But if Rome agrees to dissolve our union on other grounds, I might approve," Mary said.

Bothwell took her hands in his. "We will find a way for you to be free of Darnley. Already, the people have shunned him, and no man desires to be his friend. He is ostracized from fellowship with the lords."

"But he is supporting the Catholics in establishing their hold on Scotland and saying every person would be punished if they did not adhere to the rites of Catholicism. You must stop him, Bothwell. His actions could cause a religious war. The Protestant lords would kill him before they would let him revive the old religion." Mary paused. "Though I am Catholic, I have reassured my subjects that I would not interfere in their religious practices as long as they allowed me to practice mine, but still they turn against me at the slightest provocation. Lord Darnley's announcement has incited fear into my people."

"He does it only because he wants to be king of Scotland, not just king consort with you as ruler over him. The Catholics have promised him the crown matrimonial, which would give him full power to rule Scotland. If you should die, he would be king of Scotland for life. They have promised him full power in return for his support, but we will find a way to stop him." Bothwell kissed her hand and left.

What a cruel web entangled Mary. Queen Elizabeth had promised her if she would marry a man of her choice that she would consider Mary's claim as heir apparent to the English throne. Elizabeth had asked her to consider her cousin, Lord Darnley, but refused him passage to Scotland. When Lord Darnley decided to come to Scotland without her permission, she placed his mother, Lady Lennox, under house arrest. Elizabeth had changed her mind about Lord Darnley and instead suggested that Mary consider the Englishman Lord Dudley as her husband.

Obviously, Mary couldn't marry Dudley because Elizabeth loved him and should marry him instead of declaring that she will remain a virgin for life. Mary refused to accept him because he was inferior to her in position—he was a subject in the English court, not nobility.

She had tried to please Queen Elizabeth in choosing Lord Darnley as her husband but soon realized that Elizabeth had created a trap. She had known Darnley's personality and deliberately promoted him to Mary. Now Mary was reaping the consequences of choosing Lord Darnley as her husband.

She had chosen Lord Darnley because he also had a valid claim to the English throne, second only to hers. She had hoped the marriage would improve her chances with Queen Elizabeth, that Elizabeth would approve of her marriage and acknowledge Mary's right to succeed her as Queen of England.

Still Elizabeth refused Mary's claim. In an act of rebellion to free herself from Elizabeth's clutches, Mary had married Lord Darnley.

According to her spies, Queen Elizabeth and Cecil, her senior advisor, had agreed to the murder of Rizzio. They preferred that Moray be in charge and had funded his rebellion against Mary after she married Lord Darnley.

Before Mary had left France, Queen Elizabeth had made The Treaty of Edinburgh between England and the Protestant lords, vindicating them even when they had deposed Mary's mother, Marie de Guise, who was the lawful regent of Scotland at the time. Elizabeth had betrayed her before, and now she had betrayed Mary again by siding with Moray in arranging Rizzio's murder.

Mary refused to sign that treaty because it asked Mary to give up all her rights to the English throne. Anger rose in Mary's heart. How could Elizabeth ask such a thing of her when she had already usurped Mary's God-given right to the English throne.

Now the web grew tighter. Mary was struggling to be free of this ruse of a marriage, but there was no legal option to securing a divorce. She could only wait until Lord Darnley died or was murdered. Mary feared that murder was what Bothwell had on his mind, and she was too infatuated with him to stop him.

Mary picked up her favorite embroidery piece and entered the birthing room to wait.

Chapter Eleven

Moray's Castle, Pitlethie, Leuchars, Fife, Scotland – June 4, 1566

Pitlethie Castle in Leuchars was a two-story red sandstone with white stones at its four corners, around the windows, and around the entrance. It rested in an idyllic area with soft green rolling hills situated on the northeast coast near St. Andrews Bay.

Moray and Lethington met at Pitlethie Castle to discuss the results of Rizzio's murder. Moray handed Lethington a leather tankard of ale and directed him onto the rear veranda so they could speak privately. All the servants had been dismissed for the day, so there was no danger that their discussion would be overheard.

Lethington carried Moray's pardon papers from Mary, Queen of Scots. He gave the papers to Moray, who looked them over with suspicion and then placed them in his doublet.

"So I am safe?" Moray said.

"Yes and no," Lethington answered.

"Is something wrong? What has happened?" Moray asked.

"Our plan didn't turn out exactly as we wanted. It seems that Mary was able to draw Lord Darnley over to her side long enough for them to escape Holyrood Palace," Lethington said.

"So Lord Darnley has already betrayed us?" Moray asked.

"Yes and Laird Ty MacKenzie and his wife, Violette, who both served on Mary's Privy Council, helped them evade the guards and sneak out through a secret tunnel," Lethington said.

"I had forgotten about that tunnel. My father told me about it as a child. I never thought Mary knew about it," Moray said.

"Somehow the queen got a message to Bothwell who intercepted her near Seton Castle and took her to Dunbar Castle. They gathered more supporters and then ousted the Protestant lords from Edinburgh Castle and retook the throne," Lethington said.

"Where is Mary now?" Moray asked.

"She is at Edinburgh Castle preparing for her lying-in period awaiting the birth of her child," Lethington said.

"That's what I feared. Now we will have to contend with an heir. I had hoped the shock of Rizzio's murder would have caused a miscarriage, or even death, but my sister is resilient. Lord Darnley has failed us miserably."

"What will we do if Mary agrees to give him the crown matrimonial? We can't have that brute Darnley wielding power over us and the Protestant lords. Since he returned from Dunbar, he has been threatening to bring Catholicism back to Scotland." Lethington looked to Moray for an answer.

"He has no power without Mary's approval, and the parliament is on our side. But you are right. We have to stop him before a religious war breaks out." Moray finished his tankard of ale and stood up. He walked to the edge of the veranda and looked out upon the bay.

It was a hot summer day, and the cool waters below looked inviting. The seagulls playfully dived into the waters, catching their prey, and flying aloft to the top of the nearest mountain. He had stayed in England too long.

He had missed the rugged Scottish landscape and its unforgiving sublime beauty. Unlike the depressing rainy days in England that weakened his spirit, in Scotland he thrived. He felt more alive here than any place in Europe. It was good to be home.

"One more thing I noticed that might help." Lethington waited until he had Moray's full attention. "After we heard Mary's will, Bothwell lingered behind to talk to Mary. He touches her in intimate ways as if there was more to their relationship than a queen and her border guard."

Moray remained silent for a moment. "Do you think they are in love?"

"I cannot say, but he does have a reputation with the ladies. He has been married twice, and there were rumors he was unfaithful to both of them, especially to his first wife, Anna Throndsen. She accused him of spending her dowry and then remarrying without a divorce," Lethington said and waited for Moray's reply.

When Moray said nothing, he continued, "Bothwell is a robust man and fearless in battle. Those qualities are what brought him to the queen's attention. Most men fear him and would rather avoid crossing his path if possible."

"Has Mary shown him any favors?" Moray asked.

"Yes. After he helped her escape from Lord Darnley, Mary gave him Dunbar Castle as a reward. His quarrels with the Earl of Arran and the powerful Hamiltons landed him in prison for a time, yet he escaped and now resides at Hermitage Castle."

"I don't like Bothwell. He is too arrogant and boastful. Mary prefers his advice over mine."

"Bothwell told Mary about our plan to help her get a divorce, but we have no grounds that would be acceptable to the Pope. Either she will have to live separately from him or have him killed," Lethington said.

Moray moved closer, his face flushed with excitement. "That is perfect. My sister is foolish when it comes to men. First, she tries to force a Catholic king on us and now an arrogant fool. We could use Bothwell to serve our purposes. All we need to do is create suspicion in the people's mind, plant a doubt about Mary's honor, and accuse her, along with Bothwell as the ones who murdered Lord Darnley."

Lethington looked baffled. "What do you mean?"

"We will have Lord Darnley murdered and use Bothwell as the scapegoat. Once he is accused of the murder, if she still insists on being his lover, or worse yet his wife, it will be her downfall. The people can tolerate a man's infidelity but not a woman's, especially a woman who is their queen."

"How would we accomplish such a plan?" Lethington asked.

"First, you encourage Bothwell to free the queen. Plant the idea of murder in his mind. And I will talk with John Knox. He has hated Mary from the time she came to Scotland. He will fuel the fire of her downfall, for the people trust him."

Moray continued, "Gather the Protestant lords at Craigmillar Tavern and have them sign a bond to kill Lord Darnley. Make sure Bothwell signs it. And persuade Laird MacKenzie to sign it too."

"MacKenzie may give us trouble, but I think I can convince him."

Lethington rose. "That is perfect. But what about the heir?"

"I will be regent until the child is of age to rule. It is better being a regent than having no power at all. Besides, I have Queen Elizabeth and Cecil's full support."

After receiving his orders, Lethington left Moray alone.

Moray thought about Mary's child. It was just another obstacle between him and the throne of Scotland. He hoped the child wasn't a female. He didn't know if he could bear another queen giving him orders. He agreed with John Knox that women were weak and foolish and should keep their place at home tending to the children and the needs of their husbands. They should steer clear of politics and leadership. They did not have the intelligence or keenness of mind to rule a country like Scotland with the barbaric highlanders and the egotistical Scottish male.

If the child was a male, Moray planned to take the child away from Mary and raise it as a Protestant and serve as regent until the child came of age to rule.

The only obstacle to that plan was that Mary would never give up ruling Scotland easily. He must find a way to force her into giving up her throne, but how?

Moray cursed. "Why God, was I born an illegitimate child?"

Moray refused to accept that fact. Instead, he and his mother agreed to start the rumor that his father, James V, and she were secretly married, which made Moray legitimate and suitable to succeed Mary as king of Scots. But no one accepted the idea, or even considered it even though they wanted him to rule instead of Mary.

To rule Scotland was his divine destiny. Even though he had murdered for a place in the government, he felt God supported him. God had brought to light the truth of the Holy Scriptures, which had been hidden from the people by the Catholics for years. They promoted their own doctrines instead of obeying God's laws as set forth in the Holy Bible.

Moray felt that he had been chosen by God to establish Protestantism in Scotland and he would use every means necessary to accomplish that objective.

Chapter Twelve

Eilean Donan Castle – June 15, 1566

Violette and Ty were lying in bed. Ty propped himself up on one elbow and bent over to kiss her good morning.

"Hmm. That was nice," Violette said as she pulled him to her for another kiss.

"I have to go to Edinburgh Castle today. Mary went into labor late last night. The Protestant lords have called a meeting at Craigmillar Tavern at noon," Ty said.

"And I was hoping for a cozy day alone with you," Violette said.

"I know, my love, but I will be back this evening. Have the cook prepare a special dinner just for us." Ty kissed her once more and got up to dress.

Violette dreaded facing the day. Today she was to meet with Doralee MacRae. If Violette approved of her, Doralee would be Camden's new nanny. She groaned. She dreaded having to tell Estelle she no longer needed her services, but it had to be done.

Ty, now fully dressed came and leaned over her. "You are dreading talking with Estelle, aren't you?"

"Yes. She is so defiant it scares me sometimes. She has so much anger locked up inside her that I don't know how she will react."

"Why don't you wait until later this evening and we will talk to her together," Ty said.

Ty kissed her goodbye. "See you tonight." He rushed out the door and skipped down the stairs.

"If only I had half of his energy," Violette said out loud and got up to dress.

She was meeting Doralee at Fenella's Tavern at noon. Fenella had graciously arranged a private room in back of the kitchen for their interview. Once Violette was satisfied with Doralee's credentials, she would feel better. Still, the upcoming talk with Estelle hung like a dark cloud over her day.

When she went downstairs to the breakfast table, Ty was already gone. She ate quickly and then went upstairs to find Estelle. As she walked down the corridor, she looked in on Camden. He was awake and squirming in his bed. She picked him up, hugged him, and kissed his cheek. She walked over to the window and pointed below as they watched Ty ride across the causeway.

"Daddy." Camden pointed his finger at the figure riding on horseback.

"Yes. He's your daddy." Violette kissed him again.

Just then, Estelle slung open the door, a sour look on her face. "You shouldn't pamper him. You will spoil him. He shouldn't be up for another half hour." Estelle tried to take Camden from Violette's arms, but Violette turned away.

"I'm taking Camden with me today. Dress him in his blue outfit and have him ready to go in twenty minutes."

"But, Lady—"

"Twenty minutes, Estelle," Violette said firmly and placed Camden back in his bed. "I'll be waiting downstairs."

Estelle grunted under her breath, "You are spoiling him ..."

Violette shut the door and leaned against it as she took a deep breath. It was going to be a long day. She decided to wait until Ty came home this evening and they could dismiss Estelle together. That thought lifted her spirit and she smiled.

As she ventured down the stairs, she thought of Mary. If she was in labor, today would be hard for her too. Violette said a prayer for Mary's protection and also asked God for help in dealing with Estelle. She prayed that Doralee would be an answer to prayer. If so, she would finally be rid of Estelle.

Violette sent a servant to the stable to tell the groom to saddle Jules for a ride. Violette watched out the window as the groom tied Jules to the hitching post.

Estelle appeared carrying Camden in her arms. When she saw Jules outside her face reddened. "You aren't going to put Camden on the horse, are you? That horse is too wild for Camden to ride," Estelle almost yelled.

Violette took Camden from Estelle. "He will be riding with me, and he will be fine. Why don't you go upstairs and prepare a place for his new clothes that we will have when we return."

Estelle swore and backed away in dismay.

Violette was soon out the door into the sunshine. Camden gripped her hand as if he didn't want to let her go. Suddenly, Violette felt guilty about not spending enough time with him. It seemed that Estelle was creating a separation between them. She promised herself that she would change how much time they spent together beginning today.

The groom helped Violette into the saddle and handed Camden up to her. She placed him in front of her, and he held onto the saddle pommel as they rode. Jules kept a slow but steady canter as if he knew that he carried precious cargo. Camden laughed as the wind blew his blond hair. He pointed his finger at a herd of sheep that crossed the rode in front of them. By the time they reached the tavern, he was still in a state of amazement.

Doralee met them as they rode up. She immediately opened her arms to Camden. He leaned into her arms. Violette had never seen him do that with a stranger. She warmed at the thought.

After Violette dismounted, Fenella and Doralee were playing with Camden. The sight was beautiful to Violette and she had a premonition that Doralee would be good for Camden. Doralee was young, around eighteen, with a kindly face and demeanor. She was well-mannered and very likable.

After talking with Doralee for a half hour, Violette hired her. Doralee went with them to help shop for Camden's new clothes. She agreed to start work as his nanny the very next day. She was glad to be a part of the MacKenzie family.

It was late afternoon when Violette and Camden returned to Eilean Donan Castle. Camden fell asleep on the ride home, and the groom helped Violette carry him upstairs and put him down for a nap.

As Camden napped, Violette hung up the new clothes. Outside, she heard the sound of horses' hooves on the cobblestone veranda; Ty was home. Violette rushed downstairs to greet him.

Ty had a grim look on his face as if lost in thought. Something must be wrong. Was it Mary?

Violette waited until he dismounted and kissed her cheek. He forced a smile. "What's wrong? Is Mary all right?"

"Yes, Mary's all right. But there is something important I must tell you." Ty handed the reins of his horse to the groom. Then he caught her hand. "Let's walk." They walked across the grass down to the loch and found a seat on a nearby bench.

"Tell me Ty. What happened?"

"The Protestant lords met today. At first, everything that happened was routine. They read Mary's will and made sure everyone understood their duties if Mary should die in childbirth. After that, the meeting took on a more serious tone," Ty said and shook his head.

"You are scaring me, Ty."

"I'm sorry. It is just that I can't believe what they are planning to do." Ty hung his head. "The Protestant lords are planning to murder Lord Darnley so the queen will be free of him. They produced a bond and insisted that we all pledge our allegiance to the lords by signing it."

"That is absurd. Who put forth this idea?" Violette asked.

"It was Bothwell. He said they could find no legal way of getting a divorce for Mary, so murder was the only way. He made us all swear to secrecy. I wasn't supposed to tell you, but since you are Mary's friend and advisor and my wife, I couldn't keep this secret from you."

Violette stared at him.

"No, I didn't sign the bond. But I am certain that the lords were aware of my dissent. That decision puts me in a dangerous position. I hope that they will see the foolishness of such a venture and change their minds," Ty said.

Ty handed her a copy of the Craigmillar Bond.

> It was thought expedient and most profitable for the Commonwealth of Scotland by the whole nobility and lords under scribed, that such a young fool and proud tyrant as Henry Stuart, Lord Darnley, king consort of Scotland, should not reign or bear rule over them, and that, for divers causes therefore, these all had concluded that he should be put off by one way or another, and whosoever should take the deed in hand or do it, they should defend and fortify as themselves.

Huntly, Argyll, Bothwell, Lethington, and Sir James Balfour.

Violette thought Bothwell must be wildly in love with Mary to go to such lengths to gain her freedom. Or was there something more sinister behind the heinous act? Murder? It couldn't get more sinister than that, could it?

When Ty and Violette entered the castle, he sent for Estelle. They met in the Billeting Room, and Ty carefully explained to Estelle that they no longer needed her services.

Estelle was surprisingly quiet, but she stood with hands clenched and tight lips. Violette could almost feel the hatred oozing from her.

When Ty finished, Estelle said, "You will pay for dismissing me. I have many powerful friends in the Huntly Clan. They will avenge me." She turned and ran upstairs to pack. In ten minutes, Estelle returned, and the groom helped her onto the cart and drove her away.

Violette released a sigh of relief. Ty took her hand and they went upstairs to dine in the Banqueting Room.

Chapter Thirteen

Holyrood Abbey – June 19, 1566

Holyrood Abbey was a spacious building with stone columns supporting pointed gothic arches, which lined the interior walls of the Abbey. The end wall boasted a tall pointed arch stained glass window. The window depicted St. Andrew, a fisherman, standing with a staff and net. Behind him is the X-shaped cross or 'saltire' on which St. Andrew was crucified.

On his left was St. Margaret, Queen of Scotland, carrying a Bible and the Black Rood of Scotland, a relic of the True Cross. On his right stands St. Mungo with a salmon at his feet, alluding to his role as the founder and patron saint of Glasgow.

Above the group is the monogram of Christ and the alpha and omega. Below them are three symbols of Scotland: the saltire, the thistle, and Scotland's royal coat of arms.

Holyrood Abbey was behind Holyrood Palace and was the home of the "black rood" or "black cross" of Scotland. The ancient cross was kept in a silver-gilded casket, a holy relic believed to be an actual piece of the cross upon which Jesus was crucified. The wood piece from the true cross was set in an ebony crucifix and kept safe here in the Abbey.

Violette stood behind the back pew in Holyrood Abbey, waiting as Mary heard mass. In Violette's arms was the new heir to the Scottish throne, James VI, who was born earlier that same day. She looked into dark eyes set in a fair complexion. She pushed aside his auburn hair to kiss his forehead. When he began to cry she told him the story about the "black rood."

Violette touched the baby's lips as she spoke. "Have you heard the legend of King David I and the Holy Rood? According to the legend, the foundation of Holyrood Abbey was laid as an act of thanksgiving by the king for a miraculous escape from a hunting accident on Holy Cross Day.

"A hart was deflected from goring the king by the reflection of sunlight on a crucifix, which appeared between its antlers. The king grabbed the deer's antlers, trying to save himself, and he returned home triumphant. And this abbey is named Holyrood or 'holy cross' Abbey in honor of the king's escape on Holy Cross Day. King David's mother, Saint Margaret, had a piece of the True Cross known as the Black Rood of Scotland, and when she married King Malcolm, she brought the relic with her and placed it in the Abbey."

James gurgled and smiled at her. Then Mary was by her side, but she paid no attention to the baby.

"How are you feeling?" Violette asked Mary.

"Weak and tired but better since the weight of the baby is gone," Mary said as they walked to Holyrood Palace.

Rosa, the wet nurse, met them at the audience room door and took baby James from Violette's arms.

Mary sat on the window seat and Violette took a seat beside her. "Violette, I am troubled about Lord Darnley. He has upset the people to the point that they think I want to force Catholicism on the country, but I have tried to reassure them that I would never do that if they would let me practice my religion. But the people are unwilling to accept my right to observe my private mass."

She looked at Violette. "I cannot leave the religion wherein I have been nourished and brought up against my own conscience, but I do leave them to worship God as they please."

Mary continued, "When I first came to Scotland, Lord Moray and Lord Lethington were my advisors, but James left me when I married Lord Darnley against his wishes. Lord Lethington sided with the Protestant lords, and he receives a pension from Queen Elizabeth, so he cannot be trusted. I was content to leave the governmental decisions to them. They acknowledge my title, but they do not let me use my rights as queen. The lords in power take advantage of my gentleness and kind nature toward the people. Now I have no protector or counselor except for Bothwell." Mary grabbed Violette's hand.

"You have your son," Violette said.

"Yes, I do, but I loathe looking at him because he resembles Lord Darnley. I fear Moray will be appointed as regent over my son, if he hasn't already done so. I cannot stand against the Protestant lords by myself. They are too powerful. It seems that Bothwell is the only man they fear and the only man I can trust."

Violette told her what Ty had heard at the Craigmillar Tavern about killing Lord Darnley.

"Bothwell told me that he would find a legal way to free me from Darnley. I told him that whatever way he chose must not hinder my child from succession to the throne, nor can it do harm to my good name. Now that I have a son, he will be a threat to Moray's power. I fear they will take him from me," Mary said.

"You are considering a divorce?" Violette asked, rather shocked that Mary would be so bold.

"Yes, or even an annulment. I have many reasons that would allow a divorce. Lord Darnley has treated me badly from the beginning. Even on our wedding night, after the ceremony was over, he went off to the tavern to drink with his friends. He didn't return to well after midnight, and he was too drunk to consummate the marriage."

"Can't you arrest Darnley for trying to kill you?"

"No. The lords permitted him to protect his innocence and denounce them as his accomplices if he promised to pardon them and call them back from exile after a short time. Then they would convince parliament to give him the crown matrimonial, which would give him unlimited power and pronounce him king of Scotland. If Darnley succeeds in gaining that power, then my life is in jeopardy. He wanted to kill not only Rizzio but me and our child as well."

Mary continued, "After that announcement, the people have scorned him because they knew he was as guilty as the others. No one dares to be seen with him. He is a pariah. He has been riding through Edinburgh proclaiming that Catholicism is the only religion for Scotland and that he has returned the whole realm back to the true faith. He has torn my country into pieces."

"What are you planning?"

"My only plan is to pretend that I have forgiven him and will willingly grant him the power to become king of Scotland after the christening."

"When is the christening?" Violette asked.

Pope Pius has scheduled the christening for December 17. At that time, Darnley will be asked to acknowledge Prince James as his son and the rightful heir to the throne. Once his acceptance of Prince James is made public, then I will denounce Darnley as my husband and bar him from Holyrood Palace."

"Then you must wait for the right time and the right way," Violette said.

"I must find a way to pacify Lord Darnley until after the christening. That will not be easy." Mary sighed. "I cannot bear the idea of sharing my bed with him. He makes love to so many women and men I fear getting sick from his exploits," Mary said.

"You must feign illness. You often take ill, so it would be believable."

"I could also make the excuse that it was too soon after having the baby," Mary said. "Or I could have the Pope tell him he must wait until after the christening."

"Yes, or you could just be angry a lot or start an argument," Violette said.

Mary laughed. "Is that how you treat Ty?"

"I haven't had a reason to put him off yet, but if the time comes that I must, then I will have a few ideas of how it is done," Violette said and laughed.

Mary frowned. "Queen Elizabeth promoted Lord Darnley to me as a proper husband, but she knew about his deviate ways and didn't warn me of his lifestyle. I fear she is no longer a friend but an enemy. It seems I have no one to trust."

"You can always trust me and Ty," Violette said and stood up. "I must be going."

"I would like you to be here when I render judgments for the people in August. Could you come then? I do value your advice."

"I would love to come. I will help you as much as I can," Violette said.

Mary and Violette hugged each other.

"You cheer me up every time you visit," Mary said and hugged her. "At least, you have given me enough ideas to get me through until the christening."

Chapter Fourteen

Holyrood Palace – August 1, 1566

Violette was called by Mary to attend her while she pronounced judgment from her audience chamber. Many people came asking for judgments regarding property disputes, criminal attacks, and debt reduction. Mary rendered fair and equal judgment and often consulted with Lethington for his suggestions.

Violette stood behind Mary, along with Lethington, when the fiery preacher John Knox entered the audience chamber. John Knox was broad-shouldered and of medium height. Dressed in black pants and doublet covered with a long black cape and hat, he was an imposing figure with a long white beard.

Violette knew of his reputation as being a revolutionary firebrand that incited rebellion among the people against the Catholic faith. He was audacious and factious, causing dissention wherever he preached. He was also so eloquent that he could sway men's souls as he wished. Many called him a woman hater because of his book, *First Blast of the Trumpet against the Monstrous Regiment of Women,* written in defiance of female rulers like Mary.

Violette braced herself for this unforeseen audience with Queen Mary because she knew that the queen disliked Knox. And Mary had reason to dislike him because he had preached that Queen Mary was a Jezebel out to impose the mass on Scotland and reverse the Protestant Reformation. A cold chill ran down Violette's spine. She started to pray.

Mary's first words burned with resentment. "Why are you here,

Mr. Knox? I have heard that you caused a great slaughter in England through your preaching and the use of necromancy."

Knox straightened and spoke in a soft tone. "If to teach people to follow the truth of God was to preach sedition then I plead guilty. My book seemed to highly offend Your Majesty."

"Your book teaches people to receive another religion than what their rulers would allow," Mary said. "And since God commands subjects to obey their rulers, your doctrine cannot be of God."

"Subjects are not bound to follow the religion of their rulers, although they are commanded to give their rulers their obedience. However, if the sovereigns are exceeding their bounds and if the subjects have the means, they may then disobey their sovereign as a child who is bound to obey his father may resist him if the father is 'stricken with a frenzy' in which he would slay his own children."

Violette noticed Mary's face flush red as she clenched her fists. "So you think that my subjects should obey you and not me, their queen? That I must be subject to them and not them to me?"

"I never sought to have anyone obey me since everyone should obey God. I believe that kings should be foster fathers to God's Kirk or church, and queens should be nurses to God's people."

Mary stood up with fists clenched. "I will defend the true church, the church of Rome."

"The church of Rome is not the true church," Knox said.

"My conscience tells me it is so."

"Your conscience requires knowledge, and I fear you have none."

"I have both heard and read."

"Jesus neither said nor commanded that mass be said at his Last Supper, seeing that no such thing as the mass is made mention in the whole Scripture," Knox replied.

"If my authorities, the Cardinal of Lorraine and Pope Pius, were present, they could give you a better answer."

"I will be glad to answer them anytime."

Mary sat down. "That meeting may happen sooner than you think," Mary said in a threatening tone.

"If it happened in my lifetime, it would indeed be sooner than I think," Knox said. "Your Majesty is of a proud mind, a crafty wit, and a hardened heart against God and His truth," Knox said.

Mary broke out into tears. Seeing that the discussion had gotten out of hand, Lethington left the platform and hastily ushered Knox out of the audience room.

Knox turned to yell at Mary as he was being dragged out, "I pray you will be as blessed in Scotland as Deborah was in Israel."

Violette put an arm around Mary to comfort her.

Mary wiped her eyes. "Knox's beliefs are much like the highlanders and border people who reject being governed by a monarch. They want to rule themselves with each clan chief acting as a king over their region. They are hard to bring under control."

"And Lord James Moray?" Violette asked.

"Sadly, Moray believes the same, for he champions the Protestant lords' cause to rule Scotland," Mary said. "Knox is nothing more than a vile pest," Mary said.

Violette caught Mary's attention. "I fear he is more than a pest. He slanders your good name, your intelligence, and your honor by undermining your authority as queen. You must carefully watch him, for he is a powerful preacher who can sway people's opinions. He sways them against you and in favor of the Protestant lords."

Violette wondered if Moray had sent Knox to discredit Mary and upset her.

Lethington followed Knox out to the courtyard. "Preacher Knox!" He yelled, and Knox waited on him.

"Thank you for visiting with Mary. You have definitely upset her. Moray will certainly be pleased. Mary must be made to think that she is helpless in trying to rule Scotland. She must feel she has no power over the Protestant lords. You have helped us achieve that. Will you try again?"

Knox replied, "I promised Moray I would visit her as many times as needed. It wasn't hard upsetting her. I was just preaching her a sermon that ultimately will achieve what Moray desires, nothing more. If she relinquishes her throne, it will be because God wills it. Good day, sir." Knox walked away humming a tune.

Lethington put a frown on his face and went back inside to comfort Mary.

Chapter Fifteen

Eilean Donan – October 14, 1566

Violette and Ty were sitting on a bench near the water, watching Doralee and Camden play with Scotty. The sun was high in the sky, and the warm autumn day invigorated Violette's senses. Ty held her hand and she rested her head on his shoulder.

"Camden seems much happier with Doralee than he was when Estelle tended him," Violette said to Ty.

"I can tell the difference in him too. It was a good decision to dismiss Estelle. Besides Camden, the whole household seems livelier and more content," Ty said.

"I noticed that as well. I wish I had just made the decision sooner."

"Don't punish yourself. You are a protective and loving mother, and I trust you in matters concerning our son and our household."

A wave of contentment swept over Violette. She had a good home here at Eilean Donan. She had a great life with Ty. He was passionate and loving and treated her with tenderness and respect. She had a sweet child, and she wanted him to feel her presence in everything he did. Violette had no mother as a child, and she wanted Camden to experience the richness of a mother's love. What more could a woman want?

"How are things going at Holyrood Palace?" she asked Ty.

Ty groaned. "There is a strange feeling in the air, like the quiet before the storm. The people seem on edge as if they were disgruntled about their lives. The atmosphere is saturated with disaster."

"I understand. All the talk about murdering Lord Darnley hovers in the air like a bad omen. Have the lords approached you about signing the Craigmillar bond again?"

"Lethington has asked me twice, but I refused. I reminded him that the idea was ludicrous, immoral, and illegal, but he walked off shaking his head," Ty said.

"I think that Moray is somehow behind the discontent. I think he is using preacher John Knox to sway the opinions of the people against the queen."

"For what purpose?" Ty asked.

"He wants to discredit her in the eyes of the people so he can dethrone her and take control of the government. I believe he will seek to be appointed regent over James VI. I believe it is his plan to murder Darnley and blame it on the queen," Violette said.

"You must not speak those things in public, Violette. You could set yourself up as a target of the Protestant lord's wrath if that is what is truly happening."

"You could be a target also if you don't sign the bond. They might turn their wrath on you," Violette said.

"That is true. I know they do not like my aloofness about the matter or the way I remind them of the fact that they are considering murder, not exile, which might be a more appropriate measure."

"I told Mary about what you had heard. She believes that Bothwell will find a legal way to secure a divorce for her. She wants to believe that he is able to save her, but she is blinded by love," Violette said.

"People do foolish things for love. You could be right," Ty said and walked over to play with Camden.

Doralee came to sit by Violette. "Camden is such a good child. I love being his nanny."

Violette patted her arm. "We love having you. Since you came, Camden has been happier and heathier than ever. And I worry less about his well-being."

Just then Camden ran up to Doralee. "Doree, Can I have some juice?"

Doralee took his hand and led him to the house. "You can have some juice, and then we'll take a nap."

Violette pulled out the letter she had received from her parents this morning. She read it again. Jeanne said that the Sea Beggars, Dutch and French privateers who were winning the war at sea against

Spain in the Netherlands, had succeeded in robbing the Spanish ships of valuable cargo, food, and arms for the Huguenot cause. William of Nassau, Prince of Orange, led the attacks against the Spanish land forces. Though there were many deaths, the Huguenots were certain of victory.

Jeanne said Violette's sister, Bella, who just turned five, was growing fast and spent most of her time playing pirate down by the docks watching the ships come into port. She loves the privateers, and Jeanne fears she might marry a privateer when she got older.

Violette laughed. Her mother was getting to raise another child to replace losing Violette. Violette's heart ached. How she had longed to be raised by her mother, but things had not worked out for her and Jeanne and Pierre. Instead, Violette had been raised by her grandfather, Philippe. She found her parents later in life when she searched for them at Fontainebleau Palace where they had been imprisoned for twenty-four years.

Jeanne added a postmark from Bella. "Tell Camden I love him and want to meet him soon."

Violette sighed. She needed to make a trip to the Netherlands to see her parents. Better yet, she decided to invite them to Eilean Donan for a two-week Christmas celebration. The thought made her smile. Camden could meet Bella. Violette could see her parents.

Ty came to sit by Violette. "What are you thinking?"

Violette told Ty about the Christmas celebration.

"That would be good. We could put on a real Scottish bash." Ty laughed.

"I'll start planning today."

Ty took her hand. "Would you like to take Jules for a ride? We could ride through the mountains and view the autumn leaves."

Violette smiled. "I'd love to go for a ride."

"Wait here and I'll go get the horses." Ty jumped up and headed toward the stables.

A flash of memory rose before her eyes of her and Thomas riding furiously along the beach at La Rochelle. After the ride, they had lain on the beach, and he proposed to her. She had said yes. Then that awful accident in Vassy took away Thomas's memory, and her heart died toward him. Would he ever regain his memory?

She remembered how hard Thomas had worked to find her

parents, and he had succeeded. He found her father in Lombardy wounded but still alive after the war with Spain, and Violette had found her mother, Jeanne, imprisoned in the Guise Manor Tower, but it was Thomas that rescued Jeanne and brought her back to Violette.

Violette tamed her thoughts and focused on the ride through the Cuillin Mountains. There was snow on the ground and the treetops, but it was melting fast. The next snow would be bigger. Then there would come the days of spending all their time indoors because of the cold.

Ty often invited his highlander friends over to entertain them. The men played the bagpipes. They brought their wives and everyone danced the Scottish Fling until they ran out of breath. It was a time of great fun.

As they returned home, she thought on Celine's letter. Her heart ached over Thomas's loss of memory. Would her heart ever mend?

Chapter Sixteen

Jedburgh, Scotland – October 15, 1566

Mary's dinner table set horizontally on a dais at the front of the dinner hall. Below her, another table, positioned perpendicular to hers, ran the full length of the room. Nearest to her at the upper end, French and Scottish nobles sat according to their rank—earls, barons, knights, ladies, lairds, and French gentlemen.

At the end of the noblemen's table set the great pewter saltcellar, which divided the upper-class guests from the humble classes who sat "below the salt." These included priests, tiring women, pages, gentlemen of the chamber, falconers, laundresses, grooms, lackeys, sweepers, and the kitchen help.

The floors were covered with rush rugs upon which bones were discarded as people ate the food. Today's fare included roast pork and rabbit stew. Flagons of Grecian white wine, red claret, and amber-colored beers and ales were placed down the center of the table in close reach of all the diners.

Mary was eating alone today. Lord Darnley evidently had other plans. He was probably at the tavern drinking beer and flirting with the barmaids and pages. Mary sighed. At least she could eat her dinner in peace since she didn't have to bear Darnley's ever-changing moods and dramatic displays of anger.

She was lonely. She hadn't seen Bothwell in weeks. Someone told her that he had been wounded trying to arrest the outlaw John Elliot. She didn't know the extent of his injuries, but she wanted to see him.

Sadly, she had to present an excuse to Lethington to pacify the people. Since rumors of her feelings about Darnley were now common knowledge, she had to appear normal and at ease without arousing suspicions that she was affected by the slander. Keeping her good name was everything.

How could she get away?

A page entered and told her that a James Ogilivie wished to speak with her.

Mary finished her dinner and then met with James Ogilivie. James Ogilivie was a large, stout man and a devout Catholic supporter. He bowed when she entered the audience room.

He stood, twisting his hat in his hands and turning his head left to right as if he was expecting someone to assail him. There was a slash in his right sleeve where he had been wounded.

"Sir Ogilivie, how can I help you? Are you hurt?" Mary asked in a soft voice, putting him at ease, for he immediately calmed down.

"Your Majesty, as you know, my father, the earl of Huntly, disinherited me and adopted Sir John Gordon as his son. Gordon has broken out of prison, and he attacked me in the street less than an hour ago. I believe he is headed for Aberdeen," Ogilivie said.

"We will have to apprehend him before he hurts anyone else, but first we must attend to your wounds." Mary called for a nurse to tend Ogilivie's wounds.

While she waited for Ogilivie, she sent a page to gather an entourage for a progress through the North Country to find John Gordon. This gave her an excuse to see Bothwell. On her way, she would visit Bothwell at Hermitage Castle.

Mary had been in Jedburgh for a week holding a Justice Ayre or circuit court, which was a common practice to bring justice to her subjects who lived outside Edinburgh. Bothwell dwelt in Hermitage Castle, which was about thirty miles from Jedburgh. Hermitage Castle was haunted by a ghost of a dwarf called Redcap. It is believed that the dwarf murdered travelers who wondered into his castle.

As the entourage set out, the rain began. Mary had to admit that the road to Hermitage Castle was rough and full of hidden bogs, and fifteen miles outside Jedburgh, her horse fell into one of those bogs.

Mary treaded through the peat to dry land. She groaned. She was covered with mud and smelly grass up to her chest. She gagged at the smell. She couldn't let Bothwell see her like this.

It took over an hour to pull Mary's horse free from the swamp, but she was determined to see Bothwell. Once they arrived at the castle, Mary sent the majority of the men on to Aberdeen to apprehend John Gordon. She and a few guards remained at Hermitage Castle.

Mary was dismayed when Bothwell's wife, Jean Gordon, opened the door. She had hoped that Jean, who had served as one of Mary's ladies-in-waiting, would not be present. She wanted to see Bothwell alone.

After Jean showed her and the guards inside, she allowed Mary to wash up and put on dry clothes before she took her to see Bothwell. Jean left them alone.

Bothwell was lying on the couch with his head propped up by pillows. He smiled when he saw her.

Bothwell pushed himself up into a sitting position. He had great upper body strength and was built well. He was also enticingly handsome and strong, yet Mary knew his behavior could be vicious and erratic at times. She never knew if he would welcome her or turn a cold shoulder to her gentleness and caring ways.

A servant placed a chair near the couch so Mary could talk with him.

Bothwell nodded his head. "Welcome, Your Majesty. It seems you have caught me in a pitiful state. I apologize for my appearance."

Mary touched his hand. "There is no need for an apology. What happened to you?"

Bothwell withdrew his hand as he told her about the incident. "I raided John Elliot's camp along the border. He is a reiver, a thief known to steal cattle. I captured him, but he managed to get away on foot.

"I pursued him. He ambushed me and stabbed me in the head, my side, and my hand before I shot him. I passed out, but my servants found me and dragged me back to the Hermitage. I sent Elliot's head to Edinburgh." A wide grin spread across his face, as if to say that Elliot was no match for him.

Mary smiled. "And all the time I thought that Redcap had murdered you."

They both laughed.

"No dwarf has enough power to kill me. I am invincible," Bothwell said.

"And fearless! What were you thinking going after a murderous criminal without backup forces? You could have been killed." Tears welled in Mary's eyes.

Bothwell grabbed her hand. "But I wasn't killed. I am still alive and at your service, my queen." He kissed her hand and took a long gaze into her eyes.

A sudden sensation of sweetness swept over her. She blushed with delight, for his manner overwhelmed her.

He groaned and lay back on the pillows.

"You need to rest." Mary stood up. "I'll go find Jean. We will be staying the night, so we can talk later."

Mary and Jean spent most of the evening playing cards. Before Mary retired for the evening Jean cautioned her. "Your Majesty, I know you care for Bothwell very much, but I want you to know that I love him dearly and ask that you respect my feelings concerning him. Please no more private meetings," Jean said and walked away.

Jean's words were like hot bolts piercing her heart. A current of envy gripped her. She should obey Jean's request, but instead she hardened her heart. Her course was set.

In the morning, Mary said a quiet goodbye to Bothwell and left with her men. They had succeeded in capturing John Gordon, and together they rode home to Edinburgh.

Many gifts had arrived for the baby's christening—from Queen Elizabeth I came an enameled gold christening font weighing twenty-eight pounds. Charles IX of France sent a necklace of pearls and rubies, along with a pair of matching earrings. The duke of Savoy sent a jeweled fan worth four thousand crowns.

In December, the Pope arrived for the baby's christening, which was held in the chapel royal at Stirling Castle. The prince was christened Charles James Stuart. The christening was elaborate as befitted a Catholic ceremony. People of nobility lined the chapel from the door to the altar, all carrying candles.

None of the Protestant lords attended the christening, and Lord Darnley was forced to acknowledge James as his son before the whole congregation.

The festivities that followed the christening lasted for three days. There were banquets, masques, pageants, dancing and a huge firework display. There were also lots of singing and a ballet written by Mary's valet.

After the service, Mary moved into Holyrood Palace alone, blocking Darnley from her presence. After the christening, Lord Darnley suddenly fell ill. Some rumored he had been poisoned, but later he was treated for syphilis at Glasgow.

Hopefully, Mary could now live in peace with Bothwell by her side. She hadn't heard from him since October. Had he forgotten her?

When Mary had met him in France, he was fleeing imprisonment because of a "breech of promise" action brought by his Norwegian mistress, Anna Throndsen, concerning the return of her dowry, which Bothwell had spent and never repaid.

Then there was his illicit affair with a servant girl, Bessie Crawford. Had he found another love? Or had Jean recaptured his heart?

Mary knew what she had to do. She must be freed from Darnley and soon. She feared that Bothwell might replace her with another illicit affair. Mary could not bear that happening. She couldn't order Bothwell to spend more time with her, especially since he was out protecting the border between Scotland and England. That was his job.

He had promised to help gain her freedom from Darnley, but months had passed and nothing had been done. Maybe she had misunderstood his intentions. Of course, that was probably it. How presumptuous that she would expect him to murder for her.

Chapter Seventeen

Eilean Donan – December 25, 1566

Today was Christmas, and Violette's parents, Jeanne and Pierre de la Marne, were visiting from Antwerp, along with their daughter, Bella, who was Violette's younger sister. They had arrived on the eighteenth and were scheduled to leave tomorrow.

Violette had prepared a grand dinner of roast quail and leg of lamb. She also introduced her guests to the Scottish Haggis Pudding made from parts of the sheep. Plus, she made chocolate frangipane tarts to remind Jeanne of France. Red and white wines filled shimmering long-stemmed glasses.

Eilean Donan was dressed in green fir wreaths and red ribbon. Flaming red candles were everywhere from the upper corridors to the Billeting Room downstairs. The table in the Banqueting Room held four bouquets of ivory roses, blue thistle, and blue-green eucalyptus leaves in crystal vases. A red tartan plaid table runner ran underneath the festive bouquets. Above the table, red velvet bows with streamers hung from the three-tiered candle chandelier. The table was set.

After dinner, two bagpipe players played, "The First Noel" for a haunting, unforgettable close to the holiday.

The weeklong visit had been light and full of fun. It wasn't until after dinner when they were watching Bella and Camden play like pirates that the conversation turned to politics.

"I am Camden de la Marck of the Sea Beggars." Camden stood on a small stool with a raised sword declaring his victory over the mean Spaniards.

"I am Bella, Countess of Parma and queen of the Netherlands." Bella countered as she ran toward Camden for a confrontation.

Jeanne said, "Bella loves pirates. It troubles me what she might do if she actually met one."

Violette smiled. "I'm sure it is an innocent fantasy. She has certainly entertained Camden all week with pirate raids. They raided the kitchen for food about five times. They are having a great time."

"It is better they play pirates than imitate the raids and pillaging happening in Antwerp," Pierre said.

"How do you feel about that?" Ty asked.

Pierre shook his head. "Even though we are Huguenots and support the Huguenot cause in the Netherlands, we do not approve of all the looting and destruction of Catholic Church property. A bunch of Calvinists desecrated churches and stormed religious buildings, destroying church art and smashing statues of saints. They claim that they are smashing Catholic idols, and the government authorities are doing nothing to stop the vandalism and unrest in Belgium."

"I heard William of Orange has resigned from the Spanish rule and turned to help the Protestant Cause. Is that true?" Ty asked.

"Yes, he has. We are divided into two camps with William of Orange opposing the vandalism and Henry of Brederode supporting it. So, nothing gets done. Our only help against the Spanish troops are the Sea Beggars, who protect the Netherlands from the Spanish ships."

"You mean pirates," Jeanne said.

"Yes, they are pirates, but we need help, and it seems our sovereign Philip the second is determined to continue the inquisition against the Protestants. All we want is less taxation, more self-government, and religious tolerance so we can live in peace without persecution," Pierre said.

Ty refilled his wine glass. "Scotland is in turmoil too. The Protestant lords are vying for power over Mary, Queen of Scots. Lord Darnley, king consort and Mary's husband, has tried to kill her and Scotland's heir, Prince James sixth, even before the child's birth. Now the Protestant lords are trying to free Mary from her marriage to Darnley, but there is no legal way to accomplish their plan."

Violette interrupted. "Have you heard more about their plan?"

Ty grimaced. "Some of the lords have been talking about gunpowder and asking where they might buy substantial quantities. It may not have anything to do with an act of murder, but it sounds suspicious."

"Don't take what they say lightly. When Bothwell returns, we will know if the gunpowder is part of their murderous plans or not," Violette said.

Jeanne changed the subject. "Violette, have you made any plans to claim Camden's fourth-generation rights?"

"No, Maman. It would require a visit to France where neither I nor Ty are welcome at the moment."

"Maybe someone else could handle it for you when the time comes, someone like Thomas Montmorency," Jeanne said.

Violette nervously twisted the wineglass. "Maman, Thomas has no memory of me and our past relationship. I could never ask him to take on the responsibility of Camden's education and training for the nobility. It wouldn't be right and embarrassing."

Jeanne touched Violette's hand. "I hadn't thought about that situation clearly. You are right. I assumed he would have regained his memory by now. How sad." Jeanne took a sip of wine. "Maybe there is someone else who could arrange it for you?"

"Right now, I am focused on Camden's education. We have discussed enrolling him in a private school. He has much to learn about being a nobleman," Violette said and got up. "I'll go check on dessert." Violette disappeared into the kitchen.

Why had Jeanne brought up Thomas's name? She felt guilty over entertaining thoughts about him. Getting an outsider to sponsor Camden at the French Court was a valid idea, one she and Ty had not considered.

She took a deep breath and returned to her guests with a plate of chocolate frangipane tarts. This would sweeten the conversation a bit and turn it away from Thomas Montmorency.

The next morning, Jeanne and Pierre said goodbye and headed back to the Netherlands. Camden and Bella lagged behind the others. They were holding hands, and when it came time for Bella to leave, Camden kissed her on the lips!

Violette gasped. He should know better than to kiss his cousin on the lips. Was their affection for each other growing into something more? If so, what could she do to stop it? Then she noticed something strange about Bella. She didn't look anything like Jeanne or Pierre. Where Jeanne's hair was raven black like her own, Bella's was almost blond. Jeanne's eyes were violet like Violette's, but Bella's were cornflower blue. Surely the differences didn't mean that Bella was not Jeanne's child? It could mean that Pierre was not the father.

Violette berated herself for having such thoughts. If any two people were passionately in love, it was her parents. Yet she remembered when Jeanne told her about expecting a child. It was the next day that Violette was arrested and taken to Paris. She hadn't seen her parents again until now. She really couldn't say that Jeanne actually had Bella or when she was born. The whole situation was strange.

Violette felt Jeanne's gaze upon her.

She knows what I am thinking? She knows I've noticed Bella's differences, but why would Jeanne care if Bella belonged to someone else? Pierre had forgiven her before, and he would do so now, so why the secrecy?

Jeanne walked over to Bella and took her hand. "It is time to leave, baby," she said and gave Violette a glaring nod. They got into the cart and drove off.

After Ty had finished waving and saying goodbye to her parents, Violette grabbed his hand as they walked back inside the castle.

"Did you notice anything odd about Bella and Camden when they are together?"

Ty shrugged. "No. What is wrong?"

"They seemed overly affectionate toward each other. Camden kissed Bella on the lips when they said goodbye. It was a passionate kiss, not a childlike one," Violette explained. "Then I looked up, and Jeanne was glaring at me. She seemed to know what I was thinking."

"You are imagining things. Do not worry about a little kiss. They are children. There is no harm done. They will grow up and realize it was just a childhood thing, not true love."

Violette smiled. "You are right. I worry too much."

Ty kissed her on the cheek as they entered the castle.

Chapter Eighteen

Kirk O'Field – February 10, 1567 at 2:00 a.m.

Lord Moray and Lord Lethington, along with Archibald Douglas and several extra men, sat on horseback on a hill overlooking the Old Provost Lodging at Kirk O'Field. Waiting.

The full moon cast a blue radiance over the scene. The air was damp, and eerie night cries of the hoot owl rang out as a bad omen in the darkness.

Lord Darnley and his servant, Taylor, were inside the residence, lured here under false pretenses. The house belonged to an employee of Bothwell's, Sir James Balfour. It was a two-story building with a cellar underneath it. The first floor was where the servant's rooms were located, and Lord Darnley occupied the largest room at the eastern end. This room had a window that looked out onto an alleyway known as Thieves Row. Darnley's bed was against the far wall with a bath. There were a few tapestries, a colorful carpet, and a table.

Queen Mary had left earlier to attend a wedding celebration of Christina Hogg, one of her ladies, and hadn't returned. She had enticed Darnley here to recuperate from his outbreak of syphilis, promising him that if he came, they would be reconciled as husband and wife but not until he had fully recovered. And Darnley had come.

In the cellar, Balfour had placed several barrels of gunpowder underneath Lord Darnley's room and inserted a long fuse that ran outside the building.

Lord Moray waited in anticipation of seeing his dreams of ruling Scotland fulfilled by the dawn's light. Just a few more hours and all would be his. He had planned everything with methodical cruelty.

Once Lord Darnley was dead and Bothwell accused of his murder, then Mary would be implicated as Bothwell's accomplice. Moray would make sure that Mary's name and honor would be disgraced. He smiled. The plan had come so easily to him. He had played upon Mary's weaknesses, her foolish and coy reactions to Bothwell's restrained love advances.

Suddenly, a smoky scent bombarded his senses. In the moonlight, he saw two male figures escape from the building in a cloud of smoke using a rope and a chair to reach the ground and then running into the adjacent garden. Then an earsplitting, earthshaking boom boom exploded around them.

Moray covered his ears and fell from his horse.

Archibald Douglas and two of his men knelt beside him. Once they knew Moray was all right, they helped him stand up.

"Go. Finish the job," Moray said to Douglas.

Archibald Douglas didn't hesitate but rode quickly down the hill to the smoking building. Lord Moray and Lord Lethington watched as Douglas located Lord Darnley and his servant lying face down in the nearby garden. They were still alive and coughing.

Before Lord Darnley could get up, Douglas forced him down on the ground and strangled him until he fell limp beneath his hands. Lord Darnley was dead.

One of Douglas's men smothered the servant with a pillow he had carried from the house. Once Douglas reassured Moray that Lord Darnley was dead, Moray and the rest of the men rode away to Fife where they would hide until after the investigation.

The blast had shaken the entire town. The night watchmen and the people had already begun to gather at the explosion site. A loud warning bell was sounded and in minutes, a huge crowd with lanterns in hand had gathered, filling the air with fearful cries of agony.

They found the king's lodging place razed to the ground. The house had been blown up in an instant. The roof, floors, walls, and foundation reduced to dust. Knowing that the king was lodging here, the people began to dig frantically through the rubble with their bare hands, searching for the king's body and other survivors.

It wasn't until five in the morning that some men found the bodies of Lord Darnley and Taylor in the south garden about sixty to eighty steps from the house. Both men were dressed only in their night shirts and slippers. No one could figure out how the two had died, for there were no burns or bruises on their bodies. Only one backless velvet shoe was found near the corpses.

At Holyrood Palace, Mary was also awakened by the explosion and sent a messenger to find out what had happened. The people at Holyrood Palace ran screaming in panic, trying to find out what caused the blast that shook the palace.

Mary dressed and looked out her window to see people frantically running toward the sound of the blast. What could have caused such a huge explosion? She had heard that the Protestant lords were inquiring about buying gunpowder. Did that have anything to do with what was happening tonight?

Where was Bothwell? If anyone arranged such an explosion, it was Bothwell. Uncertainty filled her mind. She hadn't seen Bothwell since October when she rode to Hermitage Castle. Surely, he had recovered from his wounds by now. When she left him, he was feeling more like himself.

Then she remembered the embarrassing talk with his wife, Jean. Mary groaned. Jean had noticed how Mary felt about Bothwell. Mary had to suffer the embarrassment of being told by her not to steal her husband.

Jean was right in scolding Mary. Jean had been a faithful and hardworking lady in Mary's service. Mary had counted on her in vital situations because she knew Jean could be trusted. She could certainly spot disloyalty in another such as herself.

Then a knock came at the door, and a servant entered with news of what was happening. "Your Majesty, there has been an explosion at the old Provost Lodging at Kirk O'Field."

Chapter Nineteen

Holyrood Palace – 5:00 a.m. on February 10, 1567

Violette and Ty were spending some quality time together in their apartment on the Royal Mile in Edinburgh. It was early morning, and Violette couldn't sleep.

Doralee had invited several of Camden's friends for an overnight party at home so Violette wouldn't have to worry about him missing her and Ty too much while they were in Edinburgh.

Outside on the royal mile there were loud voices and a warning bell was ringing.

Violette shook Ty awake. "Something is wrong, there are people in the streets."

Ty jumped out of bed and looked out the window. He turned aside and began to dress. "I'll go down and see what has happened." Ty flung open the door and headed down to the street.

Violette rolled out of bed and quickly washed her face and slipped off her night gown and pulled on a dress. She dragged a comb through her hair and smeared a rosy lip balm on her lips and cheeks. She was ready to go.

Ty returned. "Lord Darnley is dead." Ty's lips tightened. "Just after midnight, they blew up the Provost Lodging with gunpowder." He sat down on the bed holding his head in his hands. "I should have known this was coming. I didn't believe they would execute such an audacious plan."

Violette wrapped her arms around him. "We must go see about Mary."

Violette's heart raced. Ty was grievously troubled in mind and vexed in his soul. He was feeling guilty over not acting on the information he had. She was glad that he hadn't signed the Craigmillar bond. Whatever happened, Ty would not be implicated.

When they reached Holyrood Palace, they met a huge crowd in a delirium of disorder. People were running around in a frantic rush, handing out shovels and wheelbarrows to help workers clear away the debris from the explosion site.

"I will ride over to the debris site while you visit Mary. I will be back in about an hour, and if possible, we will go home." Ty waited until Violette had disappeared inside the palace before he rode away.

Inside the palace, people and servants rushed back and forth. Some stood in corners talking in low voices about the explosion. Some whimpered. Some moaned with a hysterical note in their voices. She saw some faces with tears still glistening on their cheeks. The gloomy atmosphere shook her to the core.

She guessed that Mary would be in her audience room. She pushed through the crowd, climbed the stairs, and rapped on the audience room door. When Lady Fleming opened the door and saw her, she pulled her inside the audience room.

Violette squirmed. The red stains from Rizzio's demise were still on the floor. She took a deep breath and looked around for Mary.

Mary was seated on the window seat. Violette moved toward her, but Mary didn't react. She seemed dazed and lost in her own thoughts. Violette looked at Lady Fleming, who shook her head and left them alone.

Violette gently took Mary's hand and sat down beside her. Mary looked empty, sober, and joyless. Her face was white as paper. So Violette held her hand and sat with her. Mary never spoke. She only smiled, acknowledging Violette's presence.

When Mary finally spoke, she talked about what a lovely day it was, and she wished to be outside hunting with her falcons or riding through the woods. They sat like that for an hour. Then Bothwell arrived.

When Mary saw Bothwell, she blushed with shyness and delight, animated by his presence. Violette stood, and Bothwell nodded to her. That was his signal that she was free to go, so she went downstairs to wait for Ty.

Violette found a bench outside in the courtyard. She waited as she watched the hustle and bustle of the crowds. The guards had moved into the courtyard and began directing the people away from the palace. They asked Violette to leave.

Stunned, Violette didn't know what to do. She found Jules and left. She rode to the blast site looking for Ty. She sat on horseback surveying the crowds, but Ty wasn't there. She asked one of the guards at the site about Ty. He told her Ty wasn't at the site and hadn't been there all day. Violette headed back to Edinburgh to their apartment, but Ty hadn't returned. So she wrote Ty a note and packed their clothes and tied the luggage on Jules's back. She rode home to Eilean Donan.

It was almost noon when she arrived at Eilean Donan. The wind had picked up, and a cold breeze assailed her as she crossed the footbridge. When she reached the castle, the groom didn't come to meet her, so she tied Jules to the hitching rail and dismounted.

She entered the courtyard and turned to enter the house. The front door stood open. A quick hard pulse leapt into her throat and caused her to hesitate. Something was wrong. She slowly eased the door back. She looked around for Camden, but the Billeting Room was empty.

Violette yelled. "Camden, I'm home. Where are you? Doralee, are you here?" When there was no answer a cold chill ran down her spine. She talked to herself. "Don't panic. They are here somewhere." *But where?*

Violette ran up the stairs. When she reached the Banqueting Room, she heard a soft whimper. The sound was coming from the anteroom at the back of the room. She rushed in that direction and found Doralee lying on the floor whimpering and tossing her head back and forth.

Violette knelt down beside Doralee and touched her shoulder.

Doralee jerked herself upright and screamed. "No, don't hit me." Then she fell back onto the floor.

Violette shook her. "Doralee, it is me, Violette." That was when she spotted the wound on Doralee's head. "Your head is cut. Lie still so I can examine it."

Like a child, Doralee stiffened as Violette examined the lump on the back of Doralee's head.

"I am going to the kitchen to get some water to clean your face and head. Don't move until I return." Violette waited until Doralee promised to remain still. She ran to the kitchen and pumped some water into a pan and grabbed a cloth. She went back to Doralee and cleaned the wound.

"You will be all right. It looks like you hit your head on something, and a big lump has swelled up," Violette told her. "Let's get you to the couch."

Doralee grunted as Violette helped her stand up. As they made their way to the couch, Doralle said, "I was hit on the head with a rock." She burst into tears. She tried to tell Violette what happened, but Violette couldn't understand what she was saying.

Violette led her to the couch and had her sit down as she gave her a glass of water. In a few minutes, Doralee calmed down.

"Where are the children?" Violette asked.

Suddenly, Doralee's face contorted, that was when Violette knew something was truly wrong.

Doralee managed an answer. "Their mothers came and took them home."

"Where is Camden?" Violette asked with a lump in her throat.

"They took him."

"You mean one of the mother's took him?"

Suddenly, Doralee sobered up. "No. Estelle took him."

"What do you mean Estelle took him? She knows better than to take Camden without my permission."

"You don't understand, milady. I begged Estelle to let him go, but all she would say was that she wanted her child. That's when her boyfriend hit me on the head with a rock. She and her boyfriend, Fergus Gordon, stole Camden."

Suddenly, Violette felt as if she was in a dream and she was drowning, slowly sinking downward. Her eyes burned with tears, blinding her vision. A dead, cold, empty silence enveloped her.

How long she sat without speaking, Violette didn't know. All she knew was that Camden was gone, kidnapped by Estelle. She knew that Estelle loved Camden like her own child. Violette need not worry for his safety; Estelle would protect him, but where had they taken him? Why had they taken him?

Doralee groaned. "I want to go home."

Violette focused on Doralee's needs. "I'll find the groom, and he can take you home."

Doralee shook her head. "They're all gone."

"Where are they?"

"All the servants, including the groom, went to Edinburgh to help clean up the explosion site. They went to mourn Lord Darnley. They didn't say when they would return."

Violette had to resist the urge to panic. No servants. No groom. What could she do? She looked at Doralee who was sobbing, overwhelmed by their situation. Violette had to take courage and do something.

"Doralee, I am riding Jules to Dornie to look for help. Just remain here until I return." Her words seemed to calm Doralee.

Violette got up. She helped Doralee off the couch, and together they went downstairs to the Billeting Room. "Lock the door behind me and don't let anyone in except me or Ty," Violette said and rode off to Dornie to look for help.

It wasn't long before Violette returned with four men. One man helped Doralee onto horseback and took her home. The other three men stayed with Violette. One built a fire in the fireplace for her. Another groomed Jules and bedded him down for the night. The men spent the night in the Billeting Room guarding the castle. Violette lay on the couch next to the warm fire as she waited for Ty to come home.

The next morning when Violette awoke, she rushed upstairs to the bedchamber searching for Ty, but he wasn't in there. Then she began a methodical search of the entire castle, including the stables and the keep.

Ty hadn't come home and Violette had no idea where he could be. Something had gone wrong. It wasn't like Ty to not come home without sending a message or letting her know his plans if he planned to spend the night in Edinburgh. Could the Protestant lords be holding him because he refused to sign the bond to kill Lord Darnley? Maybe she should send someone to Edinburgh to search for him.

Violette found one of the men who kept watch over her last night. She told him that Ty had offended the Protestant lords and they could be holding him in Edinburgh. She asked him to go look for Ty. He agreed and left for Edinburgh.

Violette sat down and waited.

Chapter Twenty

Genoa, Italy – February 12, 1567

Thomas Montmorency stood on the docks at Genoa waiting for his men to unload over one thousand crates of sparkling wine from his vineyard. The vast harvest from last August had allowed him to ship his wine products throughout Europe. Today he had shipments for France and England.

As he waited, Thomas ventured to the edge of the water where a galley ship was waiting to dock. He watched as the captain of the ship steered it into the boat slip about eight feet from where Thomas stood.

As soon as the ship was moored, the captain called down to the galley slaves to unload the cargo. Men of all races, sizes, and physiques hoisted crates on their shoulders and stacked them onto the dock at the captain's feet.

One of the slaves struck a familiar note. Thomas thought he knew the man but wasn't certain. He searched his mind, ransacking his memory. Then it hit him—this slave was Ty MacKenzie, Violette's husband.

At once, Thomas realized the wrongness of the situation. He must make sure it was Ty. Thomas watched the slaves unload the cargo. Ty went below deck to fetch another crate. When Thomas saw Ty reappear, he got closer to the ship and tossed a few coins in Ty's direction. When Ty looked up, Thomas saw the recognition in Ty's eyes. Ty nodded his head, letting him know he understood who he was. Then he nodded his head toward the captain.

Thomas paused. To talk to Ty, he had to create a distraction so the captain wouldn't see the exchange. So Thomas walked over to the captain and started a conversation.

"Captain Dutetre, looks as if you have a competent crew on board," Thomas said.

The Captain, who looked rugged with brown leathered skin and wrinkled eyes, grimaced. "They will do."

"Let me introduce myself. I am Thomas Montmorency of Montmorency Vineyards," Thomas said.

The Captain grunted. "Are you looking for a cargo ship?"

Thomas realized that the Captain had given him a perfect excuse to distract him until he could talk to Ty.

"Yes, I am." Thomas pointed to the crates still being unloaded from the wagon. "I have one thousand crates to be shipped to France and England. Could you give me an estimate of the cost and how long would it take for you to deliver the crates?"

The Captain thought for a moment. "I would have to check my cargo price log, but I can't go back on the ship until the men unload the cargo. You will have to wait."

Thomas hung his head. "I have an important meeting in Genoa. I'm afraid I cannot wait." Thomas started walking away.

The Captain yelled, "Wait, if you will watch the men, making sure they don't escape, I will go inside and check the price log. Our price will be reasonable if not less than the ships docked here."

"I will be glad to watch your men. I'll wait here until you return with an estimate," Thomas said.

The captain and Thomas shook hands, and then the captain boarded the ship and disappeared into his cabin. A guard stood nearby with a pistol in his belt. When the guard moved to assist one of the slaves with a crate, Thomas acted.

Thomas rushed over to Ty. "Talk to me quickly." Thomas watched the guard as Ty talked.

"The Protestant lords kidnapped me and sold me to the galley ship. They have murdered Lord Darnley, and I knew of their plans. They are planning to capture Queen Mary and hold her prisoner. They plan to steal the baby, James sixth, the heir to Scotland's throne. When they do, Moray will appoint himself as regent and take control of the government. Violette could also be in danger, for I told her all I knew about the Protestant lord's plan to murder Darnley. They will find a way to arrest her to keep her from implicating them in the murder. Watch after Violette for me, Thomas."

Thomas reached into his pocket and pulled out the golden locket. "Here. Take this locket. If you should escape, send it home to Scotland. Write your location on the back of the picture. We will send help and bring you home." Thomas handed Ty the locket.

They both heard the captain returning.

Ty said. "Tell Violette I am alive and doing well. As soon as I escape, I will come home. Watch after her for me, Thomas."

"I will watch after her for you, Ty. God's speed."

Thomas backed away. He took the estimate from the Captain and quickly refused the offer. After his wine crates set sail for France, he rushed home, packed his bags, and, that evening he boarded a passenger ship to Edinburgh.

Things happened so fast, Thomas couldn't absorb it all. One day he was in misery because he couldn't find a way to get to Violette. Today, a way was made for him to not only see her but protect her against the Protestant lords.

As he watched the waves from the ship's deck, he thought of what he might say to her when they met. He closed his eyes and dreamed of kissing her. For years, Violette had haunted his dreams. Whenever things looked hopeless, Thomas would close his eyes and think of her. She had brought him comfort and hope every time he became downcast.

Then he remembered Ty. Could he really escape? Thomas didn't think so. That meant he could remain with Violette as long as she needed him. He determined to make their time together last as long as possible.

That night on the ship, he slept well and dreamed of Violette waiting for him on the docks at Edinburgh. When he awoke, the ship had docked and all the passengers were disembarking. On shore, he bought a horse and asked directions to Eilean Donan.

It seemed that Laid Ty MacKenzie's castle, Eilean Donan, was a good two-day ride into the highlands of Scotland near the Isle of Skye.

Thomas bought extra supplies to make the journey. The storekeeper had warned him. "Sir, you might need to take a couple of local natives with you to guide you through the rough terrain. It is winter, and some roads could be impassable."

Thomas thanked him for the advice but refused it. Besides, he had fought side-by-side with Gaspard Coligny in France against the vicious

Guise Brothers and defeated them. He was confident he could make his way through the rugged terrain of the Scottish Highlands.

After he packed the supplies on his horse, Thomas mounted and rode off to the highlands. At last, he would see Violette.

Chapter Twenty-One

Eilean Donan – Feburary 14, 1567

Thomas rode across the causeway and over the footbridge to Eilean Donan Castle. He had ridden hard from Edinburgh after seeing all the unrest in the city. His heart pounded wildly in anticipation of seeing Violette.

When he reached the castle, he jumped from his horse and loosely tied it to the hitching rail. *Oh, God, let Violette be all right.*

He pounded on the door and waited, but there was no answer, so he opened the door and entered the castle. There was no one there. He saw the stairs and hurried up the staircase, which opened onto a large Banqueting Room.

He heard movement off to his left. He followed the noise until he came into the living area. Violette was standing in front of the fireplace. She didn't see him at first, so he took the time to soak in the sight of her. Her beauty arrested his senses. Her long black tresses fell across her shoulder as she bent to stoke the fire. She appeared distraught because there was no dazzling smile on her face. He could see that she had been crying.

As if she heard his thoughts, she looked up. "Thomas?"

Thomas opened his arms, and Violette ran to him, flinging her arms around his neck. Passion overtook him, and he kissed her face, eyes, and lips, lingering on her lips until she returned his passion. They clung to each other, savoring each caress.

Violette was the first to pull away. "You remember."

"Yes, I remember everything, my love."

Violette took his hand and led him to the couch. "I'm so delighted to see you. I've thought of you often hoping your memory would return soon. And now you are here." Tears trickled down her face.

"Don't cry." Thomas pulled a handkerchief from his doublet and wiped her eyes. "Things will be all right."

Violette bowed her head as she wiped away the tears. "Ty is missing. I left him in Edinburgh the day of the explosion, and he hasn't returned. He may have abandoned me or betrayed me like the other men in my life."

Thomas bent his head down, and their foreheads touched. He placed his hands on her arms. "He hasn't abandoned you. I saw him on a galley ship in Genoa two days ago. He is fine."

Violette looked up. "You saw him?"

"I was at the docks in Genoa to ship out a load of wine. As I waited for my men to unload the wine crates, I watched a galley ship moor nearby. I noticed a man that looked familiar to me. When I got closer, I realized it was Ty."

"Oh, thank God." Violette prayed aloud.

"I distracted the captain long enough to talk to him. He told me the Protestant lords had arrested him and sold him as a slave to the galley ship captain, a Captain Dutetre, of the *Jasper Stone.* He wanted me to find you and tell you that he was strong and well able to endure the situation until he could escape."

Violette sighed in relief. "I was so frightened that they had killed him. At least, he is still alive."

"Ty told me that the lords arrested him because he knew about their plans to murder Lord Darnley. He thinks that you may be in danger of being arrested as well, for you knew about the bond," Thomas said.

"Ty let me read a copy of the bond. They wanted him to sign the bond, promising to support the murderer of Lord Darnley, but Ty refused. Now they are punishing him for his betrayal."

"Yet the charges against him are considered lawful. Ty's sentence was for five years aboard the galley ship. But don't worry about him, he will suffer much but will be all right."

Violette smiled and laid her hand on his. "I'm glad you are here. I have been so distraught not knowing what to do. I do feel better knowing Ty is alive and well, but I worry about all the horrid things that can happen to him on board that galley ship."

"You forget that Ty was a Huguenot soldier in France before he resigned and married you," Thomas said, trying to lift her spirits. "He will find a way to escape."

"But how will we know he has escaped?"

"He will let us know," Thomas said confidently as he looked into her eyes.

Thomas eased his arm around her and leaned back against the cushions. Violette laid her head on his shoulder, and in moments she was asleep.

She must have been crying for days. His heart ached for her, and he realized that he still loved her. Now that he was with her, he didn't want to let her go. He had tried living without her, yet living in the fog of a lost memory, his love for her had miraculously survived.

Thomas remembered telling Ty to send the golden locket home to Scotland when he escaped. Why had he done that? *You fool! Why did you tell her Ty was alive? You should have told her that he had died, but you didn't, so what could you do now?*

When Violette moaned in her sleep, Thomas nudged her awake.

"Sorry. I was having a bad dream about Camden." Violette squirmed and moved a safe distance away.

"Who is Camden?" Thomas asked.

"He is my son. I forgot to tell you that my nanny, Estelle, stole Camden. I don't know where he is or where to look for him."

When Violette mentioned Estelle, he immediately thought about Anne's daughter Estelle who lived in France. He didn't say anything to Violette. She was crying again. He decided to comfort her. "Don't worry. We will search for him beginning tomorrow."

"I know that Estelle loves Camden. That is the reason she stole him. She can't have children of her own, and she is desperate to have a child." Violette wiped away the tears.

The cook entered the room and announced dinner. Violette started to refuse, but Thomas encouraged her by saying, "You need your strength to hunt for Camden."

Violette relented, and together they sat down at the banqueting table and ate.

Chapter Twenty-Two

Eilean Donan – February 15, 1567

A warm stream of sunlight awakened Violette. She turned to reach for Ty, but his place beside her was empty. Where had he gone? Then she remembered that he was on a galley ship somewhere in the Mediterranean Sea on his way to France. Would he attempt to escape when he arrived in France?

She rolled out of bed and began to dress. Thomas was here. His presence strengthened her resolve, for now she had someone to help her hunt for Camden. She thanked God for sending Thomas to her during a time of need. She hummed a sweet melody while she dressed.

Thomas waited for her in the Banqueting Room as he drank a cup of coffee. When he saw her, his lips twitched with amusement. She felt a warm glow on her cheeks. He took her hand and drew her into the anteroom and caught her in his arms.

Violette pulled back. "Forgive me, Thomas, but I am a married lady with a husband and a child. I'm sorry if I gave you the wrong impression when you arrived yesterday. I was overwhelmed by the sight of you, knowing you had regained your memory. I can't return your love, but I need your support and help in finding Camden. Will you stay for those reasons?"

Thomas released her. "I apologize for acting like a rogue. I will restrain myself while I am with you. Of course, I will help you find Camden." He bowed and kissed her hand.

Suddenly, the breakfast bell rang out breaking the spell.

Violette smiled and pulled away. Together they walked to the table to eat breakfast. A servant girl, Cora, set the table with a plate of sausage-egg omelets, fresh sliced apples drenched in honey, and grape juice. After they ate, Cora refilled their coffee cups, and Violette and Thomas relaxed in the anteroom.

Thomas posed the first question. "What do you know about the nanny, Estelle?"

"She was recommended to me by Lady Fleming. I know she loves Camden almost as much as I do, but she is arrogant and dangerous." Violette winced. "She has a boyfriend, Fergus Gordon. That's all I know."

Cora returned to refill their coffee cups. Violette asked Cora if she saw Estelle the day of the explosion.

"All the servants left for Edinburgh the morning after the explosion. Estelle packed a bag and waited for her boyfriend to arrive. When Gordon walked in the door, she grabbed Camden, and they left. I supposed they were going to Edinburgh to mourn Lord Darnley. That's all I remember, milady." Cora paused. "I remember thinking how strange that Estelle wanted to take the child to the explosion site." Cora curtsied and left.

Thomas turned to Violette. "Can you describe Estelle to me?"

Violette described Estelle. "She is slender, about my height, with wavy hair the color of cinnamon and hazel green eyes. I couldn't understand why a pretty woman like her wasn't married."

"Is she Scottish?"

"No, she is French."

Thomas frowned. "Do you remember Jeanne's twin sister, Anne?"

How could she forget Anne? Anne had stalked her in La Rochelle and led Queen Catherine de Medici's army right to her door. Catherine executed Anne and imprisoned Violette in the Guise Manor Tower under the control of Henry de Guise.

Violette shivered. "Why?"

"I know it is unpleasant to think about her, but she had a daughter named Estelle living in Meaux. She was Michael Benoit's sister. I met her when Michael and I went to see his Aunt Adela to ask if she knew where Anne was staying. Do you remember?" Thomas asked.

Violette thought for a moment. "I never met her, but Celine mentioned an 'Estelle' in one of her letters. She said that she and Estelle buried Anne next to Adela in a family graveyard. She also told me that Estelle had remarried and was living in France. Do you think my nanny Estelle is the same person as Anne's daughter?"

"I cannot say for certain, but if I saw Estelle I would recognize her. And if she is anything like her mother, she imposes a true danger to Camden."

Violette frowned. "Thomas, you are scaring me."

"I don't mean to scare you, but if your nanny is Anne's daughter, Estelle, we must find her and Camden soon. Do you have any idea where she has gone?"

Violette could hardly think. An urgency to find Camden overwhelmed her. "Her boyfriend is Fergus Gordon, a member of the Clan Huntly. I don't know where they live, yet I think they would have gone to Huntly Castle to hide." Why hadn't she thought of that before? Thinking clearly was difficult when you are consumed with terror.

Thomas saw that he was losing her attention. He stood up and took her hand. "Let's walk."

He led her outside, and they walked along the footbridge where they could smell the warm wind coming off the water and the sun dazzled their eyes. Yet even the sun couldn't pierce Violette's grieving heart.

Violette held tightly to Thomas's arm as they stopped to watch the ducks glide across the loch searching for food. The birdsong clattered back and forth through the trees as the weight of grief lifted from her spirit.

Thomas talked to her in a warm tone. "After I left you in Touraine, I returned to Lombardy and began to rebuild the vineyards. The warm summer days under the Italian sun energized me. I worked from dawn to dark every day and thought of you every evening. Yet when the work was done, I felt empty because I had no one with whom to share my success."

"You have been in my thoughts ever since that night. I felt so betrayed because you didn't know me and had no feelings for me. I felt lost." The spirit of betrayal swept over her like a shadow. Why was she always being abandoned and betrayed by the men in her life? She thought that men were supposed to love and protect her.

"I decided to drown my sorrows at the tavern, so I went inside to dress, but I couldn't find my watch. I felt a lump in my doublet pocket. I thought it was the watch, but when I pulled it out, it was the golden locket you had stuffed in my pocket in Touraine."

"Mother always said that the golden locket was a curse. It always proved to be the reason for all her troubles."

"She could be right, but this time, it saved me. When I looked at the picture of Jeanne, memory flashes racked my brain. When they were over, I remembered everything."

"Where is the golden locket now?" Violette asked.

Thomas straightened. "I gave it to Ty. I told him if the worst happened, he should have a friend send the locket home to you." Thomas lied.

"You mean if he was killed or died on the galley ship," Violette said softly.

"Yes. Hopefully, it will never arrive."

"And if it does arrive?"

"Let's pray that it doesn't." Thomas paused. He regretted that what he said had cast a shadow over the moment. To lighten the mood, he asked, "How did you know I had regained my memory?"

"I knew the moment you opened your arms to me."

"I've missed you, Violette."

"And I have missed you. Could you hold me?"

Thomas opened his arms and held her. Violette closed her eyes and cherished the moment as his strong arms reassured her. Being held by loving arms was heaven. She drowned in his arms as a staggering sense of well-being swept over her and faith filled her heart.

After a few delightful moments of being close, they began to stroll along the causeway, enjoying nature's love song for lovers.

It was noon when they decided to begin their search for Camden. Thomas rode with her to Holyrood Palace.

Chapter Twenty-Three

Holyrood Palace – February 15, 1567

The palace was quiet. Lord Darnley had been buried yesterday in Holyrood Abbey. Only members of Darnley's family attended the funeral. The people continued with their usual business as if nothing tragic had happened.

Violette climbed the stairs to Mary's audience room. The door was closed, and Violette heard voices and music coming from the room. She opened the door and saw Mary and Bothwell dancing a fast galliard.

Lady Fleming and Lady Beaton were present. They sat on the sidelines watching Mary and Bothwell dance.

Violette stood still until the music ended, and Mary noticed her presence. Mary welcomed her. "Come in, Violette. Would you like to join us?"

Violette asked, "Can I speak with you and Lady Fleming in private?"

Mary turned and motioned to Bothwell. He bowed and left. Mary's face took on a sullen demeanor. She forced a smile as she joined Lady Fleming and Lady Beaton.

Violette handed Mary the copy of the Craigmillar Bond. "Did you know about this?"

Mary read the bond and then shook her head. "No, but I discussed my options for a divorce with the Protestant lords."

"Ty knew about the bond and refused to sign it. The Protestant lords arrested him and sold him as a slave to a Captain Dutetre of the *Jasper Stone.* Ty is missing."

Mary stood up, and she and the other ladies hugged her, expressing their sadness for her misfortune.

Violette let the tears stream down her face. Then she turned to Lady Fleming. "The nanny, Estelle, whom you sent me has stolen my son Camden. I need to find him. What can you tell me about her?"

Lady Fleming drew back. "I know very little about her. I met her at Fontainebleau. She worked in the royal nursery for a time, but she lost her job because all the royal children were grown. And when Mary returned to Scotland, I brought Estelle with us."

Mary spoke out. "Is she seeing Fergus Gordon?"

Violette said, "Yes. Do you know him?"

"Laird Gordon is a loyal subject. I will write you a letter to take to him. He will help you find Camden."

"And Ty. What can I do about getting Ty back?"

"I am unsure, but I will have Lethington look into the matter," Mary said as she sat down at her desk and wrote the letter. She sealed it with her royal seal and handed it to Violette.

"Take this to Laird Gordon. He will obey my instructions."

Violette left the audience room, her whole being seething with helplessness. Tears of defeat blinded her eyes. Thomas was her only help.

She felt guilty for deserting him when he lost his memory, but at the time, there was nothing else she could have done. Of course, she could have waited on him until his memory returned, but she was too impatient and angry because he had abandoned her.

Subconsciously, she must have wanted to hurt him, for she married Ty. Now Ty was gone, and she was alone again.

There must be a way to stop these urges for revenge. Then she remembered that the Lord had told her not to marry Thomas. Why? She prayed, asking the Lord to give her wisdom and show her what she should do.

Thomas was waiting for her outside the palace door. He boosted her into the saddle. He mounted his horse and pulled alongside Jules to talk to her. "I found out that Fergus Gordon lives at Huntly Castle in Aberdeenshire. One man said that he saw Fergus and his lady friend leave Edinburgh the day after the explosion. His lady friend had a young child with her."

Violette sighed. "I am so relieved. The queen couldn't help me, but she gave me a letter to give to Laird Gordon with instructions to release Camden."

"We need to write letters to my sister, Celine, and one to Michael. They might know if the nanny 'Estelle' is Anne's daughter or someone altogether different." Thomas continued, "It is getting late. Let's return to Eilean Donan, and tomorrow we will ride north to Huntly Castle to search for Estelle and Camden."

Even though Violette felt an urgent need to find Camden, she was weary from emotional exhaustion and agreed to return home.

That evening, they wrote and posted the two letters, hoping to learn more about the woman who took Camden.

After dinner, they snuggled before the warm fire. Thomas held her close.

Violette felt safe in his arms. What a mess she had made of her life. If only she had known that Thomas would regain his memory so soon. She didn't know what to say to him or explain why she had married Ty. She thought he knew and understood, for he had come to help her. They didn't need to explain. They just needed each other.

Thomas cherished every moment, knowing their time together could end any day. He was content holding her as they watched the fire. Love was simple. It was people who made it so complicated.

He had thought once he saw her again, he could help her and then return to his life in Italy. But now he realized, he could never leave her again. All he could do now was prolong his stay until she sent him home. In his heart, he hoped Ty would never return home. Violette belonged to him, and Ty knew that. But Violette was an honorable woman. She would never betray Ty unless he was killed or died. There seemed to be no way out of this dilemma. If he got his way, Thomas would take her back to Italy with him tonight. He closed his eyes and dreamed of what might have been.

Chapter Twenty-Four

On the road to Aberdeen – February 16, 1567

Thomas chose the route to Aberdeen, which was located in the northeast highlands near the Grampian Mountains. The weather was damp and cold as they left Edinburgh. Since they only had about nine hours of daylight, they lodged in Fife at the end of the day. The next morning, they left Fife and followed the coastline of the North Sea to Aberdeen.

On the road to Huntly, the fantastic mountain views inspired them to linger to take in the scenery. Aberdeenshire was mostly green grass mixed in with brown barley fields and surrounded by the snow-dusted Grampian Mountains. Herds of white sheep dotted verdant green rolling hills. At times, gusts of frigid winds chilled them to the bone, but they pressed forward.

Thomas glanced at Violette, who was covered head to toe in leather and wool-lined clothes beneath a wool-lined cape, hood, and gloves as she snuggled low on Jules's back, absorbing his warmth.

They stopped in Huntly City to get directions to Huntly Castle, the home of the Gordon Highlanders and clan chief George Gordon, the Fifth Earl of Huntly.

Thomas admired Violette's fortitude to undertake such a harsh journey, but he knew she would never have let him come alone. They had been through many trials together, including the kidnapping ruse he had arranged to gain her loyalty. That scheme had worked until she found out he was behind it, and he had almost lost her. He hadn't known then how much he truly loved her. Now he was desperate to win her back. Would his lies catch up with him again?

They stopped at a small tavern in Aberdeen to eat and warm up.

The maid served them shortbread fingers, a rectangular shaped bar treat made of butter, sugar, flour, rice flour, salt and sprinkled with icing sugar. They drank hot tea.

The maid gave them directions to Huntly Castle, which was located at the confluence of the Deveron and Bogie Rivers—a strategic defensive point against intruders.

Thomas rode ahead. They crossed a stone bridge over the Deveron River and entered the grounds of Huntly Castle. The green grassy grounds were divided into separate areas blocked off by huge chunks of granite stone creating a courtyard, a seating area, and a fountain area.

Thomas helped Violette dismount. Looking around, no one seemed to be at home. Thomas viewed the grandeur of the castle. A five-story tower of gray stone bordered the left side of the castle. The frontispiece or main entrance was marked by red sandstones, which accented the entrance and the windows. It featured carvings of heraldry of the Gordon coats of arms and family crest. It also proclaimed the Gordon motto, "Bydand—Stay and fight by courage, not by craft." The Gordons were fierce fighters and one of the richest Catholic families in Scotland.

Thomas knocked on the door.

The door opened to reveal a middle-aged man of lanky build. "Yeah," The man said, flinging the door back until it hit the inside wall. "Who are you?"

"We are looking for Fergus Gordon," Thomas said and took a step backward.

"You're looking at him. What do you want?"

Violette moved forward. "We have a letter from Mary, Queen of Scots." She handed Fergus the letter sealed with Mary's royal seal.

Fergus ripped open the letter and read it. At once, his demeanor changed. In a husky voice, he invited them inside.

Thomas expected a much rougher man than Fergus. He looked like a courtier rather than a fierce highlander. His face was long with a pointed chin and trimmed mustache and beard. His long narrow nose appeared too feminine. His attire was comfortable and loose, his hands smooth rather than calloused.

Thomas introduced himself and Violette.

Fergus directed his questions to Violette. "The queen thinks that

I have your child, Camden. Why is that?" He asked as he handed the letter back to Violette.

Violette tucked the letter into her doublet. "Your girlfriend, Estelle, was working for me as Camden's nanny. I have witnesses that saw you and Estelle take Camden from my home, Eilean Donan Castle, on the day after the explosion that killed Lord Darnley. Is that true?"

Fergus stroked his thick dark beard, thinking. "I do know a girl called Estelle, but she told me the baby was hers and she needed help taking him home. So I helped her, but I never stole your child. Why would she take your child?"

Thomas broke into the conversation. "Lady MacKenzie's child is French. He is a fourth-generation child who is to inherit nobility when he comes of age. Your girlfriend, Estelle, is childless and her mother told her about Violette's child. Estelle came from France to steal him because she is Violette's distant cousin and knows of Camden's inheritance. She wants the inheritance for herself."

Fergus shrugged. "That's quite a story, but I am not this woman's boyfriend. I only extended her a kindness unaware of any evil intent on her part. After returning home, I sent her and the child away. She is probably lodging in town. If she stole the child, it is none of my concern."

"May we speak with the clan chief, the Earl of Huntly?" Thomas asked.

"The clan is out on a raid, attacking our mortal enemies the Clan Forbes. He won't be back for days. If there is nothing more, I'll show you to the door," Fergus said and started walking toward the door.

Violette threw Thomas a worried glance and followed Fergus, who was waiting at the entrance holding the door open.

As Thomas and Violette exited the castle, Thomas heard the door shut behind them and the bar shoved into place. Fergus must be frightened. That gave Thomas an idea. When he and Violette had ridden a short distance away from the castle, he stopped and motioned Violette to the road side.

"I think Fergus was lying to us," Thomas said.

"I know he was, but what can we do?" Violette said.

Thomas looked around. "If I am correct, Fergus will go looking for Estelle as soon as we are out of sight. Let's hide over there on top of that earthen mound and wait to see if he comes out. When he does, we will follow him. I'm certain he will lead us straight to Estelle and Camden."

Violette sighed. "That is a good idea."

Violette and Thomas tied the horses to a nearby tree and climbed the earthen mound. They lay flat on the ground, hidden behind a clump of bushes where they had a clear view of the castle door.

Thomas smiled at Violette, who was laying close beside him. If the situation wasn't so dire, he would have made an attempt to kiss her, but he hesitated because she might think he was being selfish and insensitive. He needed to gain her trust so when he claimed her as his, she would not reject him. He would have to be patient. Instead of a kiss, he gently held her hand. A loving glow shone in her eyes, and she blushed.

About that time, Fergus exited the castle, and a groom walked up with his horse, which was a dapple gray stallion.

Thomas and Violette rushed to the horses and followed Fergus at a distance.

Chapter Twenty-Five

Huntly City – February 16, 1567

Violette and Thomas followed Fergus to a small cottage about a ten-minute ride from Huntly Castle. They waited behind a copse of trees as Fergus loosely tied the dapple stallion to the hitching rail and knocked on the door.

Estelle opened the door, and Fergus embraced her and slammed the door shut with one foot. Violette gasped and tried to run, but Thomas caught her.

"Wait." Thomas pulled her along to a spot near a window. From here, they could see inside and hear everything Fergus and Estelle said.

The sunlight slipped behind a cloud, darkening the atmosphere, but the bright light of the fiery torches inside the cottage fell on the snow just outside the window, painting yellow shadows on the ground near where Violette and Thomas lay hidden. They listened.

After a few kisses, the couple broke apart. Camden walked over and clung to Estelle's leg.

"That's Camden!" Violette whispered and stood up and started to yell, but Thomas tackled her down to the ground.

"Be still and listen. We need to hear what they are planning to do next in case we lose them again." Thomas clamped down on her wrist, keeping her in place.

Silent tears streamed down Violette's cheeks.

"The queen knows we have the boy. I thought he was your child, but today his real mother showed up at Huntly Castle." Violette heard Fergus say to Estelle.

Estelle picked up Camden and placed him into a makeshift playpen made with pillows and let him play with a ball. Then she turned to Fergus.

"What did you tell Lady MacKenzie?"

"Nothing. I denied knowing you and sent them away. Now we are in deep trouble." Fergus grunted. "Why didn't you tell me that the boy is the heir to French nobility? Were you trying to keep all the money for yourself?" Fergus grimaced.

"How did you find out about the inheritance? Did Lady MacKenzie tell you?" Estelle's face flushed red, and anger rose up into squinted eyes.

"No. Her friend, Thomas, told me. That's when I realized what you had done." Fergus grabbed her wrists and began twisting them.

Estelle cried out in agony until she dropped to the floor. Fergus knelt in front of her. "When I realized why you had stolen the child, I raided the family safe and took all the cash. We are going to France. Get up! Go pack your things. We have to leave now," Fergus shouted at her. He pulled her upright and shoved her backward, releasing her wrists.

"I'm not going anywhere with you," Estelle said defiantly. "We are not married and you can't make me go!"

Fergus slapped her across the face, and Estelle whimpered and backed away.

"We'll get married when and if I am ready. I want that inheritance money. If you are not ready in ten minutes, I'm leaving here with the child." Fergus pointed toward the bedroom. Then he laughed and said. "I've been the least of the Gordon's far too long. My brothers looked down on me because I wasn't a fighter. I only received a small pension from the Clan's funds while the others shared the spoils of war. Now I'm going to be rich beyond belief."

Estelle ran into the bedroom.

Thomas and Violette moved to the bedroom window. Thomas looked inside. When he turned around he nodded his head to Violette and whispered, "That is Anne's daughter, Estelle. I'd know her anywhere." Thomas and Violette returned to their spot outside the living room window.

In five minutes, Estelle appeared with two small bags. She cried as she dressed Camden in warm clothing and lifted him into her arms. She followed Fergus out the door and onto the horses.

Fergus said, "If we hurry, we can board the last ship to France." Fergus kicked his horse into a canter.

Estelle wrapped her arms around Camden and held the reins as Camden clung to the saddle pommel. She tried to keep up as Fergus increased the pace.

Violette and Thomas rushed to their horses and headed after the couple. A few miles down the road, a company of one hundred highlanders rode up behind them and surrounded them, bringing their chase to a halt. They were face-to-face with the fierce raiders of Clan Huntly. They were trapped.

Violette watched as Camden and his captors disappeared into the woods. The highlander's rode in circles around Violette and Thomas until they separated them. Now Violette faced the clansmen alone. A group of them circled her, riding around and around her and Jules, taunting her by pulling their swords. They flipped her hood back and cut the snood from her chignon, and her long back tresses fell to her shoulders. The highlanders laughed wildly and hollered insults at her.

Violette looked at Thomas; the men were doing the same to him. He mouthed the words, "Stay still." Violette took a firm hold on Jules's reins, keeping him steady. She looked straight ahead, trying not to flinch as the swordplay cut the buttons from her leather cape.

Violette looked each man in the eye as they teased her. They looked fierce in their blue and green tartans. She saw three or more daggers stuck in their belts, a dag or pistol, and a round targe or shield tied to their saddles. They wore sleeves of metal and leather boots caked in dried mud. They must have come straight from the battlefield. Weary warriors would react at the slightest provocation, so Violette held steady and tried not to scream each time one of them slashed at her clothes with his sword.

Jules got nervous and snorted, rearing up on his hind legs. Violette held on and patted his neck, trying to calm him. Then he rushed at the highlanders forcing them to split ranks and let him go.

Jules galloped along the road with Violette lying low on his back and tangling her hand in his mane to keep from falling. After a few minutes, Jules slowed down, and the highlanders surrounded them again. This time, they poked at Jules, trying to spook him again.

The horseplay seemed to go on forever and Violette's determination began to sink. She almost crumbled. Then an older man broke through the middle of the highlanders and stopped in front of Jules. He held up a long lance, and the taunting stopped. Thomas was freed and he rode to her side.

The clan chief, Laird George Gordon led the company back to Huntly Castle.

Chapter Twenty-Six

On the galley ship – February 16, 1567

The galley ship, *Jasper Stone,* plowed through the Mediterranean Sea at a fast clip. A favorable wind had caught the sails early that morning, giving Ty a break from rowing. Captain Dutetre had him mending sails. The task placed him in position to observe the captain's habits as he guided the ship to Marseille.

Jasper Stone was a sweet ship. She was 150 feet long, thirty feet wide, and stood only six feet above the water line. She carried 150 galley slaves with six rowers to one oar making the total of twenty-five oars per ship.

The comites commanded the slaves, for they carried whips, which forced the rowers not to be slack in performing their duty. They set a steady pace. During times of high winds, only a third of the slaves were required to row. They were often assigned other duties during that time.

When Ty first came aboard ship, he was stripped of his clothes and given a uniform consisting of a coarse brown tunic, a vest, two shirts, and two pairs of canvas breeches. A red cap was issued, but shoes were only given out for shore duty in case the slaves dreamed of escaping.

The food was minimal. In winter, the daily ration of soup, biscuit, water, and wine were all that Ty received. Ty learned that Captain Dutetre was a drinking man who loved red wine. He drank red wine at every meal and late into the night. He was often incapacitated from drink, especially when he played backgammon. Ty had made it known that he was an excellent backgammon player and could beat anyone on the ship. When the captain heard of his boasting, he challenged Ty to a game. Ty had spent many nights over the past weeks in the captain's cabin playing backgammon.

He noticed the captain fell asleep around midnight and didn't wake until dawn. Plus he posted a night watchman to stand guard from midnight to dawn to make sure no one escaped or stole items from the food pantry. Ty would have to make his escape at midnight, and the night watchman posed a threat to that plan. The other disadvantage of escaping at midnight was that he wouldn't be able to see unless there was a full moon. It was impossible to navigate through the dark waters without light. The next full moon was due in four weeks. That would be his only chance. He had to take it. In the meantime, he must devise a plan to get past the night watchman.

Ty felt the golden locket bounce against his chest. He moaned. The locket reminded him of Violette and Camden. He kept them at the back of his mind so he wouldn't feel the pain in being away from them. Knowing Thomas was with them put him at ease in an odd way. At other times, the thought of Thomas comforting Violette tormented him. After all, she had once intended to marry Thomas until he lost his memory.

Ty remembered how abandoned and betrayed Violette had felt when Thomas lost his memory. That was when she turned to him. Would she see him in the same light? Would she see him as a man who had abandoned and betrayed her? It didn't cross her mind that he had been kidnapped and arrested. His situation was not his choice. Yet all Violette could see was the result of being alone and unprotected.

When Ty saw the recognition in Thomas's face at the docks, he knew he had to trust him if he wanted someone to look after Violette, someone he knew would truly take care of her. Knowing that eased the mental torture. Yet he felt an urgency to return home soon, or else he might lose Violette to Thomas. How could he bear that?

Ty finished mending the two sails. He went below deck and put the mended sails in the storage locker. The kitchen pantry was only a few steps away. He looked around. No one was in sight. He slipped into the pantry and grabbed some fruit, cheese, jerky, and water pouches. He hid these in a brown sack and shoved them into his secret hiding place. He would pick them up right before he jumped overboard.

He quickly returned to the deck and started mending another

set of sails. As the time drew near to escape, he grew more excited. He stared at the blue waters ahead, which beckoned him to freedom. He would gain his freedom either through escape or through death. Either way, he would be free.

Chapter Twenty-Seven

Huntly Castle – February 17, 1567

As Violette and Thomas were escorted to Huntly Castle, a cold mist stroked their path, causing the shades of night to thicken faster than was needed. By the time they reached the castle, the moon had risen.

They dismounted in the twilight. Several clansmen gathered the horses and took them to the stables. The others surrounded Violette and Thomas, nudging them toward the castle entrance.

At the front door, Laird George Gordon halted with one hand raised. The door stood open. He sent two warriors armed with daggers inside to search the castle for intruders. When the warriors returned, they reported their findings to Gordon and stood to one side.

Laird Gordon entered the castle, and the clansmen pushed Violette and Thomas forward through the door and up the stairs to the Great Hall.

In the candlelight of the large chandelier, Violette viewed her surroundings. Huntly Castle was considered one of the grandest and most beautiful baronial castles in Northern Scotland. Violette saw why. The Great Hall glistened in the candlelight. The elongated windows with shutters swept aside filtered in the soft moonlight. A warm glow filled the room. Soon the banked fire leapt alive, and the heat cocooned her like a blanket.

Two clansmen pushed Violette and Thomas to the back of the room into a small alcove where the safe was kept. The door of the safe was wide open, and papers lay scattered on the floor.

Laird Gordon looked at Thomas. "It is empty. Where is the money?"

"We don't have your money. Maybe Fer—"

Violette interrupted Thomas's explanation. "Laird Gordon, we believe that your son Fergus took the money."

Violette straightened as Laird Gordon, an imposing man of husky build, hovered over her and glared into her eyes. Violette didn't flinch.

"That is a dangerous accusation, milady. Be careful who you are accusing," he said in a gruff voice.

"I can explain, sir." Violette related what had happened and how Fergus and Estelle took Camden and were planning to sail to France.

Laird Gordon sent three men to look for Fergus. When they came back without Fergus, he turned to Violette.

"Why should we believe you?"

Violette reached into her doublet and pulled out Mary's letter and handed it to Laird Gordon and waited while he read it. When he faced her again, he softened his tone.

"So it is true that Fergus sole your child?"

"Yes, sir. Thomas and I were following the couple to rescue Camden. By now, they should be on the last boat to France."

"Is there a special reason why Estelle wanted your baby?" Laird Gordon asked Violette.

Violette hesitated, not wanting to explain about Camden's inheritance. It must cost a fortune for the upkeep on Huntly Castle. She didn't want money-hungry highlanders after her child's inheritance. Violette glanced at Thomas. He shook his head. Then she answered Laird Gordon.

"Estelle has been married twice without bearing any children. She was desperate to have a child, and I believe she stole Camden because he was close, and stealing him would be easy. Both me and my husband were in Edinburgh at the time."

Her answer satisfied the laird's curiosity, for he stepped back and apologized for the way they had treated them.

"Tomorrow I will send men after Fergus. I will find your child and return him to you, fulfilling the queen's request. Tonight you will be my guests." Laird Gordon ordered two maids to show them to their rooms for the night.

The maids put Violette and Thomas in separate rooms across the hall from each other.

Violette glanced at Thomas, as she turned the knob to enter her room.

"Will you be afraid sleeping alone in this strange castle?" Thomas asked Violette.

She smiled, nodded her head, and closed the door. Once inside, she locked the door and went to the wash basin to freshen up. The maid had lain out a cotton shift for a night gown. She slipped into the shift, pulled back the covers, and crawled into the comfort that only riches could buy.

The last time she had enjoyed the things that only riches could buy was when she first learned that Bishop Bernard had betrothed her to an older man, Charles Gresham. She recalled the comfort of his carriage seats and how they cushioned her as they rode along the streets of Avignon.

For a moment, she was tempted to call off the search for her parents and accept Gresham's proposal, but each time she looked at him, it struck fear in her heart. She couldn't bear the thought of marrying such a man just for riches. She wanted true love and a close relationship with God. None of which Monsieur Gresham could offer her.

The strain and emotional drama of the day played on her senses. The moonlight had waned, and the fire light cast a glow over the room. The scent of heather and lavender tickled her nose. The silky bed covers were smooth to the touch. The down comforter was light but warm. Outside beneath the window, the river Deveron gurgled, luring her into a twilight sleep.

She dreamed of Ty alone amongst robbers and thieves on a wicked ship tossing on a roiling sea. Estelle laughed at she held Camden in her arms and boarded a ship flying the blue, white, and red colors of France. She ran after Estelle. Suddenly, Thomas appeared by her side, and he caught her in his arms and kissed her. He said, "You belong to me." Violette struggled in his arms, twisting and pushing, trying to break free from his arms. Then she awoke.

She set up in bed, sweat dripping from her face. It was just a dream. Violette laid her head down on the pillow. Her heart ached because even though it was just a dream, it was true. She belonged to Thomas. From the day they met, her heart had belonged to him. Even his roguish ways and wandering glances at other women couldn't persuade her heart to turn against him.

She knew he would return to Italy as soon as they found Camden. She couldn't stop him from leaving her again. When the time came for him to go, she hoped she had the courage to release him.

She turned her head into the pillow and cried herself to sleep.

Chapter Twenty-Eight

Moray's Castle in Fife – February 17, 1567

Moray and Lethington met at the ruins of St. Andrews Cathedral in Fife under the guise of going fishing at the local village. They both dressed in everyday clothes of breeches and shirts and carried fishing rods and bait.

Moray was saddened about the demise of the cathedral. The once gorgeous church had been ransacked by the Protestant lords, who destroyed the altar, images, and stained glass windows behind the altar. Shards of broken stained glass covered the floor beneath the windows. He saw the outline of glassless clerestory windows above the triforium, the panel between the arcade and the clerestory. All that remained of the church were one side wall with an arcade of pointed arches along the south wall of the nave and the adjoining entrance wall with twin turrets.

Moray understood what motivated the iconoclastic destruction because when he converted to Protestantism, he had taken part in destroying the art and images in several churches. The Protestants felt they were defending the second commandment found in the Holy Scriptures, "Thou shall not make unto thee any graven image." The Catholic Churches were full of such images. The Protestants destroyed the images in protest of being persecuted and killed as heretics. And the war raged on.

Moray saw a pile of gray sandstone ashlar piled near the back wall. He walked over to examine them. Stonemasonry tools lay next to the pile. Beside it lay a scrap of paper with the name "Wishart" visible at the top. Someone was building a martyr's memorial to the late George Wishart, who was hanged for preaching from the Holy

Scriptures in this very church. Moray grunted. Would they never be free of the papists?

Lethington joined him. "Wishart was a great man and loved by all the people. He was a true martyr of the Protestant faith."

"I agree," Moray said and quickly changed the subject. "Have they charged Bothwell yet for Lord Darnley's murder?"

"No. Lennox, his father, will deliver the bill of attainder tomorrow before Bothwell has a chance to escape town. I don't think Bothwell realizes that he is in danger."

Moray scowled, drawing his eyebrows together. "No, not yet. Mary has given him too much power, power that is rightfully mine. He controls the army. He is forceful and aggressive. He is a skilled swordsman. No lord wants to confront him for they fear him as well. I doubt that Lennox will face him either."

"I fear you may be right. Bothwell is a powerful man." Lethington bowed his head.

Moray faced Lethington. "If he should be acquitted of murder, which I am certain he will be, advise the lords to suggest that he propose marriage to Mary. Bothwell is arrogant and boastful. All he needs is a push in the right direction. If she accepts, we will have her under our power, and we can use Bothwell to destroy her credibility as a ruler of Scotland and unfit to reign. In effect, we will use Bothwell to destroy her good reputation with the people of Scotland."

"You are right, my lord. Mary foolishly thinks that she can rule Scotland as she did with France. In France, the people respect the belief that their kings and queens are appointed by God and above reproach. But in Scotland, we have taught them that our rulers must comply with the demands of the people and God's laws. If her reputation is tarnished, the people will defy her."

"How did Mary's meeting with John Knox affect her?"

"He brought Mary to tears. She loathes him and fears his influence. His presentation was as powerful as his sermons. He made us proud," Lethington said and smiled.

"Arrange another meeting with Mary and Knox. We must keep her feeling unsure and doubtful. We want her to feel weak and powerless."

Lethington nodded his consent.

"What about the situation with Laird MacKenzie?" Moray asked.

"No need to worry about MacKenzie. We sold him to Captain

Dutetre of the *Jasper Stone* galley ship. He won't cause any more trouble for us for the next five years," Lethington said.

"What about his wife, Lady MacKenzie? She is one of Mary's ladies and is quite bold. She helped Mary and Lord Darnley escape."

Lethington groaned. "She could be a problem. I'm certain that MacKenzie told her about the murder bond."

"Should I be concerned?"

"Not at the moment. Her nanny stole her son and has run away to France with the child. She will not have time to hunt for MacKenzie. She is too busy trying to find the child."

"Just keep a watch on her progress. If she tries to implicate us in any way, let me know," Moray said. "Is there anything else I should know about?"

"It could be nothing, but Sir Thomas Montmorency has arrived from Italy to help Lady MacKenzie with the search for the child. They were once engaged to be married before she married MacKenzie," Lethington said.

"An old lover perhaps?" Moray said thoughtfully. "If she gives us any trouble, I'll be able to use that information to nullify her accusations against us. No one likes a revengeful woman. She is harmless."

"I'll keep an eye on her activities just to be cautious until our plan has succeeded and Mary is no longer Queen of Scots. All I want is for us to unite with England under Queen Elizabeth's Protestant rule," Lethington said and smiled at the thought.

Chapter Twenty-Nine

Holyrood Palace – February 20, 1567

It was a gloomy day in Edinburgh. Outside Holyrood Palace, snow covered the grounds. The gray clouds loomed low, dispensing their cold white treasure.

Mary, Queen of Scots sat at her desk watching the snowflakes fall. Oh, how she missed France on days like this. Scotland made France appear as a fairy land. It was a poor land in contrast to France, and the coldness chilled her inside and out. The rugged terrain hampered her need to be outside hunting with her falcons or riding through the woods.

But the weather wasn't the cause of her depression; it was a letter from her cousin, Queen Elizabeth I of England.

Mary knew that she was the true queen of England, not Elizabeth, but Elizabeth had won the crown. Mary's grandmother, Margaret Tudor, was the sister of King Henry VIII of England. Margaret had married James IV, King of Scots, and their son was Mary's father, James V of Scotland.

Queen Elizabeth was the daughter of King Henry VIII and Anne Boleyn, whose union the Catholic Church considered illegitimate, thereby making Elizabeth ineligible to rule. But Elizabeth was Protestant, and England was no longer Catholic, so she was pronounced queen.

Times were changing. The old rules didn't apply, and the new rules changed according to the newest religious standards. Mary didn't know if she could obey the new rules or if she should even try.

The Protestant lords had perverted Mary's rule into a disastrous farce. Her good nature, kind heart, and charming manner had failed to subdue the people's idea that rulers were made to serve the people. Mary blamed John Knox for instilling that heretical idea into the people's minds.

Lord Darnley's murder incensed the people, and they were looking to blame her and Bothwell for the king's demise. Now Queen Elizabeth had joined her accusers. Mary read the letter again.

> My Dear Cousin,
>
> My mind and heart was frightened to hear of the horrible murder of your late husband and my cousin, Lord Darnley. My spirit is so low I can barely write. You have my sympathy for your great loss, for I grieve for you more than for him. I urge you to preserve your honor. Men say that instead of seizing the murderer, you have ignored your duty of seeking revenge on those who have pleased you, as though you had sanctioned the deed.
>
> I would not entertain such a thought or think less of any monarch, especially you, my cousin, to whom I desire only good and blessings. I exhort you to deeply consider this matter at once, even if the perpetrator is someone dear to your heart. Arrest the man who is guilty of this crime. Prove that you are a noble princess and a loyal wife. Please heed my advice. You have no true a friend as I.
>
> Elizabeth

Since Mary had returned to Scotland to rule, Queen Elizabeth had been a constant thorn in her side. Elizabeth was afraid Mary would marry a powerful prince and raise a vast army to invade England. She wanted Mary to marry a man with very little power or influence, so that she would be less of a threat. She was always offering advice to Mary.

Mary was finally free from Lord Darnley and was free to marry again, but if Bothwell was found guilty of Darnley's murder, her last chance of happiness would be gone.

The door to the audience chamber opened and two Skye terriers bounded across the room and jumped into Mary's lap. Not far behind, Bothwell crossed the threshold.

Mary looked up in surprise.

"Good morning, Your Majesty. The clouds have lifted, and the day has turned sunny. Would you like to go hunting?" Bothwell asked, a devious smile on his lips.

Mary didn't believe him, and then she saw the sun splashing through the window. She looked at the terriers and rubbed the head of the smallest one. "Would you guys like to go hunting?" The dogs took turns jumping up and down.

Delighted, Mary curtsied to Bothwell. "Sir Bothwell, this queen delights at your invitation, but only if you allow me to be a princess and you my prince for the day." Then she ran into his arms and kissed him.

"If you keep kissing me, I may withdraw the offer for a more enticing venture."

Mary pulled away and went into her bedroom to don serge riding breeches so she could ride astride the horse, not sidesaddle. She grabbed a warm cape, and together with the two terriers at their heels, they went downstairs.

Outside, tethered to the hitching post was Mary's favorite horse that she called Madame la Reale, a perfect choice for their hunting romp in the snow. They rode down to the falconer's cottage to fetch two of Mary's peregrine falcons.

At the falconer's cottage, Mary and Bothwell picked two hooded peregrines in a cage. Bothwell chose two pair of leather gloves, along with the mews and field jesses or leashes that restrained the birds. They refused the company of the falconer and rode out of the city to a secluded field. The snow had melted across the field and only remained in the wooded areas.

They both covered their left hands with the leather gloves and attached the field jesses to the gloves. Bothwell placed a falcon on Mary's glove and attached the field jesses with a falconer's knot to the anklet shackle on the falcon, securing the bird in place until the falconer's knot was released, freeing the bird from its shackles. Then they walked out into the field and released the falcons into the air to hunt for prey.

"That was a perfect cast. Your falcon is soaring higher than mine," Bothwell said.

"I was taught by the best," Mary said, bragging on her expertise.

Bothwell approached her. "How good are you at running?" he said in a challenging tone.

Immediately, Mary started running across the green field with Bothwell close behind her. When Bothwell caught her, he tackled her to the ground, and the kissing began. When the kissing stopped, they lay together flat on their backs, watching the falcons soar above them as they searched for suitable prey.

"Sometimes I feel like prey for the falcons," Mary said. "Between Elizabeth and the Protestant lords tearing me apart for their own gain, you are my only support." Mary sat up on one elbow. "You, my love, are my only desire."

Bothwell buried his hand in her hair and gently guided her lips to his. "My Princess Mary."

Their love making was cut short when the falcons returned with their prey. At the end of the hunt, they had three grouse and two rabbits which they gave to the falconer for his supper.

As they left the falconer's house, Bothwell caught Mary's hand. "My princess, would you care to accompany me to a beautiful site just over the hill?"

"Of course, my prince. Lead the way," Princess Mary said and rode by his side across the hill and along the stream to a secluded spot on the top of a large mound.

Mary viewed the mound. Just ahead, on top of the mound were huge stones erected to form a makeshift Celtic cross. The stones were arranged in a circle with thirteen upright stones and one stone in the center of the circle. It evoked visions of an ancient culture.

"Amazing," Princess Mary said.

"It is the Calanais Stone Circle. Let's get closer." Bothwell waved her ahead.

They dismounted at the base of the burial mound and hiked up it to stand on level ground. The stones were gigantic. She and Bothwell walked up next to one of the stones. It was much taller than her or Bothwell, almost eight feet above their heads. They continued to walk around the circle from stone to stone and then to the center stone, which marks the entrance to the burial site. There they stopped.

Mary noticed that the burial mound overlooked a large bay of water in the distance. The afternoon sun shimmered upon the waters, soothing her soul. Peace filled her heart, and she felt invigorated.

They sat for over an hour, absorbing the solace of nature's beauty. Bothwell touched her hand. "Time to go."

Before Bothwell left her at Holyrood, he showed her the bill of attainder. "It seems Lord Lennox is accusing me of Lord Darnley's murder."

Mary read the summons. "You must appear before parliament in five days," Mary said, her cheeks flaming with anger. "How can he do this to you?"

"They are jealous of us," Bothwell said.

"You are a loyal subject who has never been accused of any wrongdoing. You have faithfully kept Scotland safe and reined in the reivers on our borders. You have strengthened our army and worked tirelessly to keep England from invading our shores. This is unfair."

"I know, Your Majesty," Bothwell said.

Mary sighed and turned her back to him so he couldn't see her tears. She realized their lovely day as prince and princess was at an end. Now they were queen and subject.

He walked up behind her. His hands slipped from her shoulders down her arms, folding her arms and holding her tightly. "Do not worry, my queen. I will be gone for a few days to gather supporters who will accompany me to the trial. They will speak for my innocence. When the trial is over, I will return to claim you as my own."

Mary heard the door shut behind him, but she refused to watch him go.

Chapter Thirty

La Rochelle, France – February 23, 1567

Estelle stood in the bow of the boat. Ahead she could see the crenellated walls of Saint Nicolas Tower and the circular chain tower that marked the harbor entrance of La Rochelle, France. A delicious smell of fresh fish wafted through the air. Cheerful chatter came from the docks. She tasted the salty air.

Finally, the boat stopped, and she grabbed Camden's hand. Fergus took Camden's other hand as they pushed their way through a throng of people down the ramp and onto the docks. They found a general store where Fergus bought a cart and a horse. Estelle bought food supplies and blankets. They loaded what few belongings they had and headed to the town of La Rochelle.

Estelle's mother, Anne, had left her a map that showed the way to the house. It was a fortified house located just about three miles outside town. The house had been the home of Violette's parents that they built as a stronghold to plan war strategies for the Huguenot soldiers.

Estelle pointed toward an iron gate. "That's it."

Fergus steered the cart through the iron gates. Estelle found the hidden key over the door lintel and unlocked the door. Camden ran inside. Estelle followed and took the food into the kitchen and set the bags on a table. Fergus gathered firewood and sparked a fire in the fireplace. In minutes the house was warm.

Estelle used the blankets to make two beds near the fire. She made vegetable soup in the iron cauldron in the fireplace. Once everyone was fed, she and Camden settled into one bed, and Fergus slept in the other one. She was tired and weary from their journey and was soon fast asleep.

The next morning, Fergus shook her awake. "I'm going into town for more supplies. Stay here and don't let anyone inside." He handed her a pistol. "If anyone attacks you, pull the trigger." He showed her how to operate the pistol.

She took the pistol and laid it on a nearby table. Once Fergus had ridden through the gates, she pulled out the map that included a floor plan of the house. If she was to find the secret tunnel, now was the time to look for it before Fergus returned. She didn't want him to know about the tunnel.

Camden was still asleep. He would be all right while she explored the house. She found the planning room, and according to the map, the trap door to the basement would be hidden under the rug. The walls of the planning room were covered with maps of France, local cities, and details of fortifications used by the Huguenots. A large table in the center of the room held more maps and detailed plans for attacks on French castles.

She pulled back the floor rug and saw the trap door. She pulled the door open and let it lay back on the floor. Inside, steps beckoned her downward. Estelle eased down the stairs that opened onto a large basement filled with weapons and armor. She studied the map and found the spot where the door that led to the beach was supposed to be, but it wasn't there. For a moment, she hesitated. Maybe she just couldn't see it. She started at the top as far as she could reach and gently pressed along the wall in a horizontal pattern. She repeated the action until she felt a slight indentation that could be an outline of the door. She pressed hard on the wall, and the door popped open just enough that she could slip her hand into the crevice and pull open the door.

She looked around the room for something to prop the door open. She found a heavy block of wood and propped it against the door. It was dark inside the tunnel. She looked around and saw a lantern. She shook it; it still had oil in it. Did she have time to light it?

She decided she had to take the time to light the lantern, so she climbed the stairs and tiptoed to the fireplace, not wanting to wake Camden. In seconds, she had a bright light. In a rush, she ran back to the planning room, down the stairs, and into the tunnel.

The tunnel descended gradually down to the beach for about three hundred feet. As she neared the end, she heard the roar of the ocean waves. In another hundred feet, the exit appeared. She hurried outside. There she found a stable with tack and feed for the horses plus more weapons. She took a dagger and a powder horn for the pistol. Once she had familiarized herself with the surroundings, she rushed through the tunnel to the basement. There she hid the lantern.

Suddenly, she heard Camden upstairs in the planning room crying, "Nanny. Nanny." Then she heard Fergus's booming voice yelling for Camden. Her heart thumped wildly as she climbed the stairs. Camden stood with his back to her playing with a ball. Quietly she closed the trapdoor and lowered the rug. She walked to the door of the planning room and ran headlong into Fergus.

Camden saw her and ran and grabbed her leg. "Nanny."

"What are you doing?" Fergus demanded.

Estelle forced herself to be calm. She bent over and lifted Camden into her arms. "We were just exploring the house looking for a pantry."

"Humph. No need for a pantry, for we won't be staying here very long." Fergus shrugged his shoulders.

There came a pounding on the front door as if someone was trying to ram the door down. Then there was a crash. Fergus rushed to the front door. Estelle heard Fergus shouting, "What are you two doing here?" She had to see what was happening. She pushed Camden back into the planning room and softly closed the door. She peaked around the corner to view the living area.

Two husky men were fighting with Fergus. One man held Fergus while the other man pounded his fists into Fergus stomach and then into his face.

The man who was punching Fergus yelled, "Where is the money? Where is the boy?"

They were talking about Camden. Had Lady MacKenzie sent the men after Camden?

Fergus wouldn't answer the man. Instead, he slung his weight forward and broke free. He headed out the door. As he went, his money bag dropped to the floor, and he kicked it to one side. The two men didn't see the bag. They caught Fergus and dragged him across the yard up to the front gates.

On instinct, Estelle rushed and grabbed the money bag. A gunshot pierced the air. She saw Fergus collapse to the ground. The two men, unaware of her presence, dragged Fergus to the watchman's building outside the gate and threw him inside.

She had to flee. Get away from these men. She grabbed a blanket and snatched what food she could from the kitchen table. She ran into the planning room and locked the door behind her. She caught Camden and flung open the trapdoor to the basement, making sure the rug covered the door behind them. She located the lantern and opened the door to the tunnel. Inside the tunnel, she lit the lantern and slowly began to walk to the exit, pulling Camden along behind her.

Once outside on the beach, she kept walking, praying the two men wouldn't spot her. As darkness fell, she found a small stable where she and Camden could spend the night.

It wasn't safe to stay in La Rochelle any longer. There was no need to return to her desolate shell of a castle in Maubeuge. She had taken all the money from the castle to pay her passage to Scotland to find Camden. With Fergus dead, she was alone. As she lay down to rest, she felt the keys to Violette's apartments jingle in her pocket. First thing in the morning, she would flee to Fontainebleau Palace and sneak into Violette's apartments. She and Camden would be safe there.

Chapter Thirty-One

Edinburgh, Scotland – April 12, 1567

It had been almost a month since Violette and Thomas had been at Huntly Castle, and still there was no word on Camden. The queen hadn't contacted her about Ty's situation. Nothing was happening, so Violette and Thomas traveled to Edinburgh to consult with the queen.

Violette was shocked to see placards displayed around the city, on the tolbooth, at the Mercat Cross where proclamations were made and criminals prosecuted, and on storefront doors. Violette read one of the placards, which said, "Death to Bothwell." Another read, "I forged duplicate keys to Lord Darnley's lodging for L.B." He meant Lord Bothwell.

Violette gasped. "The people are accusing Lord Bothwell of Darnley's murder."

When they finally arrived at Holyrood Palace, the worst placard yet was nailed to the door. On it was a picture of a mermaid or siren wearing a crown and holding a whip above a hare surrounded by swords. The mermaid was protecting the hare with her whip, and no one dared to attack the hare because of all the swords surrounding it.

Thomas said, "It is a warning. The hare is Bothwell's family symbol. The people are accusing Mary of protecting Bothwell even though he may be guilty of murder."

"How humiliating." Violette pushed open the palace door. "Mary must be devastated."

Thomas waited in the gallery while Violette went to see Mary. When Violette entered the audience room, Mary and her ladies were gathered around a table having tea. She approached Mary and bowed.

Mary nodded her accent. “Would you like some tea, Violette?” Mary motioned for her to sit at the table. Mary seemed very calm.

Unsettled by the invitation to tea, Violette sat down and was served raspberry tea. Violette couldn’t look at Mary. Her eyes flitted across the table. The table before her was covered in letters. One she noticed was from Lord Lennox, another from Catherine de Medici, and another from Queen Elizabeth.

Mary noticed her glancing at the letters. “You have come at a troubling time, Violette. Lord Lennox, Lord Darnley’s father, has charged Lord Bothwell with Lord Darnley’s murder. And Queen Catherine and Queen Elizabeth have written to encourage me to prosecute Lord Bothwell. The problem is that there is no evidence against him. All of these accusations are mere gossip and hearsay.”

“But Lord Lennox has charged Bothwell with the crime, hasn’t he?” Violette said.

“Yes, he has, but he refuses to name any witnesses. Of course, Lord Bothwell will face trial, but unless Lord Lennox can produce witnesses, today’s trial will be a ruse,” Mary said.

Mary smiled. “Have you found Camden?”

Violette sipped the tea and placed the empty cup on the table. “Actually no, Fergus refused to return my child. He has fled the country. Yet, Laird Gordon has sent men to search for Camden. It has been almost a month now, and there is no word on their progress.” Violette related the details of her trip to Huntly Castle.

“I will have to consult with Lethington to see if he has any information on Ty and Camden, but now I must leave to attend Lord Bothwell’s trial. I will contact you if anything significant is found.” Queen Mary stood.

Violette realized she was being dismissed and rose to leave. She joined Thomas in the gallery and told him what happened.

“Let’s go to the trial,” Thomas said.

They rode down to the parliament building where it seemed the whole of Scotland had gathered.

Bothwell arrived at court with over four thousand noblemen accompanying him. He placed two hundred soldiers, all carrying arquebuses, around the parliament building and at the entrance and exit doors while the trial was in session.

In the court room, Queen Mary opened the session and then turned it over to the judge. The trial began with the queen's representatives presenting her letter of March 28 asking Lennox to bear witness against the accused. Then they read the indictment against Bothwell. It accused him of "being part of a treasonable and savage butchery of the late king, Lord Darnley, on February 10, 1567."

Bothwell then chose two attorneys, David Borthwick and Edmund Hay to represent him. The judge called Lord Lennox to the stand, but he wasn't present. He had sent his servant, Robert Cunningham, who appeared in his absence. Cunningham said that Lennox didn't have enough time to prepare his case against Bothwell. His absence was due to fear for his life, for he had heard that Bothwell was bringing thousands of men to witness on his behalf. He further added that due to his master's absence, any judgment made by this court session would be in error.

Bothwell's attorneys objected saying that Lennox had requested a "short and concise" trial and produced papers showing his request. Bothwell's attorneys also presented copies of Lennox's letter to the queen, including the one naming Bothwell and Balfour and several others as suspects in the crime. This was the only evidence offered by Lennox, the plaintiff.

Bothwell presented several witnesses that verified his whereabouts on the night in question. With this small amount of evidence, the jury retired to deliberate on Bothwell's fate. They returned a "not guilty" judgment and acquitted Bothwell of the murder, saying there was no evidence presented that supported the charges.

The judge added that if anyone accused Bothwell later and had proper evidence, the judgment of today's ruling would not hinder the new case from being executed. The trial was dismissed.

As Violette and Thomas exited the building, they overheard the people talking about the trial.

"What a travesty of justice," a nobleman cried.

One of the jurors exclaimed, "I refused to vote for fear of my life. Bothwell's men would have killed us if we found him guilty."

Violette sensed the uneasiness in the atmosphere. She felt the people's suspicions that the trial was a ruse, just as Mary had said earlier.

Bothwell exited the building with Queen Mary by his side. He had a servant post a placard on the parliament door stating, "I will fight in a single contest any man that charges me with this murder." He had the challenge posted around the town for all to see.

Mary proclaimed, "Tonight we will present a party at Holyrood Palace to celebrate Bothwell's acquittal."

The people fell silent and slowly escaped to their homes.

Chapter Thirty-Two

Holyrood Palace – April 13, 1567

Mary, Queen of Scots was holding court in the throne room. It was early morning, and the people had gathered early to present their grievances.

After last night's party for Bothwell, which lasted to three o'clock in the morning, her head hurt from all the excessive champagne. With her mind clouded and weariness overtaking her, she gave her deliberations on each issue as best she could.

When a pause came in the court's deliberations, Mary thought about last night's party. Her musicians and choir sang the most popular songs of the day, and she and Bothwell had danced and danced and danced. While he was with her, she never entertained a thought about the vicious placards and the suspicions of her people. She only wanted a few minutes of happiness without being harassed by political innuendoes, but it was not to be.

Around three in the morning, a messenger arrived telling Bothwell that his wife, Jean, had taken ill. They believed that she had been poisoned. Bothwell left to be with his wife, leaving Mary to close down the party.

After Bothwell departed, the rumors spread. "Bothwell has poisoned his wife," one courtier said. "He will do anything to gain access to the throne, even murder. Poor Mary."

Lethington touched Mary's hand to get her attention. "There is one more person requesting an audience. It is Preacher John Knox."

Mary put a hand to her temple. Could she bear to hear his complaint? Finally, she decided to see him, and she braced for the encounter. She nodded to Lethington, who opened the door to the preacher. Mary watched Preacher Knox as he greeted Lethington and walked closer to the throne. He didn't bow or kiss her hand. He waited for her to acknowledge him. He had no grace about him. She found no trace of charm in his person, being disrespectful and often rude when he addressed her, as if he were her superior. His manner was irritating. She was outraged at his belief that she could be forcibly removed from the throne because she did not worship God in the manner he suggested.

Mary opened the audience with a challenge. "I hear you are using your platform in the church to tarnish my reputation before my people. You preach that I should be removed from the throne for my religious beliefs and because I am a woman."

"I believe that women are not fit to rule for I find them weak, frail, feeble, and foolish creatures whom God considers repugnant. It is an act of obedience to God to remove and imprison a ruler who is disobedient to the will of God. Such a ruler should be confined until the ruler returns to her senses. But that is not why I am here today."

Mary clinched her fists, and the heat of anger flushed her face. She gritted her teeth. She decided to end this audience as fast as possible. "Why are you here?"

"I approve of the way you have recently handled matters of business, but your frolics with French fiddlers and married men are not for honest women. Dancing is a form of devil worship. Pleasure in dancing should not come before the Christian faith of the dancers. I fear you were dancing in celebration of your uncle's Catholic victory in France where thousands of Huguenots were recently slaughtered in Rouen."

Mary stood. "You are mistaken, sir. We danced in celebration of Bothwell's acquittal, nothing more. In the future, you are not to preach about me in public but bring your complaints directly to me. Is that understood?"

"Your Majesty, it is not my vocation to stand at your door and beg audiences with you. Rather, you should listen to my sermons."

"Remove Him!" Mary shouted to the guards.

How could a minister be so arrogant? She saw nothing of God in Knox. He sounded more like Moray every time he came to court. Was Moray advising Knox what to say to her so she would be upset and unsure of herself? Violette was right. Moray was trying to undermine her popularity with the people, and he had succeeded. It was getting more difficult for her to handle political matters.

After that fiasco, she retired to her bedchamber and slept through the day and night, barring all visitors, including her ladies.

Chapter Thirty-Three

Ainslie's Tavern, Edinburgh, Scotland – April 19, 1567

Bothwell and the Earl of Argyll met for dinner at Ainslie's Tavern in the district of Canongate on the lower eastern half of the Royal Mile. They had met in response to the request of the Earl of Moray. Bothwell and Argyll were eating when the other Protestant lords arrived. Along with the lords, there were several earls and bishops joining them for the meeting.

Moray had the chairs, benches, and tables rearranged to create a formal meeting. Other diners were invited to finish their food and leave. The tavern door was barred, allowing no one to enter without Moray's permission.

Bothwell remained calm. He expected a fight; tension fumed inside him. He gulped down the last of the ale and stuffed the remaining food in his mouth. He cleaned his fingers on the napkin cloth slung over his left shoulder and laid it on the table. His eyes narrowed as he scanned the room, assessing his enemies. He liked nothing better than a nasty tavern brawl.

Finally, Lord Moray addressed the noblemen. "Tonight, we gather to affirm and congratulate Lord Bothwell on his acquittal."

All the earls, lords, and bishops stood on their feet and hefted tankards of ale, shouting, "Hail Bothwell! Hail Bothwell! Hail Bothwell!"

Bothwell blinked with surprise. And then he hefted up his tankard in return to acknowledge their toast. "All Hail to the Lords of Scotland." All the men chugged their ale.

"We are grateful that you rid us of the intolerable Lord Darnley and henceforth, we support your acquittal against all accusers," Lord Moray said.

Moray looked at Bothwell. "Lord Bothwell, we commend you on

a job well done, but with the death of Darnley, another problem has arisen. We have deprived our queen of a husband. We need a man up to this gallant task. That man would be you, Lord Bothwell."

A bitter taste of absurdity filled Bothwell's mouth. He smirked. "You forget, Lord Moray, that I already have a wife. I am not free to marry another."

The earl of Morton shouted, "That has never stopped you before." He slapped his knee and the entire room burst out in laughter.

Lord Moray quieted the crowd. A rich and warm silence filled the room. "We are prepared to sign our names to a bond that expresses our support for you as king consort of Scotland. All you have to do is convince Mary that your intentions are sincere and have her sign the bond agreeing to our request." Moray pointed around the room. "We, the Protestant lords of Scotland, are a powerful alliance, and we will annul your present marriage if you accept this agreement."

Intoxicating suspense filled the atmosphere. Bothwell sensed the request was a setup, but his arrogance got the better of him, making him think that he could handle any situation. Besides, he wanted Mary, and he deserved to be king over this feeble lot of phony aristocrats.

Bothwell rose and lifted his tankard. "Line up, men. I'm the man for the job."

The men lined up to sign the bond.

Morton whispered in Bothwell's ear. "You are a dead man, friend."

"I'm up for the challenge." Bothwell smirked and called for refills for all. Before Bothwell signed the bond, he read it.

> By the decease of the king, her husband, Her Majesty is now destitute of a husband, living in the state of widowhood which she is willing to continue if her subjects permit. But since, as Queen, her people believe it best that she be coupled with a husband, she is inclined to marry. Since many are opposed to her marrying a foreign prince from a strange nation, Her Highness has decided to yield to one of her own subjects, James Hepburn, Earl of Bothwell—he being one of her most trusted and reliable men in her service. He also has a heart of love and affection for her, and she takes the said earl of Bothwell as her lawful husband and promises that after his divorce from Jean Gordon be ended, Her Majesty shall take the said earl to be her husband.

Bothwell signed his name to the bond next to the signatures of the others present. Now that business was done, each man returned to their own homes. Bothwell decided to visit Mary. When Bothwell arrived at Holyrood, he handed Mary the bond for her to sign. After reading it through, she frowned.

"I know the lords have good intentions, but even if they secure your divorce from Jean, what about the people? You have seen the placards, which display their disgust of you and me being a couple. Our motives are suspect. We are watched closely. If I accept this arrangement, my honor will be tarnished, and regaining the people's trust will be impossible," Mary said.

Bothwell pulled her into his arms and kissed her. He felt her surrender, and that was all he needed. He released her.

"Would you sign the bond if I made it appear that you married me against your will? That you had no choice but had to marry me to save your honor and good name?" Bothwell asked.

"But how?"

Bothwell placed one finger against her lips. "Trust me. I will arrange everything."

Mary smiled. "You always take care of everything. That is one of the things I love about you." Mary took the pen and signed the bond.

"I'm yours!" Bothwell drowned her in passionate kisses, and then he was gone.

After Bothwell left, Mary wondered how he would make it appear that she had been dishonored and had to marry him. But she had no doubt that he would accomplish what he had promised.

He had always done the impossible for her. He secured Scotland's border with England and brought the vicious reivers under government control. No one else had ever succeeded at those two things.

Bothwell was the strongest and most resourceful man she knew. She felt safe when he was near. She only wished that he would come to see her more often. She sighed. She was leaning on him too much. As queen, she needed to be more independent of all the Protestant lords, for they were a ferocious group that lusted for power and domination.

Once she and Bothwell were married, she would revise her Privy Council with wiser men with lesser ambitions.

Chapter Thirty-Four

Marseille, France – April 20, 1567

It was nearly midnight, and Captain Dutetre hadn't fallen asleep as was his usual custom. Tonight he seemed to possess a surge of stamina. Could he know about Ty's plans to escape? They had been playing backgammon for three hours. Ty had let Dutetre win several games except for the last eight games. Would he never tire?

A knock came at the door.

"Enter!" Captain Dutetre yelled.

It was Arno Petit, who was the captain's head mate. "Captain, sir. I need MacKenzie's help below. The wind has calmed, and we need to move closer inland if we are to dock at Marseille in the morning. It won't take long."

"Very well. MacKenzie, return to your bench." Captain Dutetre waved him away. "I'll get some sleep."

Ty followed Petit below deck. Petit directed him to the food pantry. What was he doing? When they entered the food pantry, Petit closed the door behind them. He reached down and pulled out Ty's secret food stash.

"I believe this belongs to you," Petit said. "The cook said he thought some rations were missing. I searched the ship and found this in your secret hiding place. Can you explain?"

When Ty didn't answer, Petit smiled. "I will bargain with you MacKenzie. I won't reveal your escape plans if you will let me come with you."

Ty couldn't believe what Petit was offering him. Was he serious? "Sir, I truly don't know why you would think that I planned to escape. The stash must belong to someone else." Ty lied.

"Don't lie to me, MacKenzie. You are different from the other slaves. You are strong and intelligent. You are competent at backgammon and chess. Only noblemen learn such things. Now can I come, or shall I inform the captain?"

"Very well. Give me the sack." Ty took the sack of food and tied it around his waist. He filled another sack with food for Petit. "Now let's go on deck and check on the captain."

They returned to the deck. Petit eased the door open to the captain's cabin. They both could hear the snores. He eased the door shut. Then Ty slipped overboard into the water, thanking God for the full moon glowing in a cloudless sky. Petit did the same.

Ty looked ahead. He had calculated that the docks of Marseille were about one and a half kilometers away. He moved into a gentle breast stroke and eased away from the galley ship. When Ty was certain they were out of hearing distance, his strokes became more vigorous. He alternated between ten minutes of overhead strokes, ten minutes on his side, and ten minutes of floating with the waves.

Suddenly, Ty heard excessive splashing behind him. He stopped and saw Petit floundering in the water. He swam back to him and caught him under his arms.

"Calm down," Ty whispered in his ear. "Take your time, or you will never make it ashore." Ty released him and began to swim on his side. "Copy my movements."

Petit followed his instructions and swam on his side. After an hour, they had reached the wave crests near the shoreline. Ty stopped, treading water. "We must swim stronger here to cross the crests. Once you are over the crest, you can ride the wave down the other side. Ready?" He asked Petit.

"Yes," Petit answered.

"We will make for the beach away from the docks. We can't be seen there." Ty swam parallel to the shore for a short distance before he attacked the wave crests.

Ty rode crest after crest, stopping between swells. Petit was right behind him. Ty helped Petit onto the shore, and they both fell flat on the sand, gasping for air. Ty stripped off his wet shirt and wrung out the excess water. Before he could put on the shirt, Petit pointed to the golden locket around Ty's neck.

"Where did you get the locket?" Petit asked.

Ty thought a moment. Should he tell him about the locket? What if he gets killed or dies before he made it home to Violette? He decided to confide in Petit. "The locket belongs to my wife. I am to send it home if I escape and write my location on the back of the portrait so she can send help." He glared at Petit. "If I should perish before I get home, will you send the locket to Scotland for me?"

Petit grunted. "Of course, my friend. I owe you a debt for helping me escape with you. I would have never made it on my own. Tell me where to send it."

Ty gave him the address. "Thank you, Petit," Ty said.

"We will need to get some more clothes. We can't walk around Marseille looking like galley slaves," Petit said.

"I know a place where we can get everything we need, that is, unless you want to go on alone." Ty waited.

"No, I will wait until we get the clothes, then I will go find my friends."

"Good. We will have to use as many backstreets as possible until we reach the outpost. Follow me," Ty said. He slipped his shirt on and led the way off the shore. He was headed to the nearest Huguenot camp in Marseille.

Once they reached the Huguenot camp, Ty and Petit were handed a horse, two changes of clothes, boots, and enough money to buy food for a week. Ty took two daggers and stuffed one into each boot.

"Will you ride with me to meet my friends? They live a short way outside Marseille," Petit asked.

Ty hesitated. He didn't want to take any extra time to escort Petit home, but the man was weak and needed help, so Ty consented to go with him. When they arrived at a large manor house on the outskirts of Marseille, several men ran out of the house. Petit rode up to them and dismounted, taking time to embrace each one, and whispered something into the largest man's ear. The man looked at Ty.

Ty turned to ride away, but the men were on him too fast. He tried kicking the men off of him, but they were too strong. Ty fought until one of the men clobbered him on the back of the head, and he fell into darkness.

While Ty was unconscious, Petit jerked the golden locket from around his neck. The big man who had hit Ty on the head glared at the locket. Petit bit the locket.

"It is solid gold." He laughed. "This is worth a lot of money." He put the locket into his doublet for safekeeping.

"What are we to do with your friend?" the big man asked.

"Take him to England and sell him to the highest bidder," Petit said. "Now I'm going to Fontainebleau Palace and see this female 'escadron volant' of which all the men talk."

"The Italian queen's flying squadron? They are spies. They will take all your money." The big man protested.

"I will give it all to them for a few moments of pleasure!" Petit yelled as he rode off to the court at Fontainebleau.

Chapter Thirty-Five

Eilean Donan Castle – April 21, 1567

It was a warm spring day. A light misty "haar" or fog rose from Lochalsh, forming white fluffy clouds as it floated up and across a pink and gold sky. Early morning in the Cuillin Mountains invigorated one's senses. Buds of purple heather and blue thistle peeked out from the garden, their sprouts pushing higher and higher as the weather warmed. Lavender scent blew over the land on gypsy winds, wrapping Violette in its haunting aroma.

The last time Violette had been outside on the lawn was the day Camden had almost fell into the water. Scotty had saved him. Today Camden was missing, and Violette's heart ached for his return. He would be missing her by now. Violette breathed a prayer for his safe return.

She and Thomas were sitting in the garden. They had received two letters—one was from Michael Benoit and the other from Celine, Thomas's sister.

Thomas read both letters before saying anything. "Michael says we would be wise to find Camden as soon as possible. Estelle was distraught and could be dangerous to Camden. Celine says that Estelle is unpredictable and she was living in a castle in Maubeuge, France which belonged to her mother, Anne."

"You were right. It is Anne's daughter. Do you think Estelle took Camden to the castle in Maubeuge?"

"That seems to be our only lead," Thomas said.

"But Huntly's men claim they have no idea where in France Estelle is headed."

"Maybe they are lying to us," Thomas said.

"I wonder how Estelle found out about Camden's inheritance. She must have known about it when she first abducted him. I have been careful not to mention private matters to our servants. She must have known about it before she became his nanny. Or maybe that is why she became his nanny."

"It's possible that Anne could have told her. After all, she has been living in Anne's castle. She must have left Estelle money and other papers of her affairs."

"What should we do now? If Huntly is lying to us, we need to act soon."

Just then, Doralee arrived and met them in the garden. Violette and Thomas rose to greet her.

"What are you doing here, Doralee? You should be enjoying your free time, not worrying about us," Violette said.

"Lady MacKenzie, I had to come. I have important news you need to hear."

"Tell us Doralee," Thomas said.

"My mother works in the kitchens at Huntly Castle. She told me that Fergus is dead. Laird Gordon brought his body home yesterday. They are keeping his death secret. They buried him in the family cemetery at Huntly Castle without a decent ceremony. Laird Gordon was complaining that the woman got away with the child and all the clan's money. They are sending the men back to France to hunt for Estelle," Doralee said.

"Thank you, Doralee. Your message was very important. Now we can decide how to get Camden back." Violette gave her a hug, and then Doralee left.

"I believe that the Huntlys know of Camden's inheritance. Fergus must have told them when he was begging for his life. They will be after Camden. They will most likely kill Estelle," Thomas said.

"Give me a minute. I want to check something." Violette disappeared into the castle. Violette went upstairs to her bedroom and rifled through the bureau where she kept important papers. The money she had saved for Estelle to take Camden to the Netherlands in case she or Ty died or was killed was not in the drawer. Neither were the keys to her apartments in Fontainebleau Palace. She rejoined Thomas in the garden.

"What is it?" Thomas asked. "Something is wrong. Tell me what it is."

"I think Estelle has fled to Fontainebleau Palace. She took the keys to my apartments there. Maubeuge is where she wants us to look for her, but she is taking Camden straight to the Queen Mother, Catherine de Medici who is my mortal enemy."

"But Camden is not her child. How can she possibly make Catherine believe she is his mother?" Thomas asked.

"Look, Thomas. All she has to do is tell Catherine that Camden is her child. She is Anne's daughter and has a rightful claim to her own child's inheritance to nobility. Catherine cannot prove her wrong. Even if she investigates Estelle's claim, she would find no evidence that refuted her claim."

"Then we must go to Fontainebleau and stop her."

Violette sighed. "As soon as I set foot in Fontainebleau, Catherine will have me arrested and thrown back into the Guise Manor Tower. How can I take the risk?"

Thomas put his hands on her arms. "How can you not take the risk? You must go for the sake of your son."

He took her in his arms, and she clung to him for comfort.

Chapter Thirty-Six

Eilean Donon Castle – Later that night

Violette was frightened, more so than she had been when she was locked in the Guise Manor Tower before Mary rescued her. She might never see Camden again. Ty would never forgive her if she lost Camden because she feared for her own safety. She didn't have a choice. She must find Camden and bring him home.

She knelt on the floor before her wardrobe and opened the bottom drawer, which held all of her night gowns. The lavender negligee Sister Maggie had made for her wedding night with Thomas lay on top. She pulled it out and sniffed the erotic scent of violets and ran the silky fabric across her cheek.

Suddenly, she burst into sobs. Why couldn't she have waited for Thomas? No. She had to rush into a marriage with Ty and push Thomas out of her mind. She hated being alone, but now that Thomas was here, she realized her vulnerability.

She had tried to tell him that she couldn't return his love. She had chosen Ty, but Thomas knew she was lying. She had thrown herself into his arms at every turn since he had arrived. He wouldn't wait forever. He would push her to the limit of restraint, and she would yield. She never thought of herself as a promiscuous woman; she wanted to be pure and faithful, but it would take all her strength to fend off Thomas's advances. She folded the lavender gown and put it back into the drawer. Then she pulled out a warm cotton nightshirt. She undressed and eased the shirt over her head and then crawled into bed.

Fear gripped her heart. Going back to Fontainebleau Palace was as good as signing her own death warrant. If she was recognized or if anyone reported seeing her there, Catherine would seek to have her arrested.

She thought about Camden. He must be scared too. She couldn't leave him with Estelle. There was no question, she had to rescue him. She imagined him crying himself to sleep wishing he could come home. He probably had to spend his days in the nursery playing with the other children while Estelle spent her time at dances and dinners to entertain the nobility.

The thing that caused her the most pain was if she didn't find him soon, he would forget her. That she couldn't bear.

There was only one place she could go for true courage and comfort. She took her Bible from the nightstand and began to read. "The Lord is my Shepherd, I shall not want ..."

Chapter Thirty-Seven

Eilean Donan Castle – That same night

Thomas lay in bed awake. Violette filled his thoughts. She was scared. The risk of returning to Fontainebleau could mean arrest and imprisonment, but they had to go.

He truly loved her, but what could he do? Ty is alive and would return eventually. Would she wait faithfully for her husband for the full five-year sentence? He moaned. "I hope not." But if time lingered without Ty being released, he was sure Violette would consent to go with him to Italy.

Ty may not ever escape, or he could get killed. There was no guarantee that he would return before his five-year sentence was completed. After being absent for five years, Violette may not want him back. She was a very impatient woman and needed constant warmth and reassurance of being loved and wanted.

When he returned to Italy, he wanted Violette with him. How could he convince her to forsake Ty and marry him? Then he remembered lying to her about the locket. When Ty escapes, he would send the locket home, letting them know he had escaped and needed assistance. But Thomas had made sure that Violette thought otherwise.

How could he have lied to her? She thought that when the locket was returned, it meant that Ty was dead. All he had to do was keep reminding her of the false meaning of the locket, and she would belong to him. But if she ever discovered his deception, she would never forgive him.

"Oh," he said aloud. "I don't think I can hurt her like that." He wrestled with his conscious for a time, and then he jumped out of bed and headed to Violette's room. He would tell her the truth, apologize, and hope for her forgiveness.

In minutes, he stood outside Violette's bedroom door. He lifted his hand to knock, but he hesitated. Strange sounds were coming from the room. Violette was sobbing. She still loved Ty. He had thought from her actions that she loved him, but he was mistaken. He backed away in anger.

She would not get away from him so easily. If and when the cursed locket arrived, he would find a henchman to do away with Ty MacKenzie.

Chapter Thirty-Eight

Linlithgow Palace, Scotland – April 24, 1567

Mary, Queen of Scots looked outside the palace window to the city below. This was her birthplace, but it didn't feel like home. She always thought of France as her home. Even now, she yearned to be in France. It was there she had learned to enjoy being a queen. She missed the celebrations, the parties, and the dancing. No worries; she had thrived there.

A servant entered to announce that her entourage was ready to depart for Edinburgh. "Thank you," Mary said and headed down to the courtyard. Where was Bothwell? She hadn't seen or heard from him in days. Had he changed his mind about marrying her?

Yesterday, she had brought her son, James VI, to Stirling Castle where he would have his own household under the supervision of the earl of Mar as his guardian. There were five ladies who acted as James's personal rockers of his cradle and musicians who played to soothe his spirit.

As for Mary, public opinion had turned against her and the Protestant lords wrestled her for power. Afraid the lords might kidnap him, she decided to bring him to Stirling Castle, a fortress not easily breached. He would be safe in the custody of the earl of Mar, a trusted friend. She couldn't resist stopping at Linlithgow Palace for the night. Maybe she would find Bothwell in Edinburgh. He hadn't shared his plans of how he would arrange their marriage. He had only asked that she trust him, and she agreed.

Mary's entourage was small, numbering only thirty guards, three of her ladies, and three members of her Privy Council—Lethington,

Huntly, and Melville. Once Mary was settled on her horse, the head guard motioned them forward toward Edinburgh.

The Ainslie Tavern Bond was proof of the Protestant lords' consent for Mary to marry Bothwell. Why was he taking so long?

The entourage was now only six miles outside Edinburgh. Ahead was the Almond Bridge crossing, which they crossed, and then as they rounded a curve in the road, they were met by Bothwell and a force of over eight hundred men with swords raised and ready to attack.

Mary's men pulled their swords. Bothwell rode up to Mary and snatched the bridle from her hands. "Your Majesty, there has been an insurrection in Edinburgh. For your own safety, you must come with me."

One of Mary's men rode up to Bothwell with sword drawn. "Release the queen or be killed."

"No!," Mary cried. "Can't you see we are outnumbered? Besides, Bothwell is a trusted ally." She turned to face her entourage. "There will be no fighting here. Return to Linlithgow and tell the authorities what has happened. I will go peacefully with Bothwell."

Bothwell held on to the bridle of Mary's horse and led her away to the fortress of Dunbar Castle.

When they reached Dunbar Castle late that evening, Bothwell dismissed half of his men, keeping the others to protect the castle if the Protestant lords besieged the castle in an attempt to rescue the queen.

As Bothwell reached up to help her dismount, Mary whispered, "So this is what you had in mind? You plan to ravish me? It is perfect. No one but you could have thought of it."

Once Mary was inside, he barred the castle doors and led Mary upstairs to his bedroom and tossed her on the bed.

Mary smiled and welcomed him into her arms.

Chapter Thirty-Nine

Edinburgh Castle – May 7, 1567

Violette and Thomas rode to Edinburgh Castle when they heard about Mary's return. Many rumors ran rampant throughout Edinburgh that Bothwell had abducted the queen and took her to Dunbar Castle and forcibly raped her. Yesterday evening, he returned with Mary, and they took up residence at Edinburgh Castle, and he had posted over two hundred men armed with arquebuses outside Mary's rooms.

Violette dreaded the visit with Mary. How would she console Mary after being raped? It was a woman's greatest fear. The Protestant lords were doing nothing to oppose Bothwell. It seemed every man was afraid of his power and influence.

When they arrived at Edinburgh Castle, the gates were open, and hordes of people filled the courtyard. Armed guards were posted at all entrances and exits. Would Violette be allowed to talk to Mary? She and Thomas dismounted and tied their horses at the gates. They had to shove their way through the crowds to reach the castle entrance. Miraculously, when Violette told the guards she was a member of Mary's Privy Council, they allowed her and Thomas to enter the castle.

When they reached Mary's audience room, only Violette was allowed to enter.

"I'll wait here," Thomas said and took a seat near the door.

Violette took a deep breath as the guard opened the door for her. Inside, there were several or more ladies tending to Mary. A quiet hush permeated the room. The ladies talked in whispers. Violette spotted Mary sitting frozen in a chilly composure, with Lady Fleming leaning over whispering in her ear.

When Mary saw Violette, she whispered something to Lady Fleming, who immediately ushered all the women outside the room, leaving Violette alone with Mary.

Lady Fleming whispered to Violette, "Lock the door behind us."

Violette locked the door and sat down beside Mary. She rehearsed in her mind what she might say to comfort Mary but stopped. Mary's chilly composure had changed into a light-hearted demeanor, like ice melting into warm sea waters. What was happening? Violette couldn't speak.

Mary greeted her warmly. "I am glad you came, Violette. I desperately need to talk with someone I can trust."

"I am confused," Violette said. "I heard rumors that Bothwell had abducted you and forcibly raped you. I came to comfort you thinking you would be devastated, but I find you happy and well."

"All is well, my friend. I have been longing to tell you the truth about what has happened. I know you will understand."

Mary went to a desk across the room and pulled out a piece of paper and brought it to her "Read it," she said.

It was the Ainslie Tavern Bond. Violette read the bond and realized that the Protestant lords, earls, and bishops of Scotland had suggested that Mary consent to marry Bothwell. All their signatures appeared at the bottom, along with Mary's consenting signature.

Violette instantly knew the lords had wooed Mary into a vicious trap. "Listen, Mary, this is not what you think—"

"Bothwell and I are in love. We want to be married. But with the people's ill opinion of us, we had to find a way to gain their support of the marriage without dishonoring my position as queen. Ingenious, don't you think?"

Violette couldn't believe what she was hearing. "So there was no abduction or rape?"

"No. Whatever happened at Dunbar, I did willingly and without coercion. I am deliriously happy. Bothwell is the type of man I have always dreamed about ruling alongside me. He will help me defy the Protestant lords whom I cannot control alone. Scotland needs a strong man to rule it, and that man is Bothwell. And the lords agree."

"What about his wife, Jean?" Violette asked.

"The Protestant lords promised to acquire an annulment of their marriage. The banns for our marriage will be read next Sunday."

"The Protestant lords can only secure a protestant dissolution of Bothwell's marriage. The Pope will not recognize the validity of such a marriage. You would be considered an adulterer and probably excommunicated. Can you live with such a decision?"

"The whole of Scotland is Protestant. They will accept our union because it will relieve their fear of being ruled by a Catholic monarch. The marriage will instill peace in the nation."

"The people gossip, saying that you and Bothwell planned Lord Darnley's murder together so you two could marry. Marrying him would only confirm suspicions of your guilt."

"The court acquitted Bothwell because he is innocent."

"That trial was a farce. The people feared he would retaliate against them if they testified otherwise. You know he would have killed anyone who defied him."

Mary held up another letter. "I received news from Lord Arygll proving that Lord Darnley wasn't killed by the gunpowder blast but was strangled to death. That proves that someone else murdered him and his servant. Bothwell is only guilty of attempted murder, nothing more."

"The proof comes too late." Violette stood up. "Mary, I believe the lords are trying to trap you into a marriage that will bring disrepute upon you. Moray wants only to be ruler in your stead. I beg you have nothing to do with Bothwell or this marriage. You still have time to repent—"

"Repent. Never. You sound like Queen Elizabeth." Mary picked up a letter and waved it in the air. "She wants nothing more than to humiliate me. She is afraid I will marry a strong, capable man who can wage war on her precious England. Well, I have found such a man. Now she has a real reason to worry about losing her throne to me," Mary said with fire in her eyes.

Violette moved closer to Mary and softened her voice. "Mary, please. You cannot trust Moray and the Protestant lords. They will turn against you as soon as you marry Bothwell, and you will be ruined."

"Bothwell will save me."

Violette backed away. *She hasn't heard anything I've said.* "I hope you are right." She unlocked the door and went in search of Thomas.

Chapter Forty

London, England – May 8, 1567

The jostling of the cart shook Ty awake. A pain shot through the back of his head. He tried to raise his hand to his head, but he realized his hands were tied together. He moved his head to see that he was lying inside a cart. Above him blue skies and clouds passed by as the cart moved past tall buildings bearing signs saying, "Weavers of London."

He was in London.

"Bayard, how much do you think the slave will bring?" one of the drivers of the cart asked.

"Maybe five hundred pounds. We can do more than rebuild our homes. We could build a new one for each of our families."

Bayard pointed forward. "There is the weaver's shop." He drove the cart into an alley. "Check on our passenger," Bayard said.

Ty shut his eyes. A hand shook him rather hard.

"He is still out. He isn't going anywhere soon," Edgar said.

Ty waited until he heard a door slam, and then he cautiously peered over the side. The alley was empty. He pushed himself to his knees and slowly raised his head. When he moved to climb over the side of the cart, pain erupted inside his head. He stopped and waited. Finally, the pain lessened, and he slipped over the side of the cart. He started walking toward the crowds of people on the street.

Some stared when they saw him with hands tied and dressed in pirate's clothes. Before long, they started pointing. He walked faster until he found a tree to hide behind. He drew his dagger from his boot, the one he got from the Huguenots in Marseille, and sliced the ropes, freeing his hands. He checked his other boot for the second dagger, it was still there.

Ahead a group of street vendors lined the street. He bargained with one of them, claiming the dagger was a "genuine Scottish dirk." He sold it to the vendor for thirty pounds. Then he bought some cheese, apples, and bread. He found a bench on the sidewalk and devoured half the food and saved the other half for the morning. Now for a place to spend the night.

He had several hours before nightfall, and he wanted to put as much distance as possible between him and the slave runners. He walked hard for over three hours until he spotted a barn behind one of the houses that lined the street. He slipped past the house and hid in the barn.

When Ty entered the barn, he almost collided with a table, which set just inside the door. Ty groaned. It was a table for the mysterious brownies who were believed to dwell in people's barns. The table was full of bread, butter, cheese, and ale.

Ty was not superstitious, and he was still hungry, so he ate everything on the table. When he left, the people who owned the barn will be pleased that the brownies accepted their offering. Now they could look forward to a bright future.

After the candles in the house went dark, he washed himself in the cow's water trough and rinsed out his shirt and pulled it over his head. The wet shirt felt cool on his skin. He made a bed of straw near the back entrance to the barn and lay down to rest.

As he rested, he thought of Violette and the seductive look in her eyes as she twiddled with a golden locket—

He jolted upright. Where was the locket? He ran a hand around his neck, but the locket wasn't there. He searched the pockets of his doublet, but the locket wasn't there. Petit must have taken it.

Ty lay back on the straw. The locket was all he had that connected him to Violette. Now he had no way of letting her and Thomas know where he was. He cried, feeling lost and alone.

After he regained control of his emotions, he coerced himself to think logically. He needed money and food plus a horse. He thought for a long time but couldn't think of anyone whom he could trust that lived in London. And then he remembered a night in La Rochelle when Violette's friend, Sister Maggie, was forced to flee

France. Her parents wrote her a letter asking her to come home to London. Her family owned a silk shop near Spitalfields. He forgot Maggie's family name, but he was determined to find her. She was his only hope.

Chapter Forty-One

Fontainebleau Palace, France – May 9, 1567

Estelle dressed for the evening festivities. She wore a periwinkle blue dress with puffed sleeves that were slashed, revealing a cream white color beneath and a matching petticoat. A single long string of white pearls hung from her neck to her waist. The low-cut bodice of the dress revealed her creamy skin, and the periwinkle color highlighted her bouncy cinnamon curls, hazel green eyes, and curvy figure.

She felt at home at the Fontainebleau court. Catherine, the Queen Mother, took a liking to her immediately, though Estelle sensed Catherine did so because she felt guilty of having Estelle's mother, Anne, killed by mistake. So they had bonded.

Estelle joined Catherine's notorious *escadron volant,* or the flying squadron, who spent their time coaxing noblemen to reveal their military plots and secrets, which might affect France negatively. Spies. Yes. Estelle found it exciting being involved in espionage. Plus, she loved all the handsome noblemen who fell vulnerable to her charms and whispered their inmost secrets in her ear for a few kisses.

Estelle felt her life was transformed being among the educated women at court. The women here were valued for their contribution to courtly society. All of them were required to be good conversationalists and have knowledge of different languages, history, and poetry. They spoke well and could easily engage their guests with witty speech. These skills drew the attention of noble families from France, England, Germany, and the other surrounding countries. It was high society at its best.

All the ladies were skilled in music, dancing, needlepoint, and embroidering. They used these skills to make gifts and to adorn the lackluster dark rooms of the palace and to enhance the bedcovers, table cloths, and tapestries. Most of them sang and played an instrument, such as the lute or harp.

Queen Margot and Queen Mother Catherine de Medici also set the fashion trends of the day. Catherine made certain that all her ladies were dressed in the height of fashion, which drew crowds of noble ladies to court to view and copy the latest French fashions. Such an atmosphere helped the ladies of the court to find rich and suitable husbands.

Estelle loved being at Fontainebleau. Now she understood why her mother, Anne, had given everything to be part of this glittering court. The air here was intoxicating, glorious, and mesmerizing. After only two months, Estelle was addicted.

Catherine had taken Camden under her wing and supervised his education for life as a nobleman. She was actively searching for a proper wife for Camden, although it would be several years before he reached the age to marry. He was just five. He had a lot of fun friends to occupy his time. He had almost forgotten about Violette.

Estelle smiled. It was good he had forgotten his mother, Violette. She needed to suffer after what she had done to Anne, letting Catherine mistake Anne for her twin sister, Jeanne. If Violette had told Catherine the truth, that she was arresting the wrong person, Anne would still be alive. Estelle still mourned her mother's death. Tears filled her eyes, but she wiped them away quickly. She couldn't go to the party with teary streaks down her cheeks.

Recently, she had met an older man named Arno Petit. He was too old to be attractive, but he had a mysterious air about him, as if he was carrying a deep dark secret. Tonight she hoped to find out what kind of secret was so heavy that it weighed down a man's spirit, even to despair of life.

Just then, Camden walked into her room. She pulled him onto her lap.

"You are pretty, nanny," Camden said as he twiddled her blue earrings. "Can I go to the party?"

"You are going to a party with your friends. You will have as much fun as I will at the grown-up party."

He bowed his head. "I want to go home. I miss my mother. When are we going home?" Camden started to cry and laid his head on her shoulder.

Estelle rang a bell for a servant who came and took Camden to the kid's party. Angry, Estelle took a cloth and wiped Camden's tears from her dress. Why couldn't he love her as his mother? She flew into a rage, swiping all the perfume bottles from her dressing table.

By the time she walked to the ballroom, she had a wide smile across her face. She held her head high as she took the arm of a handsome nobleman who escorted her to the ball. Estelle strutted into the ballroom, turning male heads as she moved onto the dance floor to dance with her current partner. As she danced, she spotted Arno sitting alone. He looked sickly and pale.

She caught his eye and he smiled. He looked as if he might drop dead at any moment. So after the dance ended, Estelle strolled across the room and sat beside him.

"Monsieur Petit, I am so glad to see you." Estelle extended her hand.

Arno kissed her hand and held it as he looked into her eyes. "Could we go somewhere private? I have something important to tell you," Arno asked.

"Of course, sir." Estelle waved for two men to help her. She directed them to a small anteroom two doors away from the ballroom. She was not going to waste all of her time on this man, who appeared to be weakening by the minute. She made sure the men remained outside the door, in the event Arno collapsed.

After Arno was settled on a chaise lounge, she lay down beside him and curled up within his arms. Without any coaxing, he began to tell her his story. "I am dying, milady," Arno said.

"Oh, no. Stay with me," Estelle said, and then she saw death creep into his eyes. She fought an impulse to run. She hadn't come to the ball to entertain death. She came to enjoy life. She forced herself to lay still. He was going to tell her his secret.

"I am a wicked man, Estelle. I have killed men in the past, and they sentenced me to life on a galley ship. I escaped from that galley ship two months ago with the help of a man called Ty MacKenzie."

Estelle gasped and started to speak, but he placed one finger over her lips.

"Let me finish, my dear. I don't have much time left." He took a deep breath. "The night of the escape, MacKenzie helped me as I floundered in the water. I would have drowned if I had been alone. But I sensed he was a good man. If he let me go with him, I would be saved. And I was. But after I was free, I turned on him and handed him over to English slave traders."

Arno reached into his doublet and pulled out a golden locket. "I took this locket from around his neck. It is solid gold, and I hoped to sell it for a good price, but I couldn't bear to part with it until now. I want you to have it."

Estelle held the locket in her hand. "It's gorgeous." She started to put it on, but she sensed there was more to the story.

"MacKenzie said that he must return the locket to his wife in Scotland if he should escape. When she receives the locket, she will send help to bring him home. He was supposed to write his location on the back of the picture in the locket, but I stole it from him before he could write anything down."

"Do you know where he is?" Estelle asked.

Arno nodded. "He is in London, England."

Suddenly, his breaths became shorter. "Please … write 'London' … on the back … of the picture and send it to … his wife … in Scotland … Lady Violette MacKenzie at Eilean Donan Castle."

Arno was overtaken by coughing spasms. "Open it," he said. "Write the location on the back of the picture." The spasms began again.

Estelle ran to the door and sent the men for a doctor, but when she returned to Arno, he was already dead. She screamed until the men returned and took his body away. She found a pen, opened the locket, and wrote "London" on the back of Jeanne's picture. She replaced the picture and snapped the locket chain around her neck. She returned to the ball with thoughts of revenge burning in her heart.

Chapter Forty-Two

Holyrood Abbey – May 15, 1567

Today Mary was to wed Bothwell. Before she went to Holyrood Abbey where the ceremony would take place, she stood in the throne room debating this marriage.

She looked at the pair of throne chairs covered in red velvet. The chairs sat on a raised dais centered near the back wall. Yesterday, only her chair sat on the platform. Underneath the chair cushion was placed "The Stone of Destiny," which Mary sat on when she delivered judgment to her people. The weighty stone was believed to be the actual stone Jacob used while in Haran and the heavens were opened before him, and a giant stairway connected heaven and earth with angels, ascending and descending between the two spheres.

Tomorrow, Bothwell would occupy that chair and rule Scotland with a strong hand. Yesterday, Mary had dubbed Bothwell "Duke of Orkney," making him of a more suitable rank to be the husband of a queen.

As for Mary, her destiny to rule Scotland was fading fast. Once Bothwell became king consort of Scotland, she, the rightful queen of Scots, would be obsolete. Either her half-brother, Moray, would kill them both or Bothwell would destroy all the Protestant lords who defied him.

In her hand, she held another letter from Queen Elizabeth. "Forget this marriage, dear cousin. Concentrate on bringing Lord Darnley's murderer to justice. Bothwell has been implicated, and though you have evidence to the contrary, the people would never accept him as their king. You must not marry him."

She knew Elizabeth was right, but her heart yearned for

Bothwell. His wife, Jean, gave him an annulment, but Mary knew he still visited her on occasion. Mary burned with jealousy. He was already mistreating her, and yet here she was dressed in the black wedding gown of mourning. She would cast off the black gown after the ceremony, revealing the glorious white satin wedding dress that represented the new life to come.

Did she have the courage to hand over her destiny to such a forceful man? Mary was giving up everything, including her throne, her Catholic faith, and her freedom. Suddenly, she felt that the life to come would not be as glorious as she had hoped, for Bothwell would rule her and the country with a strong hand. He gained power, status, and glory.

The church bells began to ring out across Scotland. She must hurry. If she waited, she might change her mind. So she rushed to the Abbey and waited in an alcove until her time to appear.

All four of her ladies were there—Mary Livingston, Mary Beaton, Mary Seton, and Mary Fleming. They carried her white satin train decorated with white roses as Mary proceeded into the chapel and down the aisle. After a few steps, she stopped, her heart in anguish. The sanctuary was empty. None of her people came. In an instant, the full impact of the people's fury and displeasure swept over her. She turned to the left and to the right, looking for a way out. She had been certain the people would support the Protestant marriage. Obviously, she had been wrong. Tears began to fall.

Just then, Bothwell appeared before the altar. He was dressed in royal blue from head to toe, including his hat, which boasted a white feather. So debonair. So confident. So masculine. Her heart melted.

Then Adam Bothwell, Bishop of Orkney, began the ceremony. "Know now before you go further that since your lives have crossed in this life, you have formed ties between each other. As you seek to enter this state of matrimony, you should strive to make real the concepts which give meaning to both this ceremony and the institution of marriage. With full awareness, know that within this circle, not only you are declaring your intent to be handfasted before your friends and family, but also you are speaking that intent to Almighty God. The promises made today and the ties that are bound here greatly strengthen your union. They will cross the years and lives of each soul's growth." He continued, "Do you still seek to enter this ceremony?"

"Yes, we seek to enter."

"I bid you look into each other's eyes. Bothwell, will you cause her pain?"

"I may."
"Is that your intent?"
"No."

"Mary, will you cause him pain?"
"I may."
"Is that your intent?"
"No."

"Bothwell and Mary, will you share each other's pain and seek to ease it?"
"Yes."

"And so the binding is made. Join your hands."
Lady Beaton placed the first cord over their hands.

"Mary, will you share his laughter?"
"Yes."

"Bothwell, will you share her laughter?"
"Yes."

"Bothwell and Mary, will both of you look for the brightness in life and the positive in each other?"
"Yes."

"And so the binding is made."
Lady Beaton placed the second cord over their hands.

"Mary, will you burden him?"
"I may."
"Is that your intent?"
"No."

"Bothwell, will you burden her?"
"I may."
"Is that your intent?"
"No."

"Bothwell and Mary, will you share the burdens of each so that your spirits may grow in this union?"
"Yes."

"And so the binding is made."
Lady Beaton placed the third cord over their hands.

"Mary, will you share his dreams?"
"Yes."

"Bothwell, will you share her dreams?"
"Yes."

"Bothwell and Mary, will you dream together to create new realities and hopes?
"Yes."

"And so the binding is made."
Lady Beaton placed the fourth cord over their hands.

"Bothwell, will you cause her anger?"
"I may."
"Is that your intent?"
"No."

"Mary, will you cause him anger?"
"I may."
"Is that your intent?"
"No."

"Bothwell and Mary, will you take the heat of anger and use it to temper the strength of this union?"
"We will."

"And so the binding is made."
Lady Beaton placed the fifth cord across their hands.

"Mary, will you honor him?"
"I will."

"Bothwell, will you honor her?"
"I will."

"Bothwell and Mary, will you seek to never give cause to break that honor?"
"We shall never do so."

"And so the binding is made."
Lady Beaton placed the sixth cord across their hands.

While Lady Beaton tied the cords together into a knot, the bishop said, "The knots of this binding are not formed by these cords but instead by your vows. Either of you may drop the cords, for as always, you hold in your own hands the making or breaking of this union."

Bothwell and Mary removed the cords and laid them on the altar.

The bishop continued, "Today you are surrounded by your family and friends, all of whom are gathered to witness your exchange of vows and to share in the joy of this occasion. Let this be a statement of what you mean to each other and the commitment of marriage you will make." Then he prayed. "May these hands be blessed this day. May they always hold each other. May they have the strength to hang on during the storms of stress and the dark. May they remain tender and gentle as they nurture each other in their wondrous love? May they build a relationship founded in love and rich in caring. May these hands be healer, protector, shelter, and guide for each other. I will now ask you to seal the vows you share with each other by the giving and receiving of rings."

Bothwell and Mary exchanged rings.

The bishop continued, "The perfect circle of the ring symbolizes eternity. The precious metal came from the ground as a rough ore and was heated and purified, shaped and polished. Something beautiful was made from raw elements. Love is like that. It comes from humble beginnings, made by imperfect beings. It is the process of making something beautiful where there was once nothing at all."

"Bothwell and Mary, on behalf of all those present and by the strength of your own love, I pronounce you married. You may seal your vows with a kiss."

As Bothwell passionately kissed her, Mary trembled and surrendered herself into his care.

Chapter Forty-Three

Spitalfields, London, England – May 17, 1567

It was a foggy, cold morning in London. The air dripped with moisture. Ty could hardly see three feet before him, so he sat on a bench outside a local grocery store waiting for the fog to lift. He had spent the last of his money on a couple of sweet rolls and milk.

As he ate, he watched as the people clashed into each other as they fought their way through the fog. Everyone in town seemed to have a black parasol. Ty figured that it must rain a lot here in London.

For days, he had combed London in search of Sister Maggie's silk shop. He had walked for miles through Bethnal Greens, Whitechapel, and Shoreditch looking for it. There was only one area left to search and that was Spitalfields, and it was miles away from his present location.

He examined his boots whose soles were almost in shreds. He would be barefoot before he reached Spitalfields. He would have to sell his other dagger to buy new boots and hoped he found Maggie soon.

Suddenly, he heard screams. It was a woman screaming for help. Ty gulped down the last roll and swallowed the milk. He walked toward the screams. When the screaming stopped, he had to wait until the woman screamed again to adjust his direction.

"Help!"

Her screams were fainter now, meaning whoever was attacking her had almost overcome her resistance. Ty ran, and as he did, he pulled out the dagger from his boot. Several yards away, a fancy carriage came into view, and three men were ransacking it. One of the men had jerked open the carriage door and snatched the woman out of the carriage and was holding her as the others beat up the driver and tossed her luggage to the ground.

Ty appeared out of the fog and yelled at the men, "Let the lady go!"

The men looked around, and when they spotted Ty, they ignored him.

Ty moved closer and yelled again, "Let the lady go!"

The man holding the woman stopped and drew a pistol. He pointed it at Ty. Before he could shoot, Ty dropped and rolled on the ground up to the man's feet and wrapped the man's legs in a scissor hold, causing him to fall to the ground. Ty stabbed the man in the leg. The man screamed and crawled to the sidewalk, dropping the pistol.

The woman ran, but one of the other men caught her. Ty took the pistol and shot one of the men in the shoulder. The man scurried away.

The man holding the woman held a knife to her throat. "Drop the gun."

Ty dropped the gun. "Let the lady go," he said.

The man backed away, dragging the woman with him. In a flash, Ty threw his dagger, and it struck the man in his shoulder, causing him to release the woman. Then Ty grabbed her and pushed her behind him. The three thieves disappeared into the fog.

Ty turned to the lady, who was in tears. As he neared, she shrank back. "Don't be afraid. The thieves are gone. I won't hurt you," Ty said as he led her back to the carriage. He found her driver and helped him up.

"Thank you, sir," The driver said. "Miss Isobel?"

"I'm fine, Finlay. Thanks to this young Scotsman." Isobel curtsied.

"I've never seen such fine knife throwing," Finlay said.

"I'm a highlander, sir," Ty said in a matter-of-fact way.

"That explains the skill," Finlay said. "Thank you for saving Miss Isobel." He began picking up the luggage.

Ty helped him lift the luggage and secure it on top of the carriage.

Miss Isobel spoke to Ty. "Can we take you somewhere, sir?"

Ty thought a moment. "I am looking for a silk shop run by an English couple, Michael and Maggie. I don't know their last name, but I must find them. I believe the shop is somewhere in Spitalfields."

"You must be talking about Michael and Maggie Benoit. They run the Cartwright Silk Shop in Spitalfields. The queen buys all her silk materials from them. It is about fifteen miles from here. We will take you there," Miss Isobel said.

Finlay whispered in her ear.

"We will be fine," she said to Finlay. Then she turned to Ty. "Let me introduce myself. I am Miss Isobel MacRae of the Scottish Clan MacRae." She held out one hand.

Ty bowed and kissed her gloved hand.

"Ty MacKenzie, milady, of the Clan MacKenzie."

"Oh. Then we are allies. My father often talks of the escapades of the MacKenzie's and the MacRae's. Welcome to London, Laird MacKenzie."

Ty helped Miss Isobel into the carriage as Finlay took the driver's seat.

Inside the carriage, Miss Isobel talked to Ty. "Laird MacKenzie, are you in need of help? You appear to be caught in dire circumstances," she said as she examined his clothes.

Ty told her what had happened to him after escaping the galley ship.

"Yes. I heard about Lord Darnley's murder. I'm sorry for your misfortune. Of course, you must return home to Scotland as soon as possible," Isobel said to comfort him. "I am one of Queen Elizabeth's ladies-in-waiting. If you will come to court, the Queen will help you. Will you come?"

Ty groaned. "I have nothing to wear, milady."

Isobel laughed. "I'll send you some clothes. Then I'll introduce you to Queen Elizabeth. She is giving a ball next week. You can meet her then."

The carriage arrived in front of an English cottage with a thatched roof and pink climbing roses winding up one side to the roof. One knock on the door and Michael and Sister Maggie appeared at the door. Ty jumped down to greet Michael and Sister Maggie, and Miss Isobel waved goodbye.

That night after he had eaten, Ty thought about the beautiful Miss Isobel. Her hair curled into blond ringlets, her eyes the color of the sea, her laugh melodic, and her speech enhanced by her sexy Scottish brogue. A friend and an ally, he would surely attend the ball just to see her again.

Then he felt guilty thinking about another woman when Violette and Camden was waiting for him at home. Since he and Violette had been married, they had never been separated. He wasn't accustomed to being alone. But when he had talked with Miss Isobel, it seemed as if they had known each other for a long time. That was because she was a true Scottish lass who understood how he thought and felt. They were kindred spirits.

He could hardly wait until they met again. For now, he would settle for letting Miss Isobel invade his dreams.

Chapter Forty-Four

Palace of Fontainebleau – May 17, 1567

Violette and Thomas waited in an alcove outside the Palace of Fontainebleau. The courtiers were busy moving the court from Fontainebleau to Amboise. The royal carriage had just departed from the entrance. Violette drew a sigh of relief because she wouldn't have to face Catherine de Medici again. Hopefully, Camden was inside the palace with Estelle.

Thomas caught a page walking by empty-handed. "Boy, I need a carriage and a driver at the front entrance in fifteen minutes." The page nodded and smiled when Thomas handed him four pounds. He rushed off to get the carriage.

Slowly, Violette and Thomas worked through the crowds of courtiers carrying chests and arms full of precious items. They came to Violette's apartment. Thomas listened at the door. Then he slowly turned the door knob. He walked inside with Violette behind him. He looked in each room, but no one was there. He motioned for Violette to join him in the master bedchamber.

A single child's bed was the only furniture in the room. Violette recognized a couple of outfits belonging to Camden. Her heart rejoiced. "He's here. They haven't left yet, for his clothes are here. He must be in the nursery."

Thomas caught her arm, and they entered the hallway. They made their way to the nursery. Thomas pulled Violette's hood over her head. "Just to keep anyone from recognizing you." He gave her a quick kiss on the cheek. "I'm going to find Estelle. Once you find Camden, return to the carriage that will be waiting for you out front." Thomas left.

Violette entered the nursery, her heart beating wildly. Only seven or eight children remained. One young boy stood on a bench looking out the window. It was Camden. Violette felt faint. At first, she couldn't move until Camden turned around and saw her. She knelt down.

Camden screamed, "Maman! Maman!" He ran with arms open wide and threw himself into her embrace.

Violette cried tears of joy as she tightly held her son. "Oh, Camden, I have missed you so much. I'll never let you go again." She bent down to kiss him again and then she stood up. She lifted him into her arms.

Camden kissed her cheek and hid his face in the hollow of her shoulder. "I love you, Maman," he whispered.

"I love you too, my love. I've come to take you home."

"Where are you going with that baby?"

Violette shuddered; she knew that voice. She turned to face Catherine de Medici. "He is my baby, and I am taking him home with me."

Catherine moved closer. She looked at Camden. "Camden, baby, who is this woman?"

"Maman," Camden said and turned his head toward Violette. "Take me home, Maman."

Catherine stepped back.

"Estelle stole him from me," Violette said as she started toward the door, but Catherine blocked her way.

"I hear that your parents, Jeanne and Pierre, are in the Netherlands, ever the champions of the Huguenot cause as you are," Catherine said.

"Yes, I favor the Huguenot cause, but I am not your enemy, even though you are mine," Violette said. "I think you missed the royal carriage. I saw it leave."

"That was my daughter, Margot. She is Queen now. And you thought you could come in and steal your child without having to face me, didn't you?"

Violette didn't answer, she eased closer to the door.

Catherine rattled on. "I hear Mary, Queen of Scots is struggling to keep her country together. I hear she and Bothwell murdered Lord Darnley, is that so?"

Violette pressed toward the door. "Mary is not guilty. Neither is Bothwell. I heard that Queen Elizabeth and Cecil planned his demise."

"Ah." Catherine laughed. "How gullible I am. I actually believed

Elizabeth was after justice. She has not been completely honest with me."

"Now I must go," Violette said and got through the doorway and started down the hall.

Catherine yelled, "Oh, Violette, you may want to know that your husband, Laird MacKenzie, has escaped the galley ship and is in London. He has been seen with a young woman named Isobel MacRae. She is quite a beauty. Have you heard from him?"

She couldn't know that? She was lying to intimidate me. Violette couldn't move.

Catherine walked closer. "You think I couldn't know that. My dear, I have a strong network of spies. I have several in Queen Elizabeth's court, so watch your step. If an incident concerns me, I know about it."

"You're lying!" Violette screamed and ran down the hallway.

Catherine screamed out, "Guards! Guards!" but none came. They had all left for Amboise. Catherine turned and went back to her apartment to wait for her personal carriage to arrive.

Violette carried Camden outside to the carriage waiting at the entrance. She and Camden got into the carriage. The page stood on guard at the door waiting for Thomas. Where was Thomas? He should have found Estelle by now. She held Camden in her lap in case she had to run. She could feel the tension catching in her neck. She rubbed her neck and prayed for Thomas's safe return.

Chapter Forty-Five

Palace of Fontainebleau – May 17, 1567

Thomas convinced a page to find three guards. They followed him to Catherine's office. He found Estelle inside gathering papers and books from Catherine's desk. She stood behind the desk in the outer office. The three guards stood against the door as Thomas approached Estelle.

"I've almost finished packing—"

Estelle looked up to see Thomas. She froze. She let the papers in her hands fall back onto the desk. She straightened.

"Hello, Estelle. Remember me, Thomas Montmorency?"

"Slightly. What are you doing here?"

"I am here to arrest you for stealing Camden MacKenzie."

"Where is Camden?"

"He is outside in the carriage with his mother." Thomas directed the guards to take Estelle.

As the guards descended upon her, she ran into the back room and into the secret room. She slammed the door shut, and the lock clicked.

Thomas pushed the guards aside and ran into the back office. Estelle was nowhere to be seen. Thomas was baffled. Where could she have gone? The room was rather small inside, and cabinets hung on one wall. There was a desk and a chair. There was no other way out. He saw her come into this room, but where could she have gone? He walked out the door and looked on the outside, but the walls were solid, no hidden doors.

That thought resonated in his brain. It was believed that Catherine de Medici had a secret room where she kept potions and hidden files.

Violette had found it and retrieved the deed to his vineyard. There had to be a door here somewhere. But where?

He left the back room and sent a guard to ask Violette where he could find the door. As he waited for the guard to return with an answer, he felt along the wall on the right side of the room starting at the top and working his way down. About halfway down the wall, the guard returned.

"Lady MacKenzie said to look for a lever near the floor on the right wall," the guard said and waited for Thomas's instructions.

Thomas saw the lever, which was almost invisible to the eye. He bent down and pulled it. The wall began to slowly move. It opened the way into a dark room. Immediately, Thomas saw the pentagram drawn on the floor. He posted two guards behind him if Estelle should escape. Then he ventured into the secret room.

There weren't a lot of places for a person to hide. At first, he didn't see her, but as his eyes adjusted to the darkness, he saw her pressed against the far wall.

Estelle waited until he was closer, and then she bolted across the room and straight into the arms of the guards. She struggled when the guards grabbed her arms. Amazingly, she got loose and flew through the office, out the door, and down the hall.

Thomas yelled, "Catch her before she disappears from the hallway."

The guards ran after her. They soon caught up to her and grabbed her by the arms. Estelle was out of breath and couldn't move. The guards dragged her down the hallway with a pistol stuck in her side. Outside, the guards hoisted her onto a horse and tied her hands to the saddle pommel.

Thomas tied the bridle of Estelle's horse to his saddle, and they left for Scotland.

Chapter Forty-Six

London, England – May 24, 1567

Ty sat with Michael and Maggie in their dining room. During the past week Maggie told him about Estelle stealing Camden. Today Maggie held a letter from Violette saying they had found Camden and Estelle at the Palace of Fontainebleau. Camden was safe at home, while Estelle was imprisoned at Edinburgh Castle. Ty sighed in relief. The incident only increased his determination to return home.

Michael had given Ty some of his clothes to wear and offered him money, which Ty refused. "After tonight, I should have the money I need. Miss Isobel is introducing me to the queen. Hopefully, the queen will be generous and grant me a favor."

A servant from the queen had brought Ty proper clothing for the ball tonight. It was a pair of black breeches and doublet with gold accents. He was anxious to see Miss Isobel once more. Ty spent the day helping Michael repair several looms from the silk shop that had broken down. They couldn't proceed with their present orders until the looms were up and running again.

Finally, the carriage came to take him to the ball. Ty grew excited. He had survived betrayal by Petit and escaped being sold into slavery. Now he was going to a ball at Whitehall Palace. How fast life changed.

The carriage clattered down Whitehall Street and stopped at the main palace entrance. A doorman opened the carriage door. Ty eased out the door, taking in the vastness of the great white stone building that shone in the lamplight. It was overwhelming. He had heard the palace had over fifteen hundred rooms that housed its two thousand courtiers and dignitaries.

Ty joined the crowds of people all dressed in their finest clothes, surging through the doors and into the Great Hall where the ball was being held. He looked right and left, staring at the glorious white arches and magnificent paintings of kings and queens of the past. The queen's ladies were dancing with the male courtiers in the center of the room. They danced the fast steps of the Galliard. Ty stopped to watch.

Suddenly, a gloved hand touched his arm. It was Miss Isobel. He gasped. Isobel's blond hair fell to her shoulders in cascading ringlets. Her sea-green eyes sparkled with delight at seeing him. Heat rose to his face. She was lovely.

Ty took her hand and guided her to the dance floor. The musicians were playing the Viennese Waltz. The sweet violin music calmed his senses as he lost himself in the beauty of his enchanting partner.

Isobel broke the spell by reminding him of his appointment to meet Queen Elizabeth. She walked with him to the Audience Chamber where the queen was talking with guests. Ty and Isobel entered the audience chamber. The queen was the first person Ty saw because she stood out from the other courtiers.

Queen Elizabeth was dressed in a burgundy gown accented with an apple-green petticoat, white puffed sleeves with small black swirls, and white ruffs at her wrist. Around her head was a large white ruff that stood up behind her head. A string of creamy pearls adorned her neck, and a long belt with insets of rubies and pearls circled her waist and ran down along the petticoat to its hem.

She possessed alluring dark brown eyes and a cascade of curly golden red hair. Her nose ridged in the middle forming a slight bulge. Her skin was pale white, following the fashion of the day, and her lips were thin. Her hands were graceful with long fingers and nails, and her stately manner complemented a mild tone of voice—a delightful balance of majesty and modesty.

Ty bowed and waited for her to acknowledge his presence. Miss Isobel whispered in the queen's ear. Queen Elizabeth rose and motioned for Ty to follow her. Ty hesitated, looking at Isobel for direction. Isobel nodded, so Ty followed the Queen into a smaller, more private room.

The queen sat down but didn't invite him to do so. Ty stood before her wondering what was coming next.

"Laird Tyson MacKenzie, my lady Miss Isobel told me of your

unfortunate circumstances. I regret your misfortune. Your wife must suffer dearly with you being gone for so long. What can I do for you?" Queen Elizabeth asked in a caring tone.

"Your Majesty, I have been on the run for months now, trying to get back to Scotland. I only need enough money to pay for my passage home, along with a safety pass as well."

Queen Elizabeth smiled. "I see." She paused. "I understand that you are a member of Mary, Queen of Scots Privy Council."

Ty forced himself to remain calm and still. This conversation had turned to an awkward direction. He didn't know why the queen would ask about his position at Mary's court. The queen must have a hidden agenda behind this unexpected meeting.

"Yes, Your Majesty. My wife and I both serve as advisors to Queen Mary."

"I understand that you had knowledge of Bothwell's plans to murder my cousin, Lord Darnley," the Queen said.

Ty shifted his weight to his other foot. Heat rose to his face. This wasn't going well. "Yes, I read the Craigmillar bond but refused to sign it, and I was falsely arrested and condemned to a galley ship."

"Do you believe Bothwell murdered Lord Darnley?"

"Actually, Your Majesty, I examined the murder scene. I discovered that the gunpowder blast did not kill Lord Darnley. He and his servant man escaped the building just before the blast occurred. Lord Darnley died of strangulation, and his servant was suffocated."

"Who do you think was behind the strangulation?"

"I don't know. I only know that Bothwell is only guilty of attempted murder, not the murder itself."

"And your queen, was she Bothwell's accomplice? Did they plan the murder together so they could marry? Of course, you wouldn't know that Mary and Bothwell were recently married on the fifteenth of May," Queen Elizabeth said, all the time watching his reaction.

"I cannot testify to Mary's innocence or guilt. I have no direct knowledge of what happened after I was thrown onto the galley ship, but I believe that Moray and Lethington plotted the murder and used Bothwell as the scapegoat. They were jealous of Bothwell's rising authority and influence over Mary. Plus Moray has tried to take over the Regency before. I understand that he and your man, William Cecil, plotted the late king's demise."

The queen jumped to her feet. "You have strong opinions for someone who has no evidence to support such an accusation."

Ty remained calm. He just ruined his chances of getting help for his passage home.

"However, I will pay your passage to Scotland if you will agree to spend the next month here at court informing my Privy Council of the happenings in Scotland."

When Ty didn't answer, the queen softened her tone. "Please, Ty, work with us. Moray and Lethington work with us." When Ty shook his head, she continued, "We have Scotland's best interest at heart. We want to form a profitable union between England and Scotland under a solidified Protestant government with England at his head. Your queen is headed for destruction. Help us save Scotland for you and your family as well as all the families of Scotland."

Ty couldn't speak. *She is asking me to betray Mary, who is my queen.*

"Your Majesty, your request is unthinkable. I cannot do as you ask. May I leave?" Ty asked.

Elizabeth rang a small bell beside her chair, and in seconds several guards appeared. "I am placing you under house arrest. You will remain here at Whitehall for one month as part of my Privy Council. You will advise me on matters relating to Scotland." The queen ordered the guards to take him to his room.

Ty didn't struggle against the guards.

Miss Isobel waited outside. She ran to his side and walked along with him as the guards escorted him to his room. "What happened?"

"Your queen arrested me."

Miss Isobel stopped and watched as the guards took Ty away. She turned to see the queen exit the audience room. Isobel turned to confront the queen. "I trusted you to help him, not arrest him." Miss Isobel protested.

"I will help him, but first I need his council. He will be released in a month's time as I promised him." Queen Elizabeth walked past Isobel and went back to the ball.

Isobel ran to find out where they were taking Ty.

Chapter Forty-Seven

Whitehall Palace, London, England – May 25, 1567

The next day, Miss Isobel came to visit Ty. Isobel observed the luxurious room which Ty was occupying. Isobel felt the queen had betrayed her by arresting Ty. Now, she was placed in an awkward position, for she had fallen in love with Ty.

Ty stood up from the desk where he had been writing a letter to his wife. Even if Ty returned her feelings, his wife was an obstacle to any relationship she and Ty might share.

Ty handed her the letter. "Would you mail this letter for me? I want Violette to know where I am. Maybe she and Thomas can get me out of this terrifying situation."

Isobel took the letter and put in the pocket of her dress. She wanted Ty to remain here. That would give her a month to make him fall in love with her.

Ty took her hand. "Don't look so sad. I am trusting that everything will work out. Elizabeth wants information from me, but I don't desire to betray Mary. In time, Mary will destroy herself. I just have to wait until that happens, and then Elizabeth will let me go."

"I won't let her forget you." Isobel promised with tears in her eyes. "I will remind her every day of the injustice she is doing to you. Besides, I am Scottish, and our families are allies. I cannot leave you here to suffer."

Ty stroked her hair. "You are so beautiful. I wish things could be different between us, but I am bound to my wife." Ty kissed her goodbye.

Isobel stood outside Ty's door and stared at the letter. If she sent the letter, his wife would send for him, and Isobel would lose her chance to claim him for herself. She only needed a month, and his wife would never know the difference.

A vicious thought occurred to her. What if she just didn't send the letter? If Ty found out that she hadn't sent it, she could just say that she lost it and was afraid to tell him.

She tore the letter to shreds and threw it away. "Sorry, Violette, but I'll take this month to make Ty fall in love with me."

Chapter Forty-Eight

Edinburgh Castle – June 11, 1567

Violette and Thomas approached Edinburgh Castle. There were armed soldiers on either side of the road—two thousand men on horseback, including musketeers carrying muskets, foot soldiers carrying pikes, and the rest armed with claymore swords.

"Those are Morton's men," Violette said. "Queen Mary pardoned him for killing Rizzio. Who is he after today?"

"Probably, Bothwell," Thomas said.

They rode forward through the city gates. Inside the gates, about fifty men on horseback filled the courtyard. Crowds of people watched from the outskirts as Morton yelled to someone in a window on the second floor.

"He is yelling at Lethington," Violette said.

Thomas stopped the horses. "Listen."

"We are here to rescue our queen from that murderous dog, Bothwell. Send him down to us or else meet us in combat." Morton raised his sword high as shouts rose from the soldiers and the people. "We carry a legal proclamation from parliament to take Bothwell into custody."

The people chanted, "Justice for Lord Darnley!" and "Death to Bothwell!"

Morton yelled again, "Tell the queen the Protestant lords have taken Prince James from Stirling Castle. He is in our custody. We are here to execute justice for Lord Darnley."

Lethington answered Morton, "Bothwell accepts your combat challenge."

"Have Bothwell and his men meet us at Carberry Hill tomorrow at first light." Morton swung his horse around and trotted through the crowd followed by his men. They joined the army outside the gates and rode down the Royal Mile proclaiming their purpose to rescue the Queen.

"They have captured Prince James. The Protestant lords could have never taken the prince by force. The earl of Mar must have joined up with Morton. He has betrayed Mary," Violette said. "This doesn't look good for Mary or Bothwell."

"It looks like war. We must leave," Thomas said.

He and Violette rode back to Eilean Donan.

As they entered the castle, Thomas caught Violette's arm. "There is no way that Mary's army can beat Morton's. His troops are skilled fighters. It will be hard for Mary to raise enough soldiers and support to fight Morton on such short notice. This could mean civil war. If Morton wins, the lords may come after you too. They fear you might expose their complicity in Lord Darnley's murder."

"What are you suggesting?"

"I'm saying, come with me to Lombardy. You and Camden will be safe in Italy. You can't stay here any longer."

"Thomas, I am scared, but I can't leave until Mary returns from the battle. I can't desert her, not now."

"Think of Camden. He needs to be in a safe place. If you are arrested, what will happen to him? What will happen to you?"

Violette bowed her head, not wanting to face the truth of which he spoke.

Thomas pulled her into his arms and held her tightly. He whispered into her ear, "I still love you, Violette, even more now than ever before. Come home with me to Italy. It may be years before Ty is released."

Suddenly, they were kissing. At first, the kisses were gentle, but grew more heated. His scorching kisses burned her through and through.

She was at almost at the point of surrender, when Camden screamed "Maman!" breaking the spell. She pulled away, covering her mouth with the back of her hand, shocked at herself because she knew that in a few moments, she would have fallen prey to her desire. She loved him, she always had.

"After Mary returns from the battle, I will go with you to Italy." Violette rushed away to check on Camden.

Chapter Forty-Nine

Carberry Hill in East Lothian, Scotland – June 15, 1567

By first light, Mary, Queen of Scots, and Bothwell, king consort of Scotland, arrived at Carberry Hill under the banner bearing the lion rampant of Scotland and the saltire of St. Andrew. Her troops numbered two thousand. Of these, there were two hundred musketeers carrying muskets, three hundred men armed with pikes, and eight men for loading the cannons.

The Protestant lords were positioned at the base of the hill. They had the same number of forces as Mary. They carried a white banner portraying Prince James praying before his father's murdered corpse and bearing the inscription, "Judge and avenge my cause, O Lord." It was a hot day, and both factions were reluctant to fight, so they tried negotiations.

Lord Glencairn sent a message to the queen, saying, "The lord's quarrel was not with the Crown and if she would abandon Bothwell, they would restore her authority as queen of Scots."

Mary refused, saying, "The lords must yield or face combat, for they were the ones who chose Bothwell as an acceptable husband for me. He was their choice. Tell them to surrender their arms, and I will grant pardons to them for their treasonous acts."

Lord Glencairn rode back to the Protestant lord's company with the queen's message.

Suddenly, Mary remembered Violette's warning, "You cannot trust Moray and the Protestant lords. They will turn against you as soon as you marry Bothwell, and you will be ruined. It is a trap."

Despondent, Mary screamed. "Get me out of this hot sun. I need some shade."

No one responded. There was nowhere to find a shade, for the Protestant lord's troops surrounded the base of Carberry Hill.

The negotiations dragged on through the day, and some of Mary's troops slipped away without a word weakening her defense.

Lord Glencairn reasoned with Morton, but he refused, saying, "I am determined to avenge the death of Lord Darnley."

Bothwell challenged one of the lords to fight him in single combat, but there were no volunteers. Mary was hoping that reinforcements led by Huntly and the Hamiltons would arrive, but none came. By evening, seeing she was outnumbered, Mary asked the lords for their terms of surrender.

A messenger came to her, saying, "If Your Majesty would place herself in the hands of the Protestant lords, Bothwell would be allowed to go free."

Bothwell went to Mary's side. "Don't listen to them, milady. They will take you prisoner and strip you of all authority. Let's break through their ranks and return to Dunbar where we can raise another army and choose a more suitable field of battle."

Mary wouldn't accept Bothwell's solution. She told the messenger, "I too am interested in gaining justice for Lord Darnley. I have neglected my duty as queen by not pursuing the true murderer. I know Bothwell is innocent. I know that some of your lords conspired with Moray to murder Lord Darnley. All must be brought to justice. If that is your true motive, I will turn myself over to you so we can seek justice together."

The messenger returned to Morton telling him Mary's answer.

Morton told the messenger, "If I take Bothwell prisoner and put him on trial, then he could implicate me and others of our group in Lord Darnley's murder. It is safer for us if we let him go. We can always kill him later. Tell the queen, we agree to her terms."

As Mary and Bothwell waited, he handed her a copy of the Craigmillar Bond bearing all the signatures of those who took part in Lord Darnley's murder.

"If there is another trial, this bond bears evidence of all who were guilty of the act. Use it wisely." Bothwell turned and rode away. All of Mary's troops followed Bothwell.

Mary read the names: Bothwell, Lethington, Argyll, Huntly and others. Moray and Morton had also signed the bond.

Dismayed that Moray was among the conspirators, Mary thought that Violette had been right. Moray was just as guilty as all the others. He had used Archibald Douglas to do the dirty deed, but it was Moray and Lethington who had plotted the murder. Moray benefited most from the murder because now it was certain that he would be appointed regent over Prince James.

It was five o'clock in the afternoon when Argyll came and took the bridle of Mary's horse and led her away to Edinburgh. Once Mary was led to join Morton's troops, the atmosphere turned hostile. Cheers rose from the troops, and they chanted, "Burn the adulteress!" and "Burn the murderess of her husband!" Some of the troops poked her with the dull end of their pikes. Others collided their horses against hers, trying to unseat her.

Mary held fast. Her clothes were torn and spattered with mud. If she was unseated, they would tear her to shreds. Morton and Glencairn charged the molesters with their swords to placate them, but with no success.

Morton rode up to her and said, "Welcome to your new position among your subjects." He put Mary under guard like any commoner, humiliating her.

Exhaustion overtook Mary, and she had to concentrate to sit erect with head held high as they entered Edinburgh, where the crowds packed the streets.

The riotous crowds reviled her, calling her "adulteress and murderess," as they shouted "Burn her! Death to the murderess!"

Lethington confined Mary to an upper chamber, posting guards outside the door, at the Provost's residence on High Street.

Outside, Mary heard the mob raging and cursing her. No longer recognized as the rightful queen of Scots, Mary's reign was over.

Chapter Fifty

Edinburgh Castle – June 15, 1567

That evening, Moray appeared on the castle balcony before a cheering crowd.

"Protestant citizens of Scotland, today we have won a great victory. Mary, Queen of Scots has been arrested and stripped of all authority. She is being held under house arrest until she repents of her former actions. Yet still she resists denouncing the murderer Bothwell, who has fled the country. He will be treated as a fugitive and a criminal. On my honor, I tell you, my people, that everyone involved in the murder of Lord Darnley will be brought to justice."

Moray held up a silver casket. "Inside this casket are Mary's love letters to Bothwell. These letters prove Mary's guilt of conspiring with Bothwell to murder Lord Darnley so they could marry and rule Scotland under a Catholic government." Moray paused. "We have thwarted their devious plans."

Shouts and cheers rose from the crowd. Moray raised his hand to quieten the crowd. "Prince James is safe in the custody of the Protestant lords. I have been named temporary regent and will rule under the banner of a Protestant government until Mary divorces Bothwell and regains her sanity."

Shouts of approval filled the air.

Moray continued, "Go home, my people. All is well!" Moray returned the letters to the silver casket. Then he raised his arm proclaiming the Protestant lord's victory over the adulterous, Catholic queen. He turned and went inside.

Tomorrow he would be the reigning regent just as he had planned.

Chapter Fifty-One

Edinburgh Castle – June 15, 1567

Violette and Thomas had been on High Street when Argyll led Mary's horse up to the Provost Residence. The sound of hooves clattering on the cobblestone street rang out as the people held their breaths, waiting to catch sight of Mary, Queen of Scots. Regretful aahs and guilty oohs escaped their lips when Mary appeared bearing the cruel evidence of the Protestant lords' handiwork.

The sight of Mary, a defeated queen, made Violette's whole being seethe with anger and hopelessness. Tears flowed freely down her face. Look what the Protestant lords had done to the most beautiful queen of all time.

Mary rode with her head bowed, her dirty hair tousled and stringy, and tears glistening on her cheeks. Her clothes, no longer glamourous, were ragged and drenched in mud. Her sobs, barely audible in the silence.

After the Lord Provost Simon Preston took Mary inside, the crowd dispersed in the direction of Edinburgh Castle, where Moray was addressing the people. Violette and Thomas followed the people to the castle and heard Moray's victory speech.

"The people appear to be pacified and content with Moray's explanation, but once they learn the whole truth about Moray's involvement in the murder, there will be civil war," Thomas said.

"I agree. It is not safe here in Scotland anymore. Not for us," Violette said.

As she and Thomas started to leave, Lady Fleming stopped her. They hugged, sharing tears of grief over Mary's demise.

Lady Fleming handed Violette a note. "It is from Estelle. She wants to see you." Lady Fleming walked away, sobbing.

Violette looked at the note. "I need to see you. I have something that belongs to you." What could she have that belonged to her? Violette had already reclaimed her clothes that Estelle had worn while at the Palace of Fontainebleau.

Thomas touched her arm. "What is it?"

"A note from Estelle. She wants to see me."

"If you want to go, I'll go with you. It might be something important." Thomas put his arm around her. "We will talk to Estelle and then go home and pack."

Violette and Thomas waited in a small anteroom for Estelle to be brought in by the prison maid. Violette was surprised that Estelle looked healthy and well cared for since she had been imprisoned. Violette's stomach clenched. Something was wrong about this meeting.

The prison maid waited until Estelle sat down, and then she stood near the door a few feet away so they could talk in private.

Estelle spoke first. "I want to see Camden."

Violette squirmed in her seat, she started to scold Estelle, but Thomas put a restraining hand on her arm.

"Estelle, you know we won't allow you to see Camden. He is adjusting to being home again, and seeing you would disturb his recovery."

Estelle looked at Violette. "Madam, where is your compassion for a poor and destitute woman such as I. I love Camden. Please let me see him."

Thomas took Violette's arm, and they stood up. "We are leaving. If you have something else that belongs to Lady MacKenzie, give it to her now," Thomas said.

Estelle stood up. "Of course. I have one more thing that belongs to you, milady." Estelle reached behind her neck and unclasped the golden locket and dangled it before Violette's eyes. "I believe this belongs to you, Lady MacKenzie," Estelle said.

The golden locket. The thought registered in Violette's mind. The meaning struck her like a thunderbolt: Ty is dead.

Violette suddenly released a banshee-like scream and then another and another one.

Estelle dropped the locket onto the table where they had been sitting and covered her ears as Violette continued to scream. "Make her stop. What is wrong with her?" Estelle said.

Thomas grabbed the locket and stuffed it into his doublet pocket. He caught Violette and took her out of the room, leaving the prison maid to deal with Estelle. Before he left, he yelled at Estelle, "What were you thinking? I'll be back to talk with you later."

Thomas took Violette into the hallway and held her until she calmed down. Then he took her home to Eilean Donan and left her in Doralee's care.

Chapter Fifty-Two

Edinburgh Castle – June 16, 1567

The next morning, Thomas woke early and slipped out of the house and headed to Edinburgh Castle. He needed to talk to Estelle. No one was surprised as he was when Estelle produced the golden locket. How did it come into her possession? Had she seen Ty in France? Where was he now? These were all burning questions that needed answers.

What if Ty turns up today in Scotland? How could Thomas explain why he had lied to Violette about the message the locket really carried—the message that Ty had escaped the galley ship and needed help in getting home.

Thomas would have to work fast to intercept Ty wherever he was before he made his way home to Scotland and to Violette. Jealousy burned inside as he calmed the beating of his heart and took on a more controlled demeanor.

Estelle smiled as she entered the room where they had met yesterday. She sat down and stared at Thomas. She didn't say a word, forcing him to begin the conversation.

Thomas pulled the locket out of his doublet and laid it on the table between them. "How did you get this locket?" he gently asked.

"What difference does it make how I got the locket? It belongs to Lady MacKenzie. She has it now. I've returned it as I promised. What more could you want from me?" Estelle stared at Thomas, fear plainly evident in her eyes.

She's scared. Thomas thought. *But she couldn't be more scared than I am. She has nothing at stake here, but I will lose everything if I can't find Ty.*

"Who asked you to promise that you would return the golden locket to Violette? Who?" Thomas asked, still maintaining a calm manner. He didn't want to scare her too much and make her refuse to give him the information he needed. *Use your roguish charm,* he said to himself.

Estelle was shaking now. She must have realized that she had mistakenly given out too much information that raised his suspicions. "I'm sorry I scared Lady MacKenzie. I thought she would be glad to know that her husband was still alive. I hoped she would be happy enough to let me visit Camden. I certainly didn't intend to cause a panic." Estelle twisted in her seat.

She knows about the true meaning of the locket's return. She must have spoken to Ty, Thomas thought. "Did Ty MacKenzie give you the locket?" Thomas asked.

"Not exactly," Estelle said.

"Tell me."

"If I tell you, will you get me out of this cell? There were riots last night in the courtyard. I'm afraid the people will use me as a scapegoat to appease their anger towards the queen. Give me my freedom, and I'll tell you what I know."

She was right—she was in great danger confined in this cell.

"All right. Tell me what you know."

Estelle leaned forward, resting her arms on the table. She told him about the journey to France and how Huntly's men had killed Fergus. Then she told him about reaching Violette's apartments at the Palace of Fontainebleau.

"Eventually, I presented myself to the Queen Mother, Catherine de Medici. I made her feel guilty about wrongfully executing my mother, Anne, whom she thought was Jeanne de la Marne. Catherine let me join her 'flying squadron.' It is a group of beautiful women who enticed the nobility who visited her court to reveal their secret information concerning Spain, Scotland, and England's plans to wage war or to give up the names of spies in our midst. One night, I met a man called Arno Petit who was with Ty on the galley ship and had escaped with Ty. He was dying. Right before he died, he confessed to me that he had turned Ty over to a group of English slave traders. That's when he took the golden locket. He had planned to sell it for the money it would bring, but instead he gave it to me. He didn't know that I knew Ty personally and had been Camden's nanny.

"Arno told me that Ty had asked him to send the locket home with his location on the back of picture in the locket, if he should be killed. Just before Arno died, he asked me to write Ty's location on the back of the picture and asked me to send the locket home. Knowing I might be arrested for taking Camden, I kept the locket to secure my freedom should I get caught. And so here I am, needing leverage to gain my freedom."

Thomas didn't respond.

Estelle looked at him. "It is the truth. Look on the back of the picture. It says, 'London.' That is where Ty is, alive and well in London."

Thomas looked on the back of the picture and noted the location. London was handwritten on the back just as Estelle had told him. He then closed the locket and placed it in his doublet pocket.

"Why do you look upset? You can send help to bring Ty home now that you know where he is." Estelle waited for Thomas's response, but he didn't say anything.

Estelle laughed. "You don't want Ty to come home, do you? You want his wife." She laughed some more.

"Stop laughing. If you want your freedom, stop laughing!" Thomas yelled.

Estelle put on a frown. "You must have told Lady MacKenzie that the return of the locket meant he was dead. There is no other explanation for her hysterical reaction. How do you plan to keep him from coming home?" Estelle waited and when Thomas said nothing, she said. "Forget I asked that question. I don't want to know the answer. Just get me out of here."

Thomas stood up. "You must promise that you won't tell Violette about the true meaning of the locket or that Ty is alive. If you do that, I'll get you out of here today."

Estelle nodded. "I promise. I don't care about Lady MacKenzie and Laird Ty. I just want my freedom. You have my solemn promise."

Thomas went to the prison attendant and paid for Estelle's release. When the prison maid brought Estelle upstairs to the office, he handed her the release papers and enough money for her passage to France and to pay her living expenses for a year.

Estelle thanked him. "You can't keep your actions a secret forever.

When Lady MacKenzie finds out that you have deceived her, she will hate you," Estelle said.

"She is not that kind of a lady," Thomas said confidently.

"I hope she is for your sake." Estelle unexpectedly hugged him, and then she disappeared.

Thomas went to the tavern to find a henchman to track down Ty MacKenzie.

Chapter Fifty-Three

Lord Provost Residence – June 17, 1567

Mary's room at the Provost Residence was elegantly furnished. There was a four-poster bed with down comforters and plump pillows. A stool room set behind an expensive decorative screen in Chinese colors of red and black. The wardrobe was filled with a variety of expensive gowns and lingerie.

The Lord Provost had allowed his maid, Colina, to draw a hot bath for Mary. Colina stood Mary upright and stripped off her clothes and supported her as she sank into the hot lilac scented bath water.

As Colina bathed Mary and washed her hair, she spoke in tender tones. "Don't let the lords worry you, Your Majesty. They can't keep you locked up forever. Keep your hopes alive. Take encouragement from the Scriptures and freedom will come." Colina helped Mary out of the bath and wrapped her in a large sheet she had heated before the fireplace. "Feel the warmth, milady. It will help you sleep well tonight."

Next, Colina treated Mary's wounds and dressed her in a cool white cotton chemise. She led Mary to a chair in front of the fireplace, where she combed out her wet hair. As she waited for Mary's hair to dry, she picked up Mary's rag of a dress and the wet towels and dumped them in a bin beside the door. Then she chose a modest gown the color of blue bird feathers, undergarments, cape, and shoes for Mary to put on after her hair dried.

"Your Majesty, they will be moving you in a few hours to another location. Lochleven Castle, I overheard them say. If you need anything, please tell me now," Colina said.

A cold chill ran down Mary's back, and she shuddered. Lochleven

Castle was the most isolated castle in Scotland. It was run by her enemies, the Douglas family.

"You have been so kind to me, Colina. Would you send a letter for me?"

"I'm not supposed to aid you in any way, but you are my queen. I will be glad to send a letter for you." Colina turned and pointed to a small desk. "There is pen and paper in the desk drawer. After you write the letter, hide it in the drawer and I'll send it out this evening as I go home."

"Thank you, Colina. I'll not forget your kindness."

Colina bowed and left.

After her hair dried, Mary dressed in the clothes that Colina had laid out for her. She found some hairpins and used them to pin up her hair. Then she sat down at the desk to write to Bothwell.

> My dearest love,
>
> They are moving me to Lochleven Castle today. I shiver at the thought of being confined in such a lowly and small place all because I have loved you with all I am—spirit, soul, and body. I have never known such cold hatred. I try to focus on our intimate times together just lying in your arms or running through the green fields where we went hawking last spring. I long only to see the love glowing in your eyes as we embrace. You are my one desire.
>
> Mary

Mary sealed the letter and hid it in the desk drawer as Colina had suggested. She dreaded being moved to Lochleven Castle. She had stayed there in the past but only as a guest. The castle was secluded on a small island in the Lochleven near the Perth and Kincross locale. Surrounded by water, it was accessible only by boat.

The castle was owned by Sir William Douglas and Margaret Douglas. Margaret was Moray's mother. Both Margaret and Moray, Mary's half-brother, claimed that she and King James V were secretly married, but there was no evidence of any marriage taking place. It was just another way her brother tried to justify that he should rule Scotland instead of Mary. He was still considered illegitimate and disqualified to rule. Basically, Mary would be living amongst her enemies.

That afternoon, a party of twelve armed men arrived at the Provost Residence to transport her to Lochleven Castle. Mary silently thanked God that Colina had given her a warm cloak. Even though it was June, the old castle could be cold and damp. She would need it at Lochleven.

When they came to her door, she didn't resist the men but walked freely among them with her head held high as they went downstairs to the horses. When they arrived at Lochleven, Mary made no objection when she boarded the small boat used to cross the loch to the small castle. By the time they reached the dock, the wind had picked up, causing the waves to slosh against the boat. Mary disembarked on her own; none of the men offered a hand, even though they saw her struggling to get out of the rocking boat. She finally placed one foot on the dock to gain her balance. She grabbed a pylon to steady herself as she brought the other foot onto the dock.

The island had changed since her last visit. The grass was higher and scorched by the heat. Many of the flowers hung with drooped heads. The stone curtain wall that surrounded the castle grounds bore moss and lichen deposits. The iron gate, covered in spider webs, showed the evidence of neglect. Did the Douglas family actually live here?

When she entered the castle, George Douglas, Moray's brother, and Willie Douglas, a young orphaned relative, greeted her at the door. Both George and Willie were mesmerized at the sight of her, both bowing before her.

Hope rose in Mary's heart. She knew these two men could be persuaded to help her escape if she charmed them. Besides, she was still Mary, Queen of Scots, and imprisoning her was an act of treason punishable by death.

Margaret greeted her from a distance, frowning as she curtsied, showing her displeasure of having to serve Mary. Mary had expected a cold welcome because she knew that Margaret wanted Moray to rule Scotland. She had always hated having to bow to Mary as queen. There would be no favorable treatment from her.

The rich aroma of lamb stew drifted through the air. "Such a delightful smell. I haven't had lamb stew in a long time. Is that for my supper?" Mary asked with a warm smile.

"Yes," Little Willie said. "I'll bring it to you."

"That's wonderful, Willie. You certainly have grown up since I last saw you. You are almost a grown man."

Little Willie's eyes glowed as he looked down and twisted back and forth. "I'm only fourteen, Your Majesty."

"Go fetch the queen's supper, Willie," George Douglas said. He turned to face Mary. "I'll show you where you will be lodging, Your Majesty," he said to Mary and then motioned for the guards to follow them.

George took Mary to the Glassin Tower at the southeast corner of the castle grounds. It was a round tower with four levels. At the top of the tower was a small library or study. The second level was the bedchamber. The ground floor and the cellar completed the layout of the tower.

Mary walked into the living area on the ground floor. Little Willie burst through the door bearing a supper tray and placed it on the table. Mary ruffled his reddish hair. George caught Willie's arm and pulled him outside. Things seemed pleasant enough until the guards closed the door behind her. The bar was shoved into place, and the lock clanged shut.

Suddenly, the smallness of the room overwhelmed her. Disoriented, Mary turned in circles. The air stifled her breathing as she ran to the nearest window and opened it. The air filtered through the barred window. The cool air calmed her. Feeling weak, she sat down to eat supper.

After supper, Mary climbed the stairs to her bedchamber. A fire crackled in the fireplace to ward away the dampness. One small window, set in an alcove, barely lit the chamber. Mary opened the barred window and sat in the alcove. She wrapped the warm cloak around her and said a prayer for strength. "Lord, my heart is not haughty, nor mine eyes lofty ..."

She gazed out the window until weariness overtook her, and like a lullaby, the cool breeze lulled her into a restful sleep.

Chapter Fifty-Four

Whitehall Castle – London, England – June 18, 1567

Ty chose a debonair silver gray doublet, hose, and hat to wear to dinner tonight. He was meeting with Isobel. Dining with Isobel each evening since Queen Elizabeth had put him under house arrest broke the boredom of the long hot summer days.

Gigantic Whitehall Castle was full of interesting rooms, courtyards, and gardens to explore. Hundreds of activities took place each day, but Ty had soon wearied of the superficial entertainment. He always looked forward to his time with Isobel.

That worried him. Was he falling in love with her? He couldn't let that happen. It would just complicate things, but he couldn't get Isobel out of his mind. She was lovely. She was Scottish and understood him more than any other woman in France or England. He confided in her. He told her his dreams of getting home to Scotland. She often frowned when he mentioned Scotland, so he would change the conversation to suit her.

A knock at the door disrupted those dangerous thoughts, and he watched as the guards opened the door for Michael Benoit. Ty greeted Michael with a warm slap on the back, but Michael seemed distracted, his coal black eyes cool and withdrawn.

"Is something wrong?" Ty asked.

In response, Michael pulled a letter from his doublet and handed it to Ty. Ty's heart thumped in his chest. The letter was to Sister Maggie from Violette. Had she found a way to rescue him from Elizabeth's clutches?

Ty turned his back to Michael as he read the letter. Disappointment filled his heart. *Violette thinks I am dead. What nonsense was this?* Ty looked at Michael.

"I'm sorry, Ty. It seems my sister, Estelle, had the golden locket, and when she returned it to Violette, Violette became hysterical. Violette thought the locket meant you were dead, not that you had escaped."

"Thomas. This is Thomas's doing." Ty slapped the letter on the desk. "He was untrustworthy, but I had no one else to turn to at the time."

Michael looked dismayed.

Ty explained, "I saw Thomas at the docks in Genoa a few days after Lord Darnley's murder. He recognized me, and I asked him to take care of Violette until I could escape. He promised me he would. It made my stay on the galley boat easier, knowing he was watching after Violette." Ty swore. "That rogue, he is trying to claim Violette for himself."

"Thomas regained his memory?" Michael asked.

"Yes. He remembered everything, including how much he loved Violette. No wonder he was so eager to see her again. What am I supposed to do now?" Ty said.

"Estelle must have told her you were dead," Michael said.

"I don't think so. Thomas must have planted a different meaning about the locket in Violette's mind. He told her it meant I was dead. Now he will send a henchman or slave trader after me to prevent me from returning home. He knows I'm in London."

Michael looked puzzled. "What are you thinking?"

"I'm not sure, but I wrote a letter to Violette three weeks ago. I gave it to Isobel to mail for me. She may have destroyed the letter."

"And why would she destroy it? There has been so much turmoil in Scotland. It could have easily gotten lost."

Ty shook his head. "You are probably right. The letter got lost." Ty paused. "What is going on in Scotland?"

"It is rumored that Mary married Bothwell. The Protestant lords didn't accept him as king, so they called him and Mary into battle at Carberry Hill. Moray won the battle and has put Mary under house arrest at Lochleven Castle, and Bothwell fled."

Ty sat down holding his head in his hands. When he looked up he said to Michael, "I fear Violette is in real danger. She possesses evidence of the Protestant lords' involvement in Lord Darnley's murder. She just doesn't know that William Cecil and Queen Elizabeth instigated the plot from Whitehall. She hasn't tried to help Mary get released, has she?"

Michael shook his head. "No, she hasn't. It's difficult to believe that the English government would be involved in such a heinous act."

"It is, isn't it? When I met Queen Elizabeth, she was more interested in the events taking place in Scotland than in helping me get home. She asked me to betray Mary and join her and Cecil in bringing Scotland under English rule. I refused. That's why she arrested me."

"When Sister Maggie and I missed your visits, Isobel told us your confinement was more for the queen's entertainment than an arrest."

Isobel? She couldn't be trusted.

Michael rose to leave. "What can we do to help?"

"I am to be released in a few days. I will come by your house before I leave England. If you will wait a few minutes, I will write another letter to Violette and have you send it for me."

Ty sat at the desk and wrote the letter. He handed it to Michael. He tapped on the door, and the guards let Michael leave. He thought about Queen Mary confined under house arrest. He thought about Violette. Would she turn to Thomas for consolation?

Chapter Fifty-Five

Whitehall Castle – London, England – June 18, 1567

Ty and Isobel finished their dinner and took a stroll in the manicured gardens around the courtyard. The sun was low on the horizon, and the sky faded from red, to orange, to deep purple. The hotness of the day turned into a cool refreshing breeze. Soft violin melodies floated outside, adding a magical tone to the evening. When they stopped to gaze at the rising moon, the scent of honeysuckles from Isobel's perfume wafted through the air. Alluring and enticing, it drew Ty closer, and he almost kissed her. He pulled away.

Isobel laid her hand on his arm. "What is wrong, Ty?"

Ty took a deep breath and told her about Michael's visit. Then he hesitantly posed the question, "Did you mail my letter?"

Isobel turned away, a distant look shone in her eyes.

Ty's lips tightened. "You didn't send it. What were you thinking?"

Isobel responded in a trembling voice. "I'm in love with you. That's what I was thinking. I just wanted some time together so you could fall in love with me, too."

Ty shouted and waved his arms above his head in frustration. "You have endangered me and my family. Violette thinks I am dead. If I can't get home soon, she might marry her former fiancé. I will lose her and my son. They are everything to me." Ty saw tears rolling down Isobel's cheeks. He took her by the shoulders and softened his tone. "Isobel, I have feelings for you too, but our situation is impossible. I have nothing to offer you. You deserve someone who can devote themselves wholly to you, not me. Try to understand."

Isobel pulled away and avoided looking at him.

"As long as Queen Elizabeth keeps me under house arrest, I am safe. When I leave her protection, Thomas, Violette's former fiancé, will send a henchman to kill me or imprison me on another galley ship. He will chase me and destroy me because he wants Violette. He will do anything to keep her. Now that she thinks I am dead, it won't be long before she accepts his marriage proposal. And when she marries him, I will be lost," Ty said.

Isobel turned to him, looking deep into his eyes. "Can't you let her go? The world as we once knew it has changed. You said you had feelings for me. We could share a great life together. We could live in Scotland where the Protestants now rule. You could easily obtain an annulment of your marriage from the Protestant lords. Catholic rules aren't recognized in Scotland or England."

Ty gazed into her face. "I can't answer you now. Once Elizabeth releases me, I will return home to Scotland. If Violette rejects me, than I will return to you. That is all I have to offer."

"That is enough," Isobel said.

Ty drew her close and kissed her. For the first time, his passion for her took free rein.

Chapter Fifty-Six

Eilean Donan – June 19, 1567

Thomas sat outside on a bench near the water reading a note from Alastair Armstrong. Armstrong was a Scottish border reiver and mercenary whom Thomas had hired to find Ty. The report said that Ty was currently under house arrest at Whitehall Palace. He was due to be released on the twenty-fourth, which was just five days from now.

Three days ago, after Thomas had freed Estelle from her cell at Edinburgh Castle, he went to Ainslie Tavern to search for a man to locate Ty. There he had met a young man who told him about Armstrong.

Thomas followed the young man to Mangerton Tower House, a two-story stone farmhouse in the West March or county of Liddesdale, where Alastair was living. The Clan Armstrong was the largest and most powerful clan of reivers in Scotland. They practically ruled the West March of Liddesdale. They protected the border between Scotland and England and also stole cattle, sheep, and horses from county dwellers and relatives alike. That was how they made their living.

Alastair was a formidable man of tall stature and heavy weight. He wore the typical reiver's outfit of a "jack"—a leather quilted garment stuffed with horn and other hard objects to deflect sword pricks—over long sleeves, short breeches, and leather boots. On his head was a "steel bonnet" made of metal. He rode a "hobler" horse that could easily traverse the surrounding boggy and hilly terrain. He carried a sword, a dagger, and a long lance. Alastair eagerly accepted the assignment from Thomas.

Thomas returned the note with instructions to capture Ty as soon as possible and detain him until further instructions. He put money into the envelope and road into the town of Dornie and handed the communication to the young man he had met at the bar. That would keep Ty occupied for a while until he could decide what he wanted to do with him. He needed a more permanent solution.

Ever since Violette saw the locket, she had moped around the house, talking only when spoken to and wearing a forlorn look. She needed time to adjust to the news of Ty's supposed death. When Violette asked him about getting Ty's body returned home, he deceived her with another lie. "Ty was stabbed and thrown overboard by his assailant. The incident took place in very deep waters, so his body cannot be found or returned home. That is what Arno, Ty's friend, told Estelle before he died. He was likely the one who stabbed him and stole the locket."

"You are right," Violette said. "Not having his body makes the loss more difficult for me."

"Maybe this will help." Thomas handed the golden locket to Violette.

Violette clasped the locket around her neck and didn't ask any more questions.

Chapter Fifty-Seven

Eilean Donan Castle – June 19, 1567

Every time Violette thought about Ty being dead, frustration and pain leapt from her soul like a volcanic eruption. How could he be gone so quickly? Somehow, she couldn't trust what Estelle said about his death.

Surely, there is more to his death than being stabbed and tossed overboard. Maybe the Protestant lords had him killed because he knew too much about their part in Lord Darnley's murder. That was the real reason they arrested Ty in the beginning.

She knew too much about the Protestant lord's plot to murder Lord Darnley too. It was dangerous for her to live in Scotland. She would have to go with Thomas to Italy. She went into her bedchamber and began packing.

As she packed, her wedding ring kept getting into her way. She stopped to gaze at it. It was a stunning diamond ring in a gold setting surrounded by four amethyst stones that complemented her violet eyes. It reflected Ty's passionate nature and determination to win her love. She also remembered leaving Thomas's garnet betrothal ring on the ground at Vauclair Castle. She wished she had kept it. Wearing it would show Thomas that she was trying to get past the devastation of Ty's death.

Suddenly, the golden locket caught her attention. She had been wearing it ever since Thomas had returned it to her. Thomas didn't like her wearing it, but she couldn't part with it just yet. The wound of losing Ty was too fresh.

As always, the golden locket comforted her in hard times. She promised herself she would dispose of it as soon as she was ready to let go of Ty. Maybe she would give it to her younger sister, Bella. She smiled at the thought.

Next, she moved to the wardrobe to pack its contents. Inside, she found a ring box in which she placed her diamond and amethyst wedding ring and packed it in the trunk, along with her clothes.

The ring would be a keepsake to remind her of Ty.

Chapter Fifty-Eight

Edinburgh Castle – June 20, 1567

Moray sat on the throne. Even though his appointment was temporary, soon it would be permanent. He had Mary confined where she could not challenge him. Now all he needed was her abdication. Then he would reign as regent until Prince James was of age.

He loved Edinburgh Castle. For centuries, it had been the seat of the most powerful rulers of Scotland. Moray could feel the power seeping into him as he sat upon the Stone of Destiny. The ancient castle could be seen from anywhere in Edinburgh. It rested on the high craggy hill of Castle Rock situated in the center of the city. The castle actually rested upon the smaller of two ancient volcanoes, a virtual fortress surrounded by medieval walls. It could only be approached from the East.

Today Moray was meeting with Lethington to discuss the next step in getting rid of Mary so she would no longer be a threat to Moray and the Protestant lords' rule of Scotland. Moray reluctantly left the throne room and walked to the nearby St. Margaret's Chapel to meet Lethington.

Outside, it was a sunny hot day with clear skies—an omen of sorts affirming Moray's spirit. The coolness of the chapel felt good on his skin as he entered the sanctuary. Lethington was seated on the front pew.

Moray sat down beside him. "Is anyone else here?"

"I've seen no one. It is safe to talk."

"Great. How is the queen doing?" Moray asked.

"She is not happy and constantly complains about not having her own bed brought to the tower. She is nervous. I believe she is planning an escape."

"We must obtain her abdication. Then if she wants to escape, it will mean nothing, for she will be totally powerless."

"I fear she will resist giving up her throne no matter what we do."

"I know my sister. If Prince James is threatened, she will surrender to our plans rather than deny him his legacy as king of Scots."

"Queen Mary is a vulnerable woman who wants only to enjoy being at court. She loves hawking, riding, and dancing at parties. She has no desire for politics, but she is stubborn about claiming her rightful place as queen of Scotland and England. It will be difficult to get her to agree to abdicate her throne. The throne is her life," Lethington said.

"I have a plan. Tell Morton to gather several lords he can trust. Let him threaten Mary's life and the life of her son if she refuses to abdicate."

Moray stood to leave.

"You can't murder the queen," Lethington said.

"What is murdering the queen? I've already murdered the king."

"But—"

"Get it done quickly. I'm tired of waiting."

Chapter Fifty-Nine

Lochleven Castle – June 24, 1567

Mary settled into her bedchamber alcove to read Bothwell's letter. His words of love and encouragement poured off the page into her heart. He was trying to gather troops to arrange her escape.

"Be patient my love. I am on my way to Denmark-Norway to gather your supporters. It won't be long until we are together again. Then I will hold you in my arms and never let you go. I am still the king consort of Scotland.

Yes. He was still king consort of Scotland and she was still queen of Scots. Yet today she didn't feel like a queen. She had been imprisoned for over a week, and she was getting impatient. She had been working on little Willie Douglas. He seemed to be more receptive to her cause than George. Yet George was falling in love with her. Each day, he sought her out, and they spent hours talking.

Their talks were usually about George and his ambitions, which included a coveted position at court. She promised him that position as soon as she could get back to Edinburgh Castle. It wouldn't be long before he succumbed to her charm. She missed her ladies and the singing and dancing at Holyrood Palace. Those were happy times, but they were long gone now.

As the loneliness seeped in, she heard a familiar voice downstairs—a voice that sparked memories of Rizzio's murder and chilled her bones. Dread like a dark cloud descended upon her, and she waited as footsteps of several men tromped up the staircase.

She quickly tossed Bothwell's letter into the fire and stood erect as the door opened and several Protestant lords entered the room.

Lord Morton led the pack. The sudden urge to scream rose, but she swallowed it hard and stood steadfast.

Mary noticed a paper in Lord Morton's hand. He moved closer to her while the others barred the door with their bodies.

"What is that?" Mary asked as she pointed to the paper.

"This, my dear—"

"You will address me as 'Your Majesty.' I am still your queen," Mary answered defiantly.

The other men bowed, but Lord Morton remained still.

"Your Majesty," he said, "these are papers for your abdication."

"You are wasting your time, gentlemen. You tell my brother I have no intention of abdicating. If that is what you are here for, it is time for all of you to leave."

Morton moved closer. "We came for your abdication, and we are not leaving until you sign the paper." He motioned to the others to move closer.

Two of the men grabbed Mary by the arms and held her fast. Mary struggled to free herself.

Morton pulled a pistol from his belt and held it to her stomach. "I've heard you are having Bothwell's bairn. It would be horrible if I accidently pulled this trigger all because you refuse to submit to the will of the people, now wouldn't it."

Mary refused to back down. "I will have all your heads chopped off for treason." She fought the captor's grasp, but the men tightened their hold on her arms.

"I don't think so, milady. You forget we have your son, Prince James. Would you deny him his rightful succession to the Scottish throne?"

A heavy silence filled the room as they awaited her response. Mary's resolve weakened. Her head bowed like a rose wilting under the scorching sun, and she became faint.

"I thought not." Lord Morton handed her the pen.

Mary straightened. "Remember, all of you, that I sign this paper against my will while under extreme duress." Mary signed the papers. Legally, she was no longer the queen of Scots.

After the men left, she vomited and almost fainted before she got to her bed. She had experienced some weak spells during the past few days, but she wrote them off to the hot weather. She had suspected a baby but couldn't believe it.

A thrill of joy ran through her heart. She was pregnant with Bothwell's child. That gave her something to live for.

Little Willie brought up her supper. When he saw her condition, he ran to tell George. Little Willie sat by her bed day and night.

A midwife was called. When she delivered two dead fetuses, only then did Mary began to recover.

Chapter Sixty

Whitehall Palace – June 24, 1567

Ty met with Queen Elizabeth in her audience room. She and Cecil were the only two officials present. Ty stood before the queen and bowed. He remained quiet and composed, knowing how the queen liked confident men.

The queen spoke first. "Laird Ty MacKenzie, I want to express my condolences upon the abdication of Mary, Queen of Scots. I admire your loyalty and your willingness to suffer on her behalf. Today I am releasing you from my custody, as I promised. I am giving you a safe travel pass to Scotland, along with funds to pay for your passage aboard the next ship to Scotland."

A page handed Ty the documents.

"Thank you, Your Majesty." Ty bowed again. "Your kindness is overwhelming."

The queen blushed. "If, at any time, you wish to join my Privy Council, I would welcome your appointment. You have proven to be a kind, confident, and loyal servant."

"Thank You, Your Majesty."

"I know you are anxious to return home, but seeing that your ship doesn't sail until tomorrow, I would like for you and Miss Isobel to join tonight's festivities. Will you stay?"

Ty swallowed hard. "Of course, Your Majesty. I would be delighted to stay."

The queen nodded her head and dismissed him.

When Ty exited the queen's audience chamber, Isobel was waiting for him. Ty smiled. "I'm free, but she asked me to stay for tonight's gala, and I agreed. Will you go with me?"

Isobel hugged him. "I would love to. It may be the last time I will see you." Isobel frowned.

"Don't say that. I won't be gone but just a few weeks." Ty pulled her close.

Isobel trembled in his arms. "You don't know that. Violette may not let you return to me." Isobel pulled away.

"Please cheer up. I don't want to leave you in tears. I couldn't bear it."

"I'll try."

Ty hugged her again. "Meet me at the Great Hall tonight."

"All right. I'll wait for you at the door," Isobel said.

Ty returned to his room. He started to pack what few clothes he had, but most of them were too formal for life in Scotland. Instead, he decided to wait and pack his old clothes which he had left at Michael and Sister Maggie's house. He couldn't leave London without saying goodbye to them.

Later that evening, Ty dressed in a black doublet and trousers. He donned a black captain hat, made stylish by King Henry VIII. The hat was made of soft felt. It had a rounded crown and narrow brim. Ty thought the hat made him look debonair. He smiled as he thought of tonight.

Leaving Isobel behind troubled him. Yet he must see Violette and confront Thomas. He had no choice but to return to Scotland.

Ty found Isobel waiting for him at the door of the Great Hall. Tonight, she was lovelier than he had ever seen her. She wore a long white silky dress. Her long soft hair was braided and interlaced with sparkling diamonds and rubies. Spiral blond curls surrounded her warm radiant face. A ruby necklace adorned her neck. Ruby and diamond bracelets on her wrists made her sparkle from head to toe.

Ty's heart skipped a beat. He took a deep breath as she clasped his elbow. How could he leave her? He must go home to Violette and Camden.

Through the evening, he danced with Isobel, dreading the moment they would stop and move to the banquet table for dinner. He immersed himself by focusing on the moment—a moment he could relive in his memory for years to come. Before the dancing stopped, his heart was broken into pieces.

As the dancers dispersed, a tall, rugged man caught Ty's attention.

The man looked out of place among the suave courtiers. He simply didn't belong here. The large man looked up and nodded his head. Ty knew him, but from where did he know him?

The page announced dinner, and Ty took Isobel's elbow and maneuvered her to their assigned seats at a long banquet table near the queen's dinner table. The familiar man sat at the nobility table facing Ty. A cold feeling swept over Ty, and his stomach clenched. He recognized Alastair Armstrong, the border reiver and mercenary from Scotland's West March district. He must be the one Thomas had chosen to hunt him down and kill him.

Ty surveyed the room until he spotted Russell, one of the guards that had protected him for the past month. They had developed a friendly relationship, and even played cards together on occasion. He could trust Russell. He made an excuse to Isobel and stood up. Before he could go too far, Russell was at his side. He followed Ty out the door into the hallway.

"Laird Ty, where are you going?" Russell asked. Then he hesitated. "I'm sorry, Ty, you are a free man now, and I have no right to question your movements."

"You are fine, Russell. Can you help me with a problem?"

"Of course, sir. What can I do?"

"There is a large, heavyset man from Scotland who is here to arrest me. Have you noticed him? He speaks with a Scottish accent much like myself."

"In fact, I did notice him. He seemed very nervous."

"Isobel and I are going to get up and leave in a few minutes. The man's name is Armstrong. He will try to follow us, can you detain him for a while?"

"Anything for you, Laird MacKenzie. I will get several guards to help me. I'll accuse him of insulting the queen and throw him in a cell, but I can only keep him for forty-eight hours."

Russell instructed a page to bring Isobel's carriage around to the side door.

"Thanks. My ship sails tomorrow at two o'clock. I'll be gone before he realizes it."

Ty returned to the table and sat down beside Isobel. She was talking to a young gentlemen on her left. When she finished she continued eating.

Between bites of veal and green peas, Ty talked to Isobel. "We must leave."

"Why?" Isobel gulped down some peas.

"There is a mercenary from Scotland seated across the room. I recognized him as Alastair Armstrong a border reiver and mercenary. I believe Thomas sent him to detain me, or even kill me."

Isobel stared at Ty, faking a smile. "What do we do?"

"Finish your food. While the dessert is being served, we will get up and go out the side door. Your carriage will be waiting for us. My guard, Russell, will detain Armstrong until we can get away."

Then the kitchen maids, all dressed in black and wearing white aprons and caps, entered the dining room with trays of apple pie topped with whipped cream.

Ty waited until the maids stood in front of Armstrong. He tapped Isobel's arm, and they got up and exited out the side door. Ty took her hand, and they ran down the hall to exit the palace. Outside stood Isobel's carriage. They jumped inside. Finlay cracked the whip, and the carriage lunged from a full stop into a canter.

Neither of them spoke as they rode to Sister Maggie's house. They just held hands, and Isobel laid her head on his shoulder.

Ty was the first to speak. "My ship leaves tomorrow afternoon. Will you be at the docks to say goodbye?"

Isobel groaned. "I can't bear watching you sail away without me. Can't you reconsider?"

"I have to let Violette know I am still alive. I promise that we will see each other again. Tell me you will be at the docks in the morning."

"Yes, my love, I will be at the docks." Isobel promised.

The carriage stopped at Michael and Sister Maggie's house, and Ty went inside to pack.

Chapter Sixty-One

London, England – June 25, 1567

By noon, Ty had his one bag packed. He dressed in his highlander clothes, which Maggie had washed for him. As a precaution, he stuck his pistol in the waistband of his breeches and a dagger in his boot. The reivers were a flexible bunch. He dared not underestimate Armstong's ability to escape from the castle guards. He wanted to be prepared.

Maggie fed him one last meal, an English meal of potatoes, beef steak, bread, and tea. Ty longed for shepherd's pie and ale, but he could wait until he got home. Isobel's carriage arrived around one and he said farewell to Michael and Sister Maggie. He told them they didn't have to go to the docks with him. They understood that he wanted to say goodbye to Isobel alone.

When they arrived at the docks, Ty and Isobel sat alone inside the carriage. With curtains drawn, Ty kissed away her tears, and they shared their last embrace. No words were needed. Words would only bring more tears, and he might not have the strength to leave, but he knew he must go. At the sound of the ship's bell, Ty left Isobel and walked down to the docks, not looking back. In minutes, the ship set sail. Ty watched as the London shores faded from sight, his heart heavy laden with longing.

Isobel cried all the way back to Whitehall Palace. She went straight upstairs to her room and took a hot bath and changed her clothes. She covered her red eyes with makeup. Then she went to the dining hall for an early dinner.

She sat in the dining hall for about an hour, not wanting to go upstairs. She thought of Ty. What was she going to do? She couldn't let him go. Isobel got up to leave when she heard a ruckus outside the dining hall near the front entrance. Out of curiosity, she walked toward the noise. She caught a glimpse of three guards struggling with the Scottish mercenary Armstrong.

Armstrong must have escaped the cell, and now he was fighting with the guards, and he was winning. Isobel watched as he put down two of the guards single-handedly. He was strong. He was asking the guard where Ty lived. The guard told him that Ty had sailed on the afternoon boat to Scotland.

Armstrong crashed through the entrance doors, and Isobel ran to the guards to see if they were all right. All of them were bruised. She found three other guards to help the men up and into the sickroom. The guards were supposed to hold Armstrong for forty-eight hours, yet Ty had only been gone for two hours. If Armstrong followed him, he would overtake Ty before he could get to Eilean Donan. Isobel had to do something.

Queen Elizabeth just entered the dining room, and she caught Isobel by surprise. "What is wrong, Isobel? Won't you join me for dinner?"

"I'd be delighted, Your Majesty." Isobel followed the queen to her table. She ordered dessert. Over dessert, she told the queen what had happened.

"My dear, you must go after Ty. The border reivers are a dangerous and cruel lot. They will surely kill him and torture him. My guards are at your disposal. The crown will pay your passage, so go pack your clothes." The queen waved her away and ordered dinner.

Isobel did as the queen suggested, and within the hour, she was on a boat to Scotland. She acquired the help of two of the queen's guards to rescue Ty. She had family in Scotland who were also suited for the dangerous task of raiding the West March to rescue Ty. The MacRaes had fought for the MacKenzies many times in the past. They were ruthless and well able to save Ty from the Armstrongs.

Isobel felt better already. At least, she was doing something to help Ty. She could hardly wait to see him again.

Chapter Sixty-Two

Eilean Donan – June 26, 1567

Violette, Thomas, and Camden were having dinner.

Camden was five years old now and had insisted he eat "at the big table" with Violette and Thomas. So Camden began joining them for dinner each night. The cook was exasperated because Camden would only eat beef stew, bread, and milk. Every night, he ate the same thing.

Violette enjoyed having Camden at the table. He was growing up so fast. Thomas had eagerly taken on the role of substitute father. Camden called him Uncle Monty. At least with Camden at the table, Thomas couldn't prod her with romantic advances and beg her to marry him. She wasn't ready yet.

While Camden played with his stew, Thomas admired her appearance. "You look lovely tonight. The violet dress complements your eyes." Thomas paused. "I notice you are wearing the golden locket."

Violette laid down her fork and looked at Thomas. "I know you don't like for me to wear it. It has caused a lot of bad feelings in my family, both for me and my mother, but I can't let it go just yet." She laid her hand over his. "I am trying, Thomas, to put the past behind me. It just gets difficult sometimes."

Thomas kissed her hand. "I can be patient." He kissed her hand. "I see you aren't wearing your wedding ring."

Violette pulled her hand back. "I packed it away with the other things we are taking when we move."

"I'm glad. It shows me you are trying to put the past behind you."

Camden started tossing bread into his stew and making strange noises.

Violette said, "Camden stop. Finish your stew."

Thomas stood up and said to Camden, "Do you want to help me feed the horses, Camden?"

Camden jumped up. "Yes, Uncle Monty. Can I brush Jules's coat?"

"Sure thing." He took Camden by the hand, and together they headed down to the stables.

Violette helped Doralee with the dishes. By the time she finished, Thomas had already put Camden to bed. Before he went to sleep, Violette crept upstairs to tuck him in. She sat down on the edge of the bed and took Camden's hand. She kissed him on the forehead.

Camden wiped away the kiss. "I'm too big for kisses, Maman."

"Oh, of course. I forgot," Violette said and smiled.

Camden looked into her eyes. "Where is my dad?"

Violette was shocked. At first, she didn't know how to respond. Camden had never shown any signs of missing Ty, or even knowing that he once existed. Violette reached for her Bible. "Camden, your dad died … which means … that even if we can't see him … he is with us in spirit."

Violette read the verse from Ecclesiastes 12:7 "'Then shall the dust return to the earth as it was, and the spirit shall return unto God who gave it.' Camden your dad is with God, and he is fine. It is just that he can't be here with us except in spirit. We keep him alive here … in our hearts." Violette touched her heart and she touched his. "Here in your heart."

"Is Uncle Monty my new dad?" Camden asked.

Violette nodded. "Uncle Monty is your new dad. He loves you and will take care of you and me from now on."

Camden raised up and hugged her neck. "Good night, Maman." He lay down and closed his eyes. Before she left the room, he was asleep.

Thomas was waiting for her downstairs in the Billeting Room. He was playing billiards by himself. When she walked in, he looked up.

She told him about Camden's question. "He asked me the same question and I told him you would have to answer it for him."

"Coward," Violette said with a smile.

He lay down the cue stick and moved toward her. Violette's heart jumped with joy as he pulled her into his arms and gently kissed her.

After several steamy kisses, he released her. "Have you got everything packed?"

"Yes. I am excited about leaving. I fear we are not safe here, and I want to see Mary." Violette moved to the sofa. "It is unforgiveable that the lords forced her to surrender her throne. I've heard about the riots in Edinburgh, and they seem to be getting worse."

Thomas sat down beside her and put his arm around her shoulders. "We will leave early in the morning at first light. No one will notice us leaving. We will find a place to stay near Lochleven so you can see Mary."

"I hate to abandon her, but I worry about staying here too long. When Moray is appointed regent, he will be looking for me. I must think about Camden's safety as well as mine and yours."

Thomas smiled. "Mary will understand."

"Have you written Celine letting her know we are coming?" Violette asked.

"Yes. She is excited to have you. She is preparing a special bedroom for you in shades of violet. Plus she is excited to have another woman in the house. She always enjoyed your company and longs to see you again."

"I'll do my best to help with the wine parties. When I was at Fontainebleau, she helped me learn all of my duties as a lady-in-waiting. Now I can return the favor." Violette smiled.

Chapter Sixty-Three

Lochleven – June 27, 1567

At dawn, pinpoints of daylight peaked above the horizon. An indigo sky boasted fluffy white clouds. The music of birdsong floated on the wings of the wind, and the trees murmured as a breeze filled the woods.

Thomas was up first. He carried Camden in his arms and laid him in the back of the cart, which was packed and ready to go. He covered Camden with a blanket. He returned inside to get Violette.

Violette was saying goodbye to Doralee. "Thank you for watching after the castle. Please make it your home, for I don't know when we will ever return."

Doralee shed a few tears. "I will miss you, milady."

"And Camden will miss you as much as we will," Violette said.

Thomas touched her arm, reminding her they must leave. Violette hugged Doralee once more and then followed Thomas out the door to the cart. She checked on Camden, and he was fast asleep. Thomas helped her up onto the driver's seat and took his place beside her. Then he gently nudged the horses forward.

"It is going to be a hot summer day," Violette said.

When the cart crossed the footbridge, and turned south, Violette looked back at Eilean Donan Castle. A haunting sense of longing and farewell filled her heart. What a satisfying life she could have had if not for Ty's death. Would she ever get rid of her heart's yearning to see him just once more?

Thomas touched her arm, bringing her back to reality. Violette smiled. How could she be sad? She was with the love of her life. She moved to sit closer to him, and Thomas put one arm around her as they made their way to Lochleven.

As the day wore on, Camden woke up and came to sit beside Violette. They reached Lochleven around noon and began their search for a place to stay. They found a small cottage inn near the docks with a view of Lochleven Castle across the loch on the island beyond.

What a lonely place. She saw the Glassin Tower where Mary was imprisoned, and her heart ached for Mary. It was almost as if Violette could feel Mary's anguish floating on the waves, longing for freedom like a bird in a cage crashing against the cage bars. Such beautiful creatures were made to be free.

Violette spent a restless night. She feared the worst for Mary. She dreaded leaving her, but it was too painful to see her in such dire circumstances.

Chapter Sixty-Four

Edinburgh, Scotland – June 27, 1567

When Ty arrived in Edinburgh, he rode to Holyrood Palace to see if Mary was confined there. When he arrived, the palace courtyard was empty. He had no trouble entering the palace and walking up to Mary's audience room.

The audience room was empty except for boxes stacked to one side. He looked into Mary's bedchamber. Her bed had been dismantled, and the pieces laid on the floor. Her wardrobe emptied of clothes, and he looked for her jewelry box.

A page startled him. "You won't find any jewelry or anything of value. The lords ransacked all of the queen's belonging and sold her expensive jewelry at auction. It seems that Queen Elizabeth won the bid for Mary's lustrous black pearls. In fact, she and Catherine de Medici bid against one another, and Elizabeth won."

"Is it true she abdicated?" Ty asked.

"Sadly, yes. The lords threatened the life of Prince James. She had no choice."

"Where is she being held?"

"At Lochleven Castle."

Ty knew Lochleven. It was a small island approachable by boat or ferry. As soon as he could, he would check on Mary, but first he had to get to Eilean Donan and secure his family. He couldn't do anything here. He headed home.

As he rode home, he thought about Armstrong. He hadn't noticed anyone following him, but he had forty-eight hours before Alastair would be released. He had plenty of time to get to Eilean Donan.

A few hours later, he arrived at the village of Dornie. As he approached the footbridge leading to Eilean Donan, he noticed several strange men guarding the bridge. Armstrong was thorough; he had planned ahead.

Ty rode past the bridge and out of sight of Armstrong's guards. He tied his horse in a copse of trees and slipped into the water. He swam across the loch and came up behind the castle. Were Armstrong's men holding Violette and Camden hostage?

Ty crawled up on the bank and checked the pistol in his belt; it was ready to fire. He pulled out the dagger from his boot and then entered the castle near the keep. All was quiet. He didn't see any guards. The guards were only at the bridge. Slowly, he made his way to the kitchen, hoping to find Violette or Camden. Instead, he found Doralee. Before he could grab her, Doralee turned around and saw him. She screamed.

He ran up to her and clapped his hand over her mouth. "Doralee, it is me, Ty." He waited for her to calm down. Her eyes were wide with fear. "It is really me. I am taking my hand from your mouth. Don't scream or Armstrong's men will hear you and come to investigate." Ty waited until she nodded.

He took her by the hand and pulled her along behind him. He walked to the window to check on the guards, making sure they hadn't heard Doralee scream. He looked for the guards. They hadn't moved. "They didn't hear you. We are safe."

He looked down at a small table with a basket that held the mail. The letter he had sent by Michael was lying in the basket, unopened. *Violette still thinks I am dead.* Fate seemed to attack him from every side, thwarting every attempt to get to Violette. He released Doralee's hand and sat down in a nearby chair, holding his head in his hands.

Doralee knelt before him. "Are you feeling all right, Laird Ty?"

Ty didn't look up. How could he be all right? He would never be all right until he found Violette. Doralee was slow in answering his questions. He had to calm down. He took a few deep breaths.

He kept her quiet until they walked to the inner courtyard where they could talk.

"Where are Violette and Camden?"

"You are supposed to be dead. You gave me quite a fright." Doralee wiped a hand across her face and smoothed her apron. "This cannot be happening to me. I didn't recognize you in those highlander clothes. I'm sorry, Laird MacKenzie. Give me a moment."

Ty paced around the courtyard. Time was running out. "Please Doralee, where are Violette and Camden?"

"They left with Thomas—"

"Where did they go?"

"Oh my. They left for Italy."

Ty shouted, "No! Are you sure?"

"I am very sure. It was too dangerous for them to remain here after the queen abdicated. Lady MacKenzie was afraid the lords might come after her. She had no choice. She had to leave. She said they would never be back."

Ty's heart pounded in his chest. He was too late. They must have left about the same time he had arrived. "Doralee, it is important that I find Violette and Camden today. Can you remember which route they took when they left? Were they planning any stops on the way?"

Doralee frowned. "I almost forgot. Lady MacKenzie said she had to visit with Mary before they sailed for Italy. They planned to spend a couple of days in Lochleven."

Ty sighed with relief. "Thank you, Doralee. I can catch them at Lochleven."

"Please be easy approaching Lady MacKenzie. She might die of fright when she sees you."

Ty instructed Doralee to go home and do not return to Eilean Donan unless he came for her. "Don't tell anyone you have seen me. Promise me."

"I promise I won't tell a soul." Doralee promised.

"I'm leaving now. Give me twenty minutes and then tell the guards you are going shopping. Then go home. Can you do that for me?"

"Yes, Laird MacKenzie. I'm glad you are still alive. I don't like that Thomas guy. I don't see how Lady MacKenzie could marry such a rogue."

Marriage. Ty shook his head. Anger heated his face. He had to get to Lochleven.

Chapter Sixty-Five

On the road to Lochleven – June 28-29, 1567

Ty slipped back into the waters of Lochalsh and swam across the loch until he reached the location where he had tied his horse. He used a bamboo reed at times to swim underwater until he passed the guards posted at the causeway.

The water was warm, and swimming was easy. He could see the shadows of the men reflected in the water as he swam past. When he reached the water's edge, he gently lifted himself out of the waters to avoid making noisy splashes. He untied his horse and led him into a sunny spot so Ty could dry off.

In minutes, his clothes were dry, and he mounted his horse and rode away from Eilean Donan. As he passed the guards, they noticed him but didn't move. Then a black snake scurried across the path, nearly touching his horse's feet. The horse whinnied and reared up, catching the guard's attention. Then shots rang out, and the guards rushed to their mounts.

Ty kicked his horse in the side, pushing the horse into a gallop. Ty lay low on the horse's back and whipped the horse to gain more speed. He looked back. The guards were gaining on him.

Ty decided he couldn't keep this speed for too long; his horse was already snorting. He looked for a place to hide. Up the road not far past the city of Dornie was a road that led off to the left. Not many men knew of the road unless he was well acquainted with the highlands. When the road came into view, Ty jerked the reins to the left and rode about a mile into a wooded area near a logging camp. He positioned himself behind a small hill and waited for the guards to appear.

Five minutes later, the guards entered the logging road. They stopped just before the hill where Ty was hiding and then they split up—one went to his left, the other to his right. Ty smiled. Splitting up was a grave mistake for the guards. He slipped down closer to the road, and when the first guard came by, he tackled him. Together they fell to the ground, and Ty pounded him with his fists.

The guard rolled him over and was on top of Ty. He was heavier than Ty expected, and the guard had a stranglehold around Ty's neck. With much effort, Ty used one hand to force the guard's hands from around his neck. With the other, he struggled to reach the dagger in his boot. Once he had a hold of the dagger, he stabbed the guard in the leg. The guard fell to his right.

Ty stood up just in time to be tackled by the other guard. The second guard slashed Ty's left arm, just barely missing any veins. Ty gritted his teeth and pulled his pistol from his belt and shot the second guard in the leg.

The wounds Ty had inflicted were not fatal to the guards. He mounted his horse and rode back to the main road. Once on the road, dizziness overwhelmed him, and he almost fell off the horse. He had to stop and take care of his wound, or he would never make it to Lochleven.

A mile down the road, Ty pulled over and took off his shirt. He took a drink from his water pouch and then poured some of the water over the wound, washing it clean. He fetched the knife from his boot and cut a bandage from his shirt and tied it around the wound as tight as he could manage. He was getting weaker by the moment. He must find a place to rest.

The sun was low on the horizon. Nightfall was just three hours away. He would never make Lochleven tonight. He couldn't go back to Dornie for fear of running into the guards. There could be more guards in the city.

That's when he remembered about the holy wells. Most of the Scots were superstitious and claimed that the holy wells could heal wounds, diseases, and other maladies. Ty thought the idea that water from the holy wells could heal was ridiculous. But he was in trouble. If he didn't get his wound bound up, he could easily die.

He knew where one well was located not far from here. It was the Grews Holy Well in Perthshire just a few miles ahead. He could be there before nightfall. He pulled his horse back on the road and kicked it in the side. When Ty crossed into Perthshire, he rode down into the woods behind the church. The well was down in a ravine. Not wanting his horse to fall, Ty dismounted and took the bridle and led the horse down the steep ravine.

At the bottom of the ravine, he saw the stream on his right, and another three feet down he saw the well. The well formed a small pond of water as its spring bubbled up and overflowed. Around the well were flowers and holy relics. This was it. There was a ritual to be followed, and Ty searched his memory for the details, but his mind wasn't cooperating with him. He looked around the area for clues that might jog his memory. Nothing but trees, grass, and rocks filled the ravine.

Then one tree caught his eye, and he walked over to it. The tree was a clootie tree, for it was wrapped with strips of cloth. You dipped the cloot or cloth into the well, applied it to your wound, and then tied the cloth around the tree trunk. Then you made a wish for healing. When the material disintegrated, your wish came true, and you received your healing.

Ty looked at his arm. The wound didn't look good. He decided to try the healing ritual, so he returned to the well. He cut two more strips from his undershirt, took one cloot strip, drenched it with the holy well water, and then applied it to his wound. Once the wound was clean, he went back to the clootie tree and tied the strip around its trunk.

He made a wish. "I wish for my arm wound to be healed."

Then he returned to the well and dipped the other cloot in the holy well water and tied it as a bandage around the wound. Then he cupped his hands and splashed the cool efficacious waters on his head and body. He took dry clothes from his saddlebags and put them on.

Next, he fetched his horse. A few feet down the valley, he found a small cave. He would spend the night here. He glanced at the bandage. The wound was tightly bound and he was no longer dizzy. He had plenty of strength to unsaddle his horse and tether him with a long length of rope just inside the cave opening. He retrieved a blanket from his saddlebag and, using the saddle as a pillow, lay down to rest.

As darkness engulfed the land, he could hear the tawny owl hoot his song in the treetops. A distant sparrow hawk muttered his cry to the moon. Suddenly, sleep overtook him.

The next morning, he woke with the sunrise as red hues formed the horizon and gold crests warbled their morning song. He jumped up and saddled his horse and headed up the ravine. As he passed the clootie tree, he looked at his cloot; it had deteriorated into almost nothing. Ty took off his shirt and removed the bandage. There was no sign that he had ever been wounded. Astonished, he sat for several minutes and voiced a prayer of thanks to God for his healing.

"Let's go to Lochleven," Ty said to his horse and spurred him up the hill.

Chapter Sixty-Six

Lochleven – June 29, 1567

As Violette ate breakfast, a young boy walked into the cottage inn. He wasn't more than fourteen, but he had reddish hair and a smile on his face.

"Willie, what would you like for breakfast?" the cook called out to him. Willie gave the cook his order and then he walked over to Violette.

"Are you here to visit Mary, Queen of Scots?" Willie asked.

"Yes, I am. I am one of her ladies."

"Good. She loves visitors."

About that time, the cook brought Willie his breakfast. He sat down at a nearby table to eat.

Thomas and Camden had ridden into town to get more supplies, leaving Violette alone for a few hours to visit with Mary.

Violette finished her food and walked outside to wait for the ferry to take her across the loch. As she waited, Willie came to stand beside her. Willie introduced himself and told her he lived on Lochleven Island. He bragged about taking care of Mary. He said that he was helping Mary plan her escape.

"Lady MacKenzie, we have it all planned out except for one detail—how to disguise Mary so she can reach the ferry? Would you like to help?"

"What can I do? I'm not sure I can help her."

"Actually, you are perfect for the one detail I told you about. I have some old clothes that the washerwoman wears when she comes to the island to do the laundry. All you have to do is put the old clothes on underneath yours and give them to Mary before you leave. They only search visitors on their way out. Will you do that for Mary?"

"It sounds dangerous? If I am caught, I could be arrested." Violette protested.

"It is possible but not likely. My brother George will help you get away. He is older and much bigger than I," Willie said.

Violette agreed. It was the least she could do for Mary now that she was leaving her.

Willie's face lit up. "Come with me." He led her to a small storage room beside the cottage inn. He pulled the old clothes out of a bin. They smelled like they had been freshly washed. He handed her the clothes and turned his back.

Violette slipped the thin clothes underneath her own. Outside, a bell rang, warning them that the ferry had arrived.

Chapter Sixty-Seven

Lochleven Castle – June 29, 1567

When Violette and Willie arrived at Lochleven Castle, he led the way up the bank and through the iron gates. Just inside, a bush of heavy-headed pink roses drooped under the summer heat. The brown grass on either side of the walkway was up to their knees. The door to the main house stood ajar.

She followed Willie inside to the kitchen. A lady dressed in a plain blue-gray dress greeted her with a curtsy.

Willie introduced her to Lady Douglas, and Violette returned the curtsy. "I've come to visit Mary. I am one of her ladies. May I see her?"

"Of course, milady. I will fetch George to show you to Mary's room," Lady Douglas said.

"I can show her Aunt Margaret. I know the way," Willie said.

Lady Douglas smiled. "Of course, you can take Lady MacKenzie to the tower. Please remember to stop here before you leave. We are required to search everyone that visits Mary."

"I will," Violette said and followed Willie out the door.

The Glassin Tower was smaller than Violette expected. Surely, they weren't holding Mary there, but to her horror, they were. Frustration bombarded her spirit until her head felt light and dizzy. She forced herself to appear pleasant as Willie lifted the bar across the door and pushed it open.

Mary jumped up from her chair when she saw Violette. She ran and hugged her as tears welled in her eyes. "Oh, Violette, it is so good to see a friendly face." They hugged again.

"Thank you, Willie for bringing my friend to visit." Mary rustled his hair.

Mary motioned to a nearby chair. "Come and sit with me—"

"You should take Lady MacKenzie upstairs to the library. You would have more privacy there." Willie suggested and rolled his eyes at Mary.

"I'm sorry. I forgot my manners. Come with me." Mary led the way up the stairs to the third floor to a small library.

Hundreds of books lined the circular walls. Only one small window set in an alcove barely lit the room. A stone fireplace set to the right of the window. In front of the fireplace was a square table with four chairs. Mary pulled out one chair and directed Violette to the adjacent chair. Violette stiffened.

Mary grabbed Violette's hand. "I'm so glad to see you, Violette."

Violette whispered, "I have on extra clothes for you."

"Oh?" Mary said and stood up. She waved Violette to a large chest and opened the lid. She pointed to the chest.

Violette quickly removed her outer garments and took off the washerwoman's clothing. As she pulled off each piece, Mary stuffed the clothes into the chest, hiding them under her own clothes. Then she quietly closed the lid.

Violette told her about Ty's death and how Thomas had regained his memory. "I am leaving Scotland and going home with Thomas. At least, Camden and I will be safer there. I wanted to see you before I left."

"I'm sorry about Ty. He was a brave man and gave me great advice."

"What of Bothwell?" Violette leaned closer.

Mary sighed. "I had hoped he would help me escape. He went to Denmark-Norway to gather my supporters, but he was arrested at the port of Bergen in Norway because of lacking proper exit papers from Scotland. He is being detained at Rosenkrantz Tower until he is brought to trial."

"That seems like a trivial charge to warrant imprisonment," Violette said.

"It is until you understand who arrested him." Mary waited. "Rosenkrantz Tower belongs to Danish Viceroy Erik Rosenkratz. He is Anna Throndsen's cousin."

"Bothwell's first wife?" Violette asked.

"Yes. She has had a warrant for his arrest on record since the day he left her. I fear she wants revenge. Bothwell spent her dowry, and now she wants him to repay her plus give her an annuity." Mary could hardly talk now for the tears. "His last letter was difficult to read. His pain and anguish dripped from every page. It is easier to bear one's own pain than to bear the pain and suffering of the one you love." Mary burst into sobs.

To comfort her, Violette suggested a walk along the island. Mary quickly agreed.

Outside, the sun hadn't yet reached its peak, so it was warm rather than hot, casting short shadows along their path. They walked along a line of trees near the water and toward the dock. They walked arm in arm as old friends.

At the end of the line of trees, Violette could see the docks across the water at the cottage inn. As she watched the faraway inn, a man appeared on the docks. He was waving and shouting, but Violette couldn't hear what he was saying. Suddenly, her heart clenched; the man wore highlander dress, and his blond hair was a little long as it blew in the breeze. He looked like Ty? Violette gasped. Her hand disengaged from Mary's arm and flew to her chest.

"What is it?" Mary asked as she shook Violette's arm.

Violette looked at Mary. "I'm not sure." When Violette turned to look again, the man was gone. She felt the golden locket against her chest. The locket reminded her that Ty was dead. She sighed.

She turned back to Mary. "It was nothing."

Chapter Sixty-Eight

On the Road to Lochleven– June 29, 1567

Alastair Armstrong was a patient and methodical man. He didn't leave anything to chance. When Thomas Montmorency hired him to apprehend Ty MacKenzie, he had taken the job seriously. Before he left for London, he had stationed four of his men at the docks in Edinburgh plus four men at the causeway at Eilean Donan Castle.

If MacKenzie evaded Alastair in London and made it back to Scotland, Alastair's men would intercept him in Edinburgh. Or if MacKenzie was fortunate to get to Eilean Donan, his men would intercept him there.

That was exactly what had happened. When Alastair arrived at the docks in Edinburgh, he met with his men who were stationed there. Evidently, MacKenzie had eluded capture at the docks and headed to Holyrood Palace.

When Alastair got to Holyrood Palace, MacKenzie had already left. He consulted a page who had talked with MacKenzie. The page had told MacKenzie about Mary being moved to Lochleven.

"Did you see which way MacKenzie rode when he left the courtyard?" Alastair asked the page.

"No," The page answered.

I've lost him, he thought.

Alastair had a reputation for always getting the man he hunted, yet MacKenzie had thwarted being caught twice. Were his skills lost to him? Or maybe he was getting too old to handle being a mercenary. He certainly didn't want knowledge of his failure to reach the other reivers in West March. He would be a laughingstock among the rugged reiver families.

Alastair needed a place to think, so he ventured into Ainslie Tavern. Maybe MacKenzie had stopped in for a drink or talked to some of the lairds from Edinburgh. He ordered a tankard of ale and took a seat near the door so he could watch who came and went. A young man who worked for Alastair greeted him and sat at his table. It was the same young man that got him this job of capturing Ty MacKenzie. His name was Bruce Brodie.

"Good day to you, Bruce," Alastair said and hefted high his tankard of ale in greeting.

"How is the hunt going?" Bruce asked.

Alastair lowered his voice. "Actually, I'm trying to find MacKenzie. He got away from me in London and is here in Edinburgh, but I can't locate him. Have you seen him today?"

"No, not today. But Laird MacKenzie could be home at Eilean Donan," Bruce said.

"Do you know MacKenzie well?" Alastair asked.

"Yes. Very well," Bruce said.

"If he was on the run and didn't go home, where else would he go?"

"He was on Mary, Queen of Scots's Privy Council. Since she has abdicated the throne, he could be on his way to see her."

"Is she at Holyrood Palace?" Alastair asked.

"No. Moray imprisoned her at Lochleven Castle. You might find him there."

"Thank ye lad, I will look for him there," Alastair said.

"I'd be careful if I were you," Bruce said.

"What do you mean by that warning?" Alastair asked.

"Well, there have been sightings of the old bean-nighe near Lockleven. Three men saw her this week," Bruce said.

"Ah, lad, ye are too superstitious for me. The old washerwoman doesn't scare me. You are off in the head if you believe such tales."

"The three men who made the reports are all dead. Just be on guard."

Alastair chugged down the last of the ale and stood up. "Thank ye, lad, but I plan to live for a long time." He left the tavern and headed to Lochleven, which was a few hours north of Edinburgh.

On the trip to Lochleven, Alastair bought a cart to carry MacKenzie back to West March when he caught him. When he reached the cottage inn in Lochleven, he stopped at the docks and scanned the area. There was a large clump of bushes next to the dock. Alastair decided that he would hide there and wait for MacKenzie to arrive.

Before he left the docks, he noticed a boat coming from the island back to the docks. The boat docked and three women got out of the boat. The oarsman handed each of them a wash basket filled with washing supplies. They were washerwomen.

Alastair's heart thumped in his chest. The washerwomen entered a side room at the inn where they stored their supplies. What a coincidence. He shook off a pang of fear. There was nothing to be afraid of; these women were not ghosts. They worked for the Douglas family on the island.

He led the horse and cart into the clump of bushes and settled down to wait. When MacKenzie arrived, Alastair would choose a time when he would be most vulnerable to his attack. Then he fell asleep. Suddenly, shouting startled him awake. Armstrong saw Ty shouting and jumping on the dock, so he eased up behind him and struck him on the head with a rock. He quickly dragged Ty out of sight and into the bushes. He tied his wrists and feet and dumped him into the cart and drove away. Before he left Lochleven, he drove the cart down to the loch to water his horse. Then he checked on MacKenzie; he was still unconscious.

Alastair freed the horse from the cart and led him down to the riverbank to drink. He chose a place along the loch where the water had washed away a portion of the bank. He stepped down and guided the horse to the water. As the horse drank his fill, Alastair gazed around the loch. About a hundred feet to his right, a beautiful young woman with long blond hair was washing clothes. She had three baskets and was having trouble lifting one of them back onto the bank.

Alastair ran to help her. He took the heavy basket full of wet clothes and easily tossed them on the bank. When he turned to receive thanks for his help, the young woman stood with her head bowed. Alastair heard her sobs.

"Lassie, don't cry. It will be all right." He put out a hand to lift her head.

The woman caught his hand with a grip more crushing than his own, and then she raised her head and looked him in the eye.

He screamed. “No! No!” He tried to free his hand but was unable to break her hold on him. He looked at the bony ugly face with shreds of flesh hanging from the skeleton. Yet the woman had no eyes, just empty sockets.

“Death is coming,” the old washerwoman said and released his hand. She picked up the three wash baskets and disappeared into the distance.

Alastair sat on the river bank for over half an hour, waiting for his heart to stop thumping. The thumping had gotten so rapid he feared he might die any second, but he didn’t. He wasn’t quite in his right mind when he returned to the cart, but he managed to harness the horse and begin the trip back to West March.

Chapter Sixty-Nine

West March – June 29, 1567

Ty awoke with a pounding headache. He tried to sit up, but when he did, his head began to spin. He lay back on the pillow. He opened his eyes and looked around. He didn't recognize his surroundings.

He was in a large room with sparse furnishings. There was only his bed and a couple of tables and chairs. A large fireplace was centered on the wall to his right. To his left was a screen, which probably hid the stool room. The room had a window on each wall, which suggested to Ty that this was a tower house used to fend off rustlers. The Armstrongs could watch the approach to the house from all four directions and fire at the rustlers from the windows.

Usually, the cattle were kept on the first floor. To affirm his idea, a cow mooed from below. The cows pushed against one another, causing the hay to bundle up, their hooves scratching the wood floor beneath them.

He was in the West March.

"Oh," Ty moaned. He had let his guard down for one moment, and Armstrong grabbed him. He had to get out of here before Violette left for Italy.

"What day is it?" He said aloud. How long had he been here? Where was Armstrong? He saw his clothes lying on a chair near the screen. He rose up, but his head started spinning. He forced his legs onto the floor and tried to stand. The dizziness attacked once again, but he remained standing. Slowly, he walked over to the chair that held his clothes.

When he began to fall, he fell forward and grabbed the chair back to steady himself. He waited until the dizziness subsided. Then he began a careful search of his clothes, looking for his pistol and the dagger, but they were gone. He had no weapons. It took him another ten minutes to dress himself. He walked to the nearest window and looked out on the mountainous terrain.

Below him was grassy pastureland bordered by rugged mountains. In the distance, a brook gurgled as it flowed down the mountain, across the rocks, and down into the glen. There were no houses in sight. Ty was familiar with the terrain and knew you could ride for miles before reaching a dwelling. He could smash a window and escape, but it was a death sentence. He needed to plan a way to escape, but he couldn't think due to the pounding in his head. He made a slow return to the bed and lay down and soon was fast asleep.

Then voices awakened him. There were two men in the room with him. He lay still and listened to their conversation. One man's voice had a ring of familiarity about it, but he couldn't place it. Ty peeped through half-closed lashes at the two men sitting at the table. The larger of the two was Alastair Armstrong, and he was trembling.

"Quit trembling. You know as well as I do there is no such things as ghosts. I just told you that story for amusement," the younger man said.

Alastair pounded his fist on the table. "I tell you, Bruce, that I saw the old washerwoman. She is real. She told me that death was coming. I am truly scared. I am going to die and soon."

Ty watched as Alastair began to shake uncontrollably. He then got out of bed. "Looks like you have seen a ghost," he said to Alastair.

Alastair jumped up from his chair and came to the foot of the bed. "You watch your mouth, MacKenzie. Your time to die is coming soon. I'll be alive long after you are gone."

"If you were a real man, you would have killed me by now," Ty said.

Alastair backed away. "I cannot kill you until Montmorency sends the order. When it arrives, you will see how much of a man I can be."

"It may be a long time before Montmorency sends the kill order. I suggest you sit down and write out your will before you keel over," Ty said.

Alastair pulled his dagger and ran toward Ty, but Bruce stopped him. "Don't. He is just trying to make you angry," Bruce said.

Alastair went back to the table.

Then Bruce turned to Ty. "We've brought food. You need to eat." He motioned Ty to a small table near his bed.

Ty got up and sat down at the table and ate the food. After he had finished eating, he tried to arouse Alastair to anger again. "How much is Montmorency paying you to hold me?" he asked.

An angry look crossed Armstrong's face. "Enough to make me rich so I can move to England. I'm tired of living in the backwoods of Scotland."

"Don't you think he would have sent you the money by now? What could be keeping him?" Ty asked.

Alastair jumped up and ran towards Ty. He swiped the empty dishes off the little table and placed his hands on the table and leaned forward. He was almost in Ty's face. Ty wanted to put a fist in his face but thought better.

"He is too busy planning to wed your wife. They are marrying in May. It will be the greatest event in all of Italy. You will never see sweet little Violette again." Alastair laughed and backed up.

Ty jumped from his chair and swung at Alastair but missed him. Bruce came running to stand between them. "Stop it! Both of you!" He glared at Alastair, and Armstrong went back to the other table and sat down.

Bruce pointed to the bed. Ty sat down on the bed and propped the pillow behind his back. Violette and Thomas were getting married? Of course, what had he expected? She thought he was dead. But why so soon? Was she with child? That thought tormented him. He rubbed his face in anguish.

Surely, she could stay faithful to him longer than a few months. But Ty knew how vulnerable Violette felt when left alone. He decided that Armstrong was lying to him. Violette and Thomas hadn't had time to get to Italy yet. If he could just get out of here, he would follow her to Italy and get her back. Ty racked his mind for a way to escape without getting drowned in the peat bogs that covered the West March.

Chapter Seventy

Edinburgh, Scotland – June 29, 1567

Isobel arrived in Edinburgh two days after Ty had left England. She looked around the docks for Armstrong, but he wasn't there. She stopped to think. Where would Ty go first? To Eilean Donan or to Holyrood Palace to see Mary.

She decided on Holyrood Palace. She had her two guards unload the horses, and then they rode to Holyrood Palace. The courtyard was empty except for a few pages who were sweeping debris from the courtyard.

Isobel stopped to talk to one of the pages. "Have you seen a highlander here today? He was dressed in rugged clothes and carried a pistol in his belt."

One page overheard the question and walked over to Isobel. "Milady, I saw him earlier. He came to check on Mary. I told him she was at Lochleven Castle. He left."

Isobel and the two guards rode north to Eilean Donan. If Ty hadn't talked to Mary, he would go home next. She reached the town of Dornie and saw the guards posted at the footbridge across the loch. Evidently, Alastair Armstrong thought Ty might be home, too. Isobel decided to go into Fenella's Tavern and ask if anyone had seen Ty. Her two guards stood outside protecting the entrance.

Isobel ventured into Fenella's Tavern and took a seat. The waitress came and took her order. She asked the waitress about Laird Ty MacKenzie. The waitress shook her head and ran back to the kitchen. *Did I upset her?*

In a few minutes the owner, Fenella, introduced herself to Isobel. "You were asking about Laird MacKenzie?"

"Yes. I believe he lives at Eilean Donan. The castle seems deserted. Have you seen him today?"

"No one has seen Laird MacKenzie because he died last month," Fenella said.

"Oh, I'm sorry, but I know for a fact that he is alive and well. There is a man named Alastair Armstrong hunting Laird MacKenzie to kill him. Have you seen him today?"

Fenella was taken aback. "Well, not exactly. He has some men posted at the footbridge leading to Eilean Donan." Fenella stopped to think. "Doralee, the nanny, came by earlier telling us that Ty was alive, and now you appear. What is going on?"

"Ty must have visited Doralee without Alastair's knowledge."

Isobel explained to Fenella what was happening to Ty. She shared the part about Armstrong being paid to kill Ty, but she didn't share her thoughts about Thomas's part in the scheme.

"My, my!"

"Do you know where Armstrong might have taken Laird MacKenzie?" Isobel asked.

"Well, all the Armstrongs live in the West March district. They are known as border reivers and mercenaries, and they control the border country. That part of the West March is harsh terrain. You can't go there by yourself, it is too dangerous," Fenella said.

"My family are the MacRaes, the constables of Eilean Donan, and allies of the MacKenzie family. I am Isobel MacRae."

"Welcome home, Miss MacRae."

"I thought I might find Laid MacKenzie here, but I guess Armstrong has already caught him. Since I haven't found Ty here, I will turn to my family to help me." Isobel finished her food and stood to leave. "Thank you for your help."

Isobel headed to her family home situated across the loch from Eilean Donan. She and the two guards pretended not to notice the two reivers guarding the causeway to Eilean Donan. MacRae Castle was Isobel's childhood home. It was a spacious castle built of red sandstone, and it faced Eilean Donan. Peyton MacRae had the castle built after his father died and abandoned Eilean Donan.

As a child, Isobel had sat on the edge of the loch and watched the Clan MacKenzie rebuild Eilean Donan to what it is today—the most beautiful castle in Scotland. When she viewed the finished structure, she thought it was also the most romantic place on earth. She had vowed that one day, she would be married in the beloved castle, but life had taken her to England.

Isobel broke through her reverie, and she and the two guards went inside the castle. The two guards waited downstairs as she went upstairs to locate her grandfather. Isobel found Peyton MacRae in the center courtyard killing chickens for the evening meal. Now age sixty-four, he could still ride, fight, and do daily chores with no loss of stamina. He was almost six feet tall with a lean build and rough demeanor. If Peyton couldn't actually carry out threats against his enemies, he could bluff his way, making them think he was capable of wringing their necks just like the chickens he had killed for today's meal.

When he saw Isobel, a big smile crossed his face. He pulled her into his arms and gave her a crushing hug. "You are the most beautiful person I've seen in months. What brings you home to Kintail?" Peyton asked.

"I have a pressing problem, Grandfather, and I need your help."

Peyton waved her inside, and they sat at the kitchen table while one of his servants cooked the chickens. The maid brought Isobel and Peyton a cool glass of wine.

Isobel explained the situation concerning Ty MacKenzie.

"Another MacKenzie in trouble. I've spent my whole life rescuing them from harm. I guess one more won't kill me." Peyton took a drink of wine. "I know the West March district well, and I know how the reivers operate. It will be a dangerous task, but we can manage it."

"Oh, thank you, Grandfather. I didn't know what I would do if you refused me."

"I could never refuse you, lass. Even as a child, you have always been my favorite and the most beautiful of all the Clan MacRae's offspring."

Peyton got up and went to the door and called for a few of his men to come to the Great Hall. He also sent a servant to fetch the two guards who had come with Isobel. He and Isobel moved into the Great Hall where the men had gathered to receive their orders.

Peyton gave an overview of the mission at hand. "Clan MacRae, my granddaughter's friend, Ty MacKenzie, has been captured by Alastair Armstrong and is being detained in the West March. We must rescue him. The terrain of the West March is treacherous. We will need several hobler horses to carry us across the West March countryside. Take an inventory of your weapons and prepare them for the attack. When MacKenzie's location is pinpointed, you will receive further instructions."

Peyton appointed one man to oversee the weapons inventory, and then he chose six men as scouts to locate Ty MacKenzie and lay out plans for the attack. Another man was chosen to buy the hobler horses needed to cross the terrain of West March.

After the men left, Peyton put his arm around Isobel. "The preparations will take several days. We must wait until our men have located MacKenzie, and then we will plan our attack." Peyton paused. "Will you remain here until we return?"

"When you and the men head to the West March, I will go to Eilean Donan. You can bring Ty there after you rescue him."

"As you wish, lassie."

"I will wait here until the planning is complete. The waiting will be hard, but I have waited for a man like Ty for a long time. I can wait a while longer," Isobel said.

"In the meantime, you can humor your grandfather with an entertaining game of chess." Peyton smiled as he steered Isobel toward the chess board.

Chapter Seventy-One

Town of Coccaglio in Lombardy, Italy – July 1, 1567

Violette's first impression of Italy was the colorful landscape—wild colors of melon, gold, and flaming red. The bright sun and cool breezes stroked her skin. The air was full of sweet summer scents.

When Thomas pulled the cart up to the villa, out came Celine and Fabrice. They welcomed them with hugs and kisses. Violette felt good about being here. It was like the home she had always wished for, a place among people who loved her. Here she could be her true self. Here she could express her true love for Thomas. Suddenly, the trauma of the past months faded into the background.

Celine took Violette inside and gave her a tour of the villa. Violette loved the warmth and spaciousness of the villa. Her room looked out over the rows of grape vines that spread for miles. Camden's room was next to hers, and Thomas's room was at the end of the hallway.

Violette took a warm bath and dressed for dinner. Her clothes seemed too heavy for the warmer temperatures. She would have to buy new ones to compensate for the warmer weather, but for tonight, she wore one of the summer dresses Estelle had taken from Violette's wardrobe in France. It was a soft cotton periwinkle blue dress that exposed her shoulders. The low neckline revealed the golden locket. The golden locket suppressed her excitement, so she gently pulled it off and placed it in a jewelry box. Thomas would comprehend the significance of her actions.

Her heart fluttered with expectation. She replaced the locket with a lavish necklace of diamonds and amethyst jewels to complement her violet eyes. She wore her long raven tresses loose and tousled as they fell across her shoulders. Satisfied with her appearance, she went downstairs for dinner.

As she walked down the graceful staircase, Thomas looked her way. He sat down his wine glass and met her at the bottom of the stairs. His eyes sparkled with recognition. He took her hand and pulled her into a warm embrace.

"My darling," Thomas whispered in her ear.

"My love," Violette said and saw the love spark in his eyes. She sighed with contentment.

He walked with her into the dining room and sat down for a delightful time of food and warm fellowship.

Fabrice gave a toast. "Here is to Thomas. We thank God that you made your way back to us. Here are wishes for a long and joyful life." They all drank to Thomas.

The food was fabulous, but nothing new. Violette had experienced Italian cuisine in France and enjoyed the richness and elegance of the famous sauces and desserts Catherine de Medici had brought from Italy to France. She had almost forgotten the graciousness of fine living and eating. The harsh weather and rigorous Scottish lifestyle had robbed her soul. She hadn't even realized the toll it had taken on her spirit until now.

After dinner, Thomas took her for a moonlight walk through the vineyard. The fragrant twilight brought waves of honeysuckle wafting on a cool breeze. She picked soft luscious grapes from the woody vines along the way.

"I want to show you something," Thomas said.

He led her down one of the rows in the vineyard, and on the other side was the most fabulous Italian villa she had ever seen. It was much larger than the family villa, and it set upon a higher mound. They climbed the stairs to the entrance.

Violette gasped when Thomas opened the door. The interior was exquisite. Large Italian tiles covered the floors. There were windows and French doors all around the room. The kitchen was large and flowed onto a terrace that overlooked the valley below. The ceilings were high. The atmosphere was light and airy.

"Thomas, this is gorgeous. But where is the furniture?"

"I thought you might like to choose the furnishings."

"Me?"

Thomas pulled her into his arms. "I built the villa for you, Violette. Will you marry me?"

A quick, hard pulse rose in her throat. "Yes, my love. Yes."

Violette leaned into his passionate kiss and yielded herself to the inevitable.

When Thomas had met Violette at the bottom of the stairs, the first thing he noticed was the absence of the golden locket. To make sure, he had looked into her eyes. They sparkled with anticipation. He couldn't contain himself, and he swept her into his arms. He kissed her face, eyes, and cheeks. He nuzzled her ear and tousled her hair as he lost himself in a wild longing kiss.

He could hardly eat because he wanted to show her the villa he had built for her. He wanted her to know that even when he couldn't remember her, he had thought of her constantly. She had filled his dreams from the beginning of his memory loss. Those dreams haunted him for five long years, just long enough for him to finish the villa.

His heart was full of joy and love. He would never let her go again, no matter the cost.

Chapter Seventy-Two

West March, Scotland – July 8, 1567

Ty awoke to blasts of gunfire. He jumped up and ran to the south window. A hundred men or more wearing the MacRae Tartan red plaid were firing on the Clan Armstrong. Alastair was the first to fall.

When Alastair fell, Ty remembered the prediction made by the old washerwoman Alastair had seen at the river. Was it possible that the folktale was true? Well, it came true for Alastair Armstrong.

The MacRaes were swift and ferocious in their attack like any Highlander. They shouted their war cry, "Sgurr Uaran!" or "Scure Touran!" and, without hesitation, rode down their opponents and killed them.

He remembered his father telling him that they fought so fiercely they were called "The Wild MacRaes." They were longtime friends of the Clan MacKenzie and served as constables over Eilean Donan Castle.

Their war cry referred to the tallest peak in the Five Sisters mountain range of Kintail used as a rallying point for the clan and the home of the MacRaes.

Ty was happy to see them. The battle was over in twenty minutes, for after Alastair fell, the others fled for their lives.

Suddenly, there was a shout outside the door. "Is there a MacKenzie inside?"

Ty shouted, "Yes, Laird Ty MacKenzie of Eilean Donan."

"Step back. I'm chopping down the door."

Ty walked backward until he ran into the bedrail and watched as a halberd chopped down the door. In walked a hefty man wearing the MacRae red tartan. He come over and shook Ty by the shoulders.

"Are you lost, MacKenzie? You're a long way from home," Peyton MacRae said with a laugh. "Come on. I'll take you home. Isobel will be waiting for you."

Isobel? Ty's heart warmed at the sound of her name. When he got home to Eilean Donan, Isobel was waiting for him with an anxious look on her face. As he dismounted, she ran into his arms, and he kissed her lovingly.

Peyton MacRae said to Isobel, "Take good care of him, sweetie."

Isobel replied, "I won't let him out of my sight, Grandfather."

"I don't think the Clan Armstrong will pursue Ty further, but I will leave several guards to protect you from Moray and the Protestant lords." Peyton MacRae and half of his men rode home, leaving Isobel with Ty.

Ty took a hot bath and changed into decent clothing and then met Isobel downstairs in the Billeting Room.

Ty snuggled with her on the couch. "I thought I left you in England?"

"You did, but I'm not one to give up so easily. I want us to be together." Isobel smiled. "Violette wrote Doralee a letter. She is in Italy. She and Thomas are betrothed. Are you going after her?" Isobel asked as she waited in anticipation for his answer. Would he break her heart?

Ty didn't answer for a time. Somewhere during his stay on the galley ship and then being detained in London, he had decided that fate was against his union with Violette. He should have known when Violette abandoned Thomas so easily in favor of him that she would do the same when he was arrested and forced to serve on the *Jasper Stone.*

Thomas was Violette's first love and would always be her only love. He just hadn't realized that until now. Ty wasn't the kind of man to take revenge. He had seen what it had done to Violette. She had married him to punish Thomas for deserting her, even though his actions were not under his control. It was a twist of fate. Now fate had brought them together again. He would not punish Thomas for taking Violette, who was rightfully his.

He turned to Isobel. "Would a sweet Scottish lass like you consider marriage to a wayward highlander?"

"I've wanted you since the day we met. There's no other love for me, just you."

"And you for me. I'll love you forever." They sealed the promise with a kiss.

"I heard that Moray is in France. The Protestant lords won't attempt to arrest me again without Moray's permission. Besides, they do not know I am home. I should be safe here for a month or more, but we cannot stay very long," Ty said.

"What are you suggesting?" Isobel asked, her eyes aglow with expectation.

"I suggest that we get married here at Eilean Donan," Ty said.

"Oh, Ty, Eilean Donan is the perfect place for a wedding and the most beautiful. I've always admired it as a child dreaming that one day I could be married at this castle. It would be a dream come true. We will have a true Scottish wedding," Isobel said.

Ty watched Isobel as her face flushed with delight. "Of course, I know you want to live in London. And since Queen Elizabeth offered me a position on her Privy Council, I would prefer we live in London, too."

"You won't always be an outlaw in Scotland. When that time comes, we can both move home to Eilean Donan," Isobel said, trying to comfort him.

"You are right, my love. Eilean Donan will always be waiting for us." Ty kissed her cheek. "How soon can we have the wedding?"

"With Doralee's help, give me a week," Isobel said.

"You have one week."

Isobel jumped up. "I need to get started."

Ty stood up and drew her close. "I don't know if I can wait a week?" Ty kissed her passionately.

"But you must."

Ty released her. "I'll send a guard to fetch Doralee. I will arrange the music and contact the musicians, but now I will search my room for a MacKenzie kilt."

Chapter Seventy-Three

Eilean Donan, Castle – July 15, 1567

Isobel stood outside at the end of the wedding processional, dreamily observing her surroundings. The sun was warm as it filtered through white cumulus clouds, and the air was moist from yesterday's rain shower. A rainbow glistened over the Cuillin Mountains behind the castle. Geese chattered as they glided overhead. The scent of roasted lamb wafted on the wind. A slight warm breeze caressed her neck.

She thought about the days gone by. When her father had died, Isobel moved to England where she had a relative, Caroline MacRae, who was a lady-in-waiting at Queen Elizabeth's court. She begged Isobel to come and meet the queen.

Isobel was desperate; with no relatives left in Edinburgh, she accepted Caroline's invitation and met with Queen Elizabeth. She and the queen got along well and the queen offered her a position at court. Isobel accepted the position. At least, she could now provide for herself.

But Isobel was a true Scottish lass and soon grew tired of the glitz and glamor. Most women would have gladly swapped places with her, but Isobel had her heart set on marriage, a home, and a family with a true Scottish man just like Ty.

When she first saw Ty, she knew he was the man she wanted. The thieves had attacked her carriage and tried to steal her luggage, but Ty appeared. He was dressed like a pirate in a coarse brown tunic, a leather vest, and a white shirt with billowing sleeves, and a pair of canvas breeches. He quickly subdued the thieves and rescued her like a true highlander. That was the day she decided, she would make him love her—and he had. Now they were getting married like she had hoped. She couldn't be happier.

This was her wedding day and a dream come true. She and Doralee had worked every day and night for the past week, preparing for this one splendid day that created memories for a lifetime. Doralee found the raspberry cotton fabric for Isobel's wedding dress. It was a floor-length dress with a square neckline trimmed in white lace. In Isobel's long blond hair, Doralee had woven red and white wild flowers and purple heather picked from the Highlands and made her bouquet with the same flowers to match.

In the distance, the bagpipes began to play a haunting Scottish wedding song, and the procession slowly began to move.

Doralee served as Isobel's bridesmaid. In minutes, Isobel reached the footbridge and proceeded across the loch with several of Doralee's friends as her attendants. The procession moved slowly across the long footbridge and through the Billeting Room and up the staircase to the Banqueting Room. Raspberry ribbons and bows hung from the metal chandelier. The dining table was spread with a white lacy tablecloth with an enormous center bouquet of lavender thistle and red wildflowers.

On the floor, Ty had replaced the MacKenzie Tartan rug with the MacRae red plaid. The loving gesture made her heart flutter.

As the procession filed in, Isobel came to stand next to Ty, who wore the MacKenzie kilt of blue, red, and green. He stood confidant and tall like a true highlander.

The Protestant minister had discreetly secured an annulment of Ty's marriage to Violette and acquired Isobel and Ty's marriage license.

Isobel turned to face Ty, and the ceremony began.

After the ceremony ended, everyone sat down at the table for the grand wedding feast. And after the feast, came the wild Scottish dancers who encouraged all to join the dance.

As the dancing grew wilder, Ty led Isobel away from the crowd and up the stairs to a new bedchamber he had prepared just for her. He opened the door and lifted her across the threshold into the bedchamber adorned with white flaming candles and bouquets of red roses set around the room.

Inside the bedchamber, he set Isobel down and led her along a trail of rose petals to stand before the bedside table. They shared a glass of red wine, and then Ty gently laid her on the bed. They kissed until they melted together, no longer single persons but one.

Chapter Seventy-Four

Edinburgh Castle – August 22, 1567

Moray had left Scotland after he ordered Mary's abdication, leaving Lethington in charge. He had always managed to disappear after ordering actions that might bring on a political crisis. It was a useful habit of his that freed him from any suspicions of wrongdoing. He had sailed to France and remained there until Lethington sent him word to return. Mary's abdication was completed, and Prince James was now King James VI, and the parliament was prepared to appoint Moray as the permanent regent of Scotland.

Today he stood in the court at Parliament as they pronounced him Regent of Scotland. He would rule the land until King James VI came of age to rule in his own right. Moray smiled. All his plans and dreams had come true.

Yet after the ceremony was over, fear gripped his heart. Even though Mary had abdicated, she still had many supporters in Scotland, England, and Denmark-Norway. He suspected that Bothwell's trip to Denmark-Norway was to raise Mary's supporters and return to rescue her. Moray had to prevent a rescue at all costs.

Moray had talked with King Frederick II of the Denmark-Norway alliance, who held Bothwell on charges made by his former wife, Anna Throndsen. He had received a request from Queen Elizabeth to extradite Bothwell to Scotland for trial. But since Mary was no longer queen of Scotland, Moray had convinced King Frederick not to extradite Bothwell.

To serve justice, King Frederick condemned Bothwell to Dragsholm

Castle for the murder of Lord Darnley. He left Bothwell to rot without any chance of a trial.

Moray was pleased with the King's decision. Now he could concentrate on destroying Mary, but he needed help. Talking with King Frederick gave Moray a unique idea. He had bragged to the Scottish people that he had love letters from Mary to Bothwell that would give proof of her complicity in Lord Darnley's murder. Yet when he read the letters that had been found in Bothwell's possession, none of them implicated Bothwell or Mary. In desperation to establish Mary's guilt, Moray decided to falsify the letters, adding the text needed to condemn Mary. Whoever added the text to the letters had to skillfully copy Mary's handwriting perfectly with all its flourishes and flair.

That person could be Anna Throndsen.

Anna had the education and skill to accomplish the task. She also had a spirit of revenge against Bothwell and Mary, still jealous of Mary for taking Bothwell away from her, and she had never remarried.

He sent a messenger to Anna with a verbal message. Anna had agreed, and she had been brought to Scotland and secluded in Edinburgh Castle where she would work on the letters. Then Moray had the messenger killed.

Today he gathered the letters in the silver casket and took them upstairs to Anna's suite. She opened the door with a smile and invited Moray inside. She directed him to a table in front of the window. Moray pulled out her chair so she could be seated, and Anna nodded her approval. Then he took the seat opposite her. Anna smiled at him as the maid served cold ale.

Anna Throndsen was every inch a lady. She was tall like Mary, but Anna had long blond hair and hazel eyes. Her impeccable appearance and fair, smooth skin thrilled his senses. He knew her skin would be silky to the touch, for Moray had met a few Norwegian women. They were very confident and independent. He knew they liked strong, well-mannered men who courted them with flowers and poured their wine. He kept those qualities in mind as she sat opposite him.

"Thank you for helping me secure justice for Lord Darnley. Queen Elizabeth will be most grateful and generous to us if we can accomplish this delicate task," Moray said and handed Anna the silver casket.

Anna took a sip of ale and opened the silver casket and perused a couple of the letters. She had tears in her eyes when she finally spoke to Moray. "It will take some time, but I can easily copy the handwriting. I am sorry that things have come this far. I still love Bothwell, but he loved other women too much. It is Mary I hate the most for conspiring to take him away from me, and I'm sure his second wife, Jean Gordon, hates her too. She was one of Mary's ladies, yet Mary went after Bothwell without any consideration for Jean's service and loyalty to her. No woman could compete with Mary's charm, beauty, and power she wielded as queen."

Moray handed Anna his handkerchief. "I'm sorry too. I must provide justice for Lord Darnley, for Queen Elizabeth won't let me rest until I do. I appreciate your help. Be assured that what you are doing will bring honor to the Scottish people and the Protestant lords. You will be under my protection." He lied.

Anna was an attractive woman. Maybe she would be grateful enough to receive his forthcoming advances.

Moray stood up. "I must be going. Thank you for your help, milady." Moray kissed her hand and left.

What a mockery this situation had become. He and Queen Elizabeth knew who killed her cousin, Lord Darnley. It was her and Cecil. They were the ones who gave the orders. Moray just carried them out with pleasure.

Moray sighed. Appearances were everything in politics. Truth and veracity were sacrificed in the quest for power.

Chapter Seventy-Five

Fontainebleau Palace – November 27, 1567

Estelle Benoit returned to Fontainebleau after Thomas set her free and bought her passage back to France. When she got to Violette's apartment, there was a note on her door saying that Catherine wanted to see her when she got home.

Home. That sounded nice. Estelle loved the court here, but would Catherine accept her back as one of her ladies when she discovered what she had done to Violette? Estelle opened the door and went inside to freshen up. The ship excursion had made her sea sick when the first storm hit them. As a result, Estelle felt a little shaken up. She rang the bell for a page. When he arrived she ordered hot bath water.

"Tell the Queen Mother as soon as I freshen up, I will come to see her," Estelle told the page.

"The Queen Mother is in the back courtyard. You can join her there when you are ready," the page said.

When Estelle finished her bath, she put on fresh clothes and dressed her hair. She probably wouldn't be allowed to stay. She dreaded confessing all her sins to Catherine. Yet she took a deep breath and hoped for strength to get through this meeting.

Like the page said, she found Catherine strolling in the courtyard along the path that circled the pond. Other courtiers were outside enjoying an unusually warm sunny day in November. Estelle walked up and joined Catherine as she walked.

Catherine stopped for a second and then linked her right arm through Estelle's. "I am glad you have returned, Estelle, for I have missed you."

"Queen Mother, I must tell you what happened—"

"Never mind confessing your sins to me. Besides I know about how you stole Camden from Violette. I talked with her when she came to take him home. I know you love Camden, but you also wanted his inheritance, which I could not allow."

"I'm so sorry," Estelle said.

"I know. Let's forget about that incident and think about your future," Catherine said.

"What do you mean?"

"I want to introduce you to a wonderful man I've chosen for you. His wife died a few months back and left him with a young son, Merle. His name is Taylor Moreau from Burgundy, France. He is a winemaker. He desperately needs a wife," Catherine said and pointed ahead. "There he is. He has been waiting to meet you."

"Oh," Estelle said and stopped a few feet away as she looked at Taylor Moreau. He was tall with neatly trimmed hair and mustache. He stood erect and confident. When he noticed her, he smiled and began walking her way.

Catherine said, "He will be good for you, Estelle. Don't let him go. I'll see you at dinner." Catherine left her alone.

Taylor introduced himself and kissed her hand. "Lovely Estelle, would you care to walk with me?"

"It will be my pleasure, Monsieur," Estelle said and took his arm.

As they walked, he told her about himself and the tragedy of losing his wife. "Her death devastated me, but I am trying to regain the joy of being alive. Seeing you has given me hope for a new beginning. You are much lovelier than I expected."

"You are so gracious, Monsieur, but I have been very bad recently—"

Taylor stopped her. "Catherine has told me all the details. I understand that you made some mistakes, but I have too. I've waited for months to talk to you. I'm hoping you will give me a chance to win your heart."

Chapter Seventy-Six

Fontainebleau Palace – December 20, 1567

Estelle Benoit, now Mrs. Taylor Moreau, had just returned to Fontainebleau Palace after a whirlwind marriage and honeymoon in Ireland. Her luck changed when she met Taylor. He was a nobleman and winemaker from Burgundy, France.

In Dublin, Ireland, they spent two luscious weeks at Dromoland Castle celebrating each other. Taylor was a kind man, and he treated her well. After returning from Ireland, they moved into Estelle's empty castle at Maubeuge, France. She was enjoying buying new furnishings for the once desolate castle. She wanted it to be a showplace for entertaining all her friends from Fontainebleau.

She had really turned her life around after she found Taylor. Taylor had a son, Merle, who reminded Estelle of Camden. She loved him dearly. Thinking about all of her blessings, she had made amends with everyone whom she had offended in the past, except for Lady MacKenzie. She weighed heavily on Estelle's conscience, so today she decided to write Violette a letter.

She had learned that Violette had gone to Italy with Thomas. The pact Estelle had made with him made her uneasy. Maybe she could reach Violette before she married him. She would write Celine and enclose a letter to Violette.

Dear Lady MacKenzie,

I am sorry for the way I treated you when I worked as Camden's nanny. I have set my life straight and have married a wonderful loving man. We are refurbishing the empty castle in Maubeuge that belonged to my late mother, Anne.

I have done a terrible thing to you, which I want to make right. When I gave you the golden locket, your reaction upset me. I honestly thought it would make you happy. Then I realized that Thomas had told you that the locket meant that Ty was dead. But that was a lie. When Arno gave me the locket, he told me specifically that the locket was meant to alert you that Ty had escaped and needed help getting home to Scotland. To prove what I'm saying is true, look on the back of the picture in the locket. You will see where Ty wrote his location. London. Your husband, Ty, is alive and well and living in London, England.

Thomas lied to you about Ty's location, for he wanted you for himself. He was determined to keep Ty away, even after he escaped the *Jasper Stone*.

I promised Thomas that I would never tell you the truth, but since lying and stealing was part of my former life, I could never be completely happy without telling you the truth.

Estelle

Estelle placed the letter in an envelope and sealed it with wax. She took it to the postmaster herself and went to meet Taylor.

Chapter Seventy-Seven

Lochleven Castle – May 2, 1568

May day in Scotland was a long five-day affair. It was no different at Lochleven Castle. Today was special for two reasons—first, it was the last day of the May Day festival on the island, and secondly, it was the day Mary and Willie had chosen for her escape.

Since Violette had brought the washerwomen's clothes to her last June, Mary had been preparing for the escape. Winter had come sooner than expected, and the frozen waters and icy lakes made escape impossible. The weather had slowed down vital communications between Mary and Lord Seton, who had responded to her only after Christmas. He suggested May second as the best day for her escape, and she had accepted.

The cold wintery days from January to May were hard to endure. Mary had to force herself to concentrate on one day at a time.

George Douglas had been helpful. He had ridden to Holyrood Palace and brought back Mary's embroidery basket full of her favorite *brodeur* patterns, the most expensive embroideries in Scotland. She had used them to make a couple of new headdresses for herself.

A few times, Mary had helped Lady Douglas make cotignac or marmalade to pass the time during the long dreary days. She boiled the pear-shaped quinces with honey and powder of violets until the fruit, which tasted similar to apples and pears but had a tart almost bitter aftertaste, turned red and crystallized.

Mary was too restless to think about her favorite pastimes today. Other visitors had moved into the adjacent tower for the May Day celebrations. There had been too much drinking, and eating, and too much revelry over the past five days. Tonight, would be the most boisterous celebration, and most of the guess would be drunk before nightfall. At least, Mary was counting on most of the guests and guards alike falling unconscious from drinking by then.

Because of so many guests for the May Day celebration, the Douglas family had hired several extra washerwomen for the week. Mary was glad because she planned to join the group as they left the island.

As the day wore on, Mary joined the guests at the dinner table. When the revelry began, young Willie quietly took her back to the tower. Once inside, she changed into the washerwoman's clothing and pinned her hair up and donned the usual white bonnet and apron over the dark dress.

Mary waited. A knock came at the door, and then the key turned in the lock. Mary stood up ready to go, but it wasn't Willie at the door—it was George.

"George, what are you doing here?" Mary asked.

He moved toward her and took her hands. "You make a beautiful washerwoman."

"Thanks, but I'm nervous. I hope nothing goes wrong."

"I have enjoyed having you here at Lockleven. You are the most charming woman I have ever met." He bowed his head for a moment and then looked into her eyes. "Now that you are no longer a queen, I feel I can be honest with you. Mary, I am in love with you, and I don't want you to go," George said.

Mary pulled away. Was he going to stop her escape? She glanced out the window, but Willie was nowhere in sight. She had to keep George calm until Willie arrived, or she would never escape.

"George, I am shocked. I don't know what to say. I thought we were friends," Mary said.

"I know. I led you to believe that it was just friendship I wanted from you, but it turned into something more," George said and took her hands again. "Will you marry me?"

"George, I am already married to Bothwell," Mary said.

He dropped her hands. "I forgot. What about the position you promised me at court. Is it still mine?" George asked.

"George I am no longer queen, but if I regain my throne, the position will be yours." Mary squirmed.

"And if you don't regain the throne, then what happens to me?" George asked.

Mary saw Willie approaching the tower. She had to hurry.

"There comes Willie. I must go." She took George's hand. "If I don't regain the throne, then I will arrange for Lord Seton to award you the position you seek." Mary kissed him on the cheek.

Willie unlocked the door and motioned her outside. The boat had arrived at the dock to pick up the washerwomen. He handed her a clothes basket to carry. He walked with her until she joined the rest of the group. Willie walked at the back of the group making sure no one got suspicious.

Mary looked back at the Glassin tower. George Douglas was standing in the doorway, and he gave Willie the go signal. Mary blew him a kiss.

As they neared the dock, a couple of male guests came close to watch them board the boat. They whistled at the ladies and made a few embarrassing remarks. They were definitely drunk. Mary ignored them, holding the basket a little high between her and the drunken men.

One of the men yelled, "She is a beauty." He started to grab Mary, but Willie distracted him with the offer of more ale. The two men followed Willie back to the house.

Finally, Mary was on the boat as it pulled away from the docks. It was a short ten-minute ride across the loch. Mary trembled and prayed all the way. When she reached the docks, she found the laundry room. She set her basket inside the room and followed the other women as they walked up the road to their homes.

Several feet up the road, someone whistled from the bushes. Mary turned to look—it was Lord Seton. Mary slowed her pace, letting the other women get a good distance ahead of her. Then she eased into the bushes.

Lord Seton grabbed her by the hand and led her deeper into the bushes where twenty to thirty men on horses were waiting for her. Quietly, Lord Seton boosted her onto a horse, and slowly the group slipped through the bushes and out onto a major road that led to freedom.

Once they were out of sight of the island, the group's pace increased into a canter. Free at last! Mary laughed as the wind stung her eyes and tears drenched her face. Wild and free. She enjoyed every minute of the three-hour ride to Niddry Castle where a few hundred of her supporters were lodged.

When she arrived at the castle, her supporters cheered and shouted, "God bless the queen!" Mary spoke to as many of the men as she could before she entered the castle.

Niddry Castle was a four-story tower house near the village of Winchburgh in West Lothian, Scotland. The house had a defensive corbelled parapet on the top to protect its warriors when fighting off the attacks of their enemies. It was a fortress against all intruders. Mary felt safe here. When she laid her head down to rest, she fell into a restful sleep. This night, her dreams were sweet.

The next morning, Lord Seton's wife brought her some fresh clothes more suitable for a queen. Mary dressed quickly and met with Lord Seton to plan an attack on her half-brother, Moray and retake her throne. They devised their battle strategy over breakfast.

Once the men were ready, Mary gathered what few troops she had and started a progress around the country to gather more troops for her army. After the progress, she had rounded up over six thousand troops to defy Moray. Many of these were of the nobility which included the earls of Argyll and nine other noble families.

It was made known that Mary's abdication and consent to let Moray crown James was obtained under duress and threat of death. Therefore, Moray's actions was considered acts of treason. When her supporters heard this, they all signed a bond to support Mary's restitution to the throne. They prepared to attack Moray.

Mary decided to make her home base at Dumbarton Castle and monitor the retaking of Edinburgh by degrees as supporters rallied on her behalf. She would travel by way of Langside, Crookston, and Paisley and on to Dumbarton. Unfortunately, Moray had posted his army of only four thousand, in Langside, defending every route that led to the river Mary must cross to reach Dumbarton.

When Mary's army reached Langside, they were ambushed from within the city by Moray's men, who waited behind cottages, houses, and buildings inside the city. Caught unawares, Mary's army battled thousands of Moray's pikemen. There were so many that they stood like a carpet lain over the land. Mary's army was doomed.

Mary watched from the high mound of Court Knowe as her troops fell to the ground. Moray had won. It was ironic that she had to fight her half-brother who was defending her own son, James VI.

Mary and a few of her companions rode off and found refuge at Dundrennan Abbey. There she and her companions discussed what she could do to regain her throne.

"I can't stay in Scotland. Moray will not let me abide here, he will hunt me down. I must leave. I cannot bear being confined against my will. His punishment will not be so lenient this time if I am captured."

"You could return to your castle in Touraine or to your uncle's estates in Joinville. You always loved living in France." Lord Seton suggested.

"I could, but I am the rightful queen of Scotland. I must find a way to regain my throne," Mary said.

After a few minutes, Mary made her decision. "I will go to England and throw myself upon my cousin's mercy. Queen Elizabeth is the only one who has the power to help me regain my throne."

Lady Fleming, who was among her companions, said, "But, Mary, Elizabeth has treated you shamefully during your reign in Scotland. She fears you. She would never take the chance of restoring you to your throne in Scotland. She and Cecil want Scotland to join with England under a Protestant government. She would never allow you to hold power again."

"Elizabeth would never harm me. She is my cousin and friend. I trust her completely. I will set sail immediately."

Mary, along with twenty troops, arrived by night on the shores of Solway Firth. She boarded a boat to England.

As the shores of Scotland faded before her eyes, she wept. Her long battle to rule Scotland had come to an end. So many obstacles she had faced only to be discarded like a worn-out rag-doll. The stress of the constant battle between the Protestants and Catholics had been wearisome.

She turned her back to Scotland and instead looked forward, for her destiny now lay in England.

Chapter Seventy-Eight

Coccaglio in Lombardy, Italy – May 5, 1568

Today Celine was going over wedding preparations for Violette's and Thomas's wedding. She scrutinized every detail. Everything had to be perfect. The wedding was just two hours away.

The food featured a roasted peacock with all its glorious colorful feathers, and there was also a variety of vegetables, breads and cheeses, and Thomas's famous sparkling Franciacorta white and rosé wines. The wines were served in violet wine glasses chosen by Violette.

Celine decided the food was perfect, so she started upstairs to see if Violette needed help getting dressed. As she started toward the stairs, she saw an unopened letter on the hall table. She reached over and picked it up. It was from Estelle.

Celine paused for a moment. Violette had told her how Estelle had stolen Camden and broken into Violette's apartment at Fontainebleau. What could Estelle possibly have to say to repair the damage she had already done to Violette? Celine stared at the envelope. The letter was addressed to her. Maybe it didn't have anything to do with Violette. She opened the letter and sat down at the table to read it. The first two pages were just details of how Estelle had met a wonderful man and had begun a new life. Then the last page was folded and Violette's name was on the outside.

Celine stopped. Should she read it? If the letter had been from anyone else, she would have left it for Violette, but since it was from Estelle, Celine read the last page. As she read the letter, Celine was appalled at what Estelle was telling Violette. Had Thomas really sent a mercenary after Ty and kept him confined until Thomas could convince Violette to marry him? But that wasn't the worst part of the message. Thomas had led Violette to believe that Ty was dead. That was unforgivable!

Celine knew that Thomas was a rogue and sought to win the hearts of every woman he met, but to purposely deceive the woman he loved was cruel. To steal another man's wife was not something she had thought her brother was capable of doing. When had he changed? Since Thomas had lost his memory, she hadn't noticed any visible changes in his character. She knew he was suffering, but was that the cause of such a drastic change in his personality? He had regained his memory and seemed to be just as he was before, but really that was impossible. Going through that treacherous ordeal had changed him.

Celine wished she hadn't read the letter. It put her in an awkward position. Today was the wedding; should she stop the wedding, or should she give the letter to Violette and let her decide? And what about Thomas. He was her brother. She knew how much he loved Violette. If she told Violette, Thomas would hate her forever. If she didn't tell Violette, their marriage would be based on false beliefs. Oh, Thomas!

Celine agonized over what to do. She could tell Thomas, but he would just hide the letter. Well, that was what she intended to do. She went up to her room and hid the letter in the bottom drawer of her wardrobe. No one was allowed in her room except the cleaning maid. The letter would be safe there. She would come back after the wedding and burn it.

She hurried upstairs to her room and hid the letter beneath a bunch of winter hose and scarves. Then she went to check on Violette. Celine knocked softly on the door. Then she went inside.

Violette was putting on the diamond and amethyst necklace. Her wedding gown had three tiers of lavender silk trimmed with white lace. Her long raven tresses curled into soft ringlets and flowed over her shoulders. Violette wore a dazzling smile. Celine had done the right thing. She couldn't damper Violette's spirit, not now.

"Violette, you are lovely! Thomas will be delighted," she said.

Violette smiled. "I'm a little nervous, but I guess that is usual."

"It shows that you are excited and ready for the ceremony."

A bell rang from downstairs. "That is my signal that the servants are here to carry the food to your villa." Celine kissed Violette's cheek. "Welcome to the family," she said and hurried downstairs.

As Celine rushed down the stairs, she met the bridesmaid and the other six attendants, who came to escort Violette to the wedding chapel. Italian wedding tradition dictated that the bridesmaid and the other attendants escort the bride from her old home to the chapel. At the same time, the men escorted the groom to the chapel. Then after the ceremony, the bridesmaid and her attendants, along with the male attendants, escorted the couple to their new home where the festivities were held.

Celine hurried to inspect the chapel one more time before the bride and bridegroom arrived. The chapel was near the winery. Inside, the sanctuary was decorated with lavender ribbons and bows. Before the altar stood a golden archway covered in lavender and white silk cloth accented with white roses and adorned with lavender scent that teased the senses from the altar to the entrance. The musicians were in position—it was a roving band with madrigals, lutes, and flutes.

Finally, the men arrived with Thomas at the head. They were laughing and joking until they entered the door and walked to the altar to take their places. The Protestant minister was among them. He separated himself from the group and stood before the altar with the Holy Bible in his hand.

The chapel was crowded with Thomas's friends and customers. Violette's parents couldn't make the trip from the Netherlands, for the war there had intensified. Young Camden was the ring bearer.

The musicians started to play, and the people stood as Camden and the bridesmaid walked down the aisle and took their places. Then it was Violette's turn.

When Violette entered the room, a loud "Oh" escaped from the people. She was stunning, and her face glowed with joy. Celine cried. Behind Violette, the six attendants carried the long lavender train as they walked down the aisle. When Violette reached the altar, Thomas took her hands.

The ceremony began. "Dearly beloved, we are gathered here today to unite Thomas and Violette in holy matrimony. Now for the rings ..."

Camden walked up with the rings. Thomas's ring for Violette was one large diamond with four smaller diamonds on the side, and

Violette's ring for Thomas was all gold. Then they said their vows of love, loyalty, and steadfastness.

"By the power invested in me, I pronounce Thomas and Violette husband and wife."

Thomas lifted Violette's veil, pulled her into his arms, and kissed her. After the kiss, Thomas took her hand, and they walked down the aisle and out the door into the trail that led to their new home. There were several men outside holding a white banner on poles, which they carried over Thomas and Violette's head as they walked along the trail.

Soon the musicians followed, playing lively tunes on their instruments. The men and ladies danced along, punching and pulling at one another, laughing and having a good time. Some of the men succeeded in separating the bride and groom, forcing Thomas to chase after her. They frolicked along until they reached the new villa. There the crowd dispersed into the villa.

Thomas caught Violette and led her to the table loaded with wedding presents. Together they opened gifts of lavish bedclothes for the bridal bed, sheer nightgowns, and boxes of candy. There were also more expensive gifts, like a crystal chandelier from France, and money.

After the gifts were opened, the musicians played for a time until the bride and groom had finished the wedding feast. The peacock was devoured within twenty minutes. That was when the cook brought in the quail and turkey.

Thomas and Violette began the party with a dance. They danced for a time, and then the crowd joined them on the floor. The musicians began a fast dance, and the men grabbed Violette, trying to be the first male to take off her garter. Thomas chased after them, and he finally won, catching Violette with a strong arm. Violette faced him and slowly lifted her gown, exposing her leg.

Thomas slowly eased the garter down, stopping every inch to kiss her leg. The crowd oohed and shouted suggestive innuendos. Thomas smiled and eased the garter off and tossed it into the crowds.

The bedding of the wedding couple was the highlight of the evening. After the garter was caught, the couple proceeded to the bedroom followed by the crowd. As space narrowed, only the bridesmaid and best man was near enough to open the door for the couple.

The bridal bedchamber was draped in lavender silk, including the curtains and bedclothes on the four-poster bed. Over a hundred candles lit the room, creating a soft glow. Around the room, crystal dishes held candy and fruits, including grapes from the vineyard. Lavender scent wafted across the room as Thomas closed the door and turned the key.

Inside the bridal bedchamber, Thomas and Violette fell onto the bed and closed the bed curtains.

At last, the satisfaction and joy for which they both had longed for was finally fulfilled.

THE END

Resources

Website Resources

Beaty, Mary. Humanist Chaplain. Celtic Wedding Ceremony. info@weddingsofnewyork.com

www.marie-stuart.co.uk The official site of the Marie Stuart Society based in Scotland.

Other Resources

Knox, John. The History of the Reformation of Religion in Scotland – including Knox's Confession and The Book of Discipline

Nicholas, Christy. 2014. Scotland, Stunning, Strange and Secret: A Guide to Hidden Scotland. Tirgearr Publishing

The Scottish Clans 2014

The Scottish Clans: A Guide to the Clans and armigerous families of Scotland. 2003-2010, 2011. First published as "The Clans and Tartans of Scotland" on CD Rom, 1995. Revised on www.scotClans.com. Written and published by ScotClans, 3 Restalrig Road, Edinburgh, Scotland. www.scotClans.com.

Bibliography

Abbott, Jacob, Mary Queen of Scots, Didactic Press (2014), eBooks

Bell, Henry Glassford, (a public domain book), Life of Mary Queen of Scots, Volume II

Byrd, Elizabeth ©1955, Immortal Queen, A novel of Mary, Queen of Scots, (New York City)

George, Margaret ©2006, Mary Queen of Scotland and The Isles, (Macmillan USA)

Graham, Roderick ©2008, An Accidental Tragedy, The Life of Mary, Queen of Scots, (This eBook edition published in 2012 by Birlinn Limited, West Newington House, Newington Rod, Edinburgh EH9 1QS, www.birlinn.co.uk.)

Guy, John ©2004, Queen of Scots. The True Life of Mary Stuart. (First Mariner Books edition 2005, Houghton Mifflin Harcourt Publishing Company 215 Park Avenue, South, New York, New York 10003) www.hmhco.com.

Marshall, Rosalind K. ©2010 Mary, Queen of Scots: Truth or Lies. Saint Andrew Press, 121 George Street, Edinburgh EH2 4YN

Meyer, Carolyn©2012, The Wild Queen, The days and nights of Mary, Queen of Scots (Houghton Mifflin Harcourt Publishing Company 215 Park Avenue South, New York, New York 10003).

Plaidy, Jean ©2006, The Captive Queen of Scots, Three Rivers Press, Imprint of the Crown Publishng Group, a division of Random House, Inc., New York, www.crownpublishing.com.

Plaidy, Jean © 1955, 1968, 1996, Royal Road to Fotheringhay, Three Rivers Press, Imprint of the Crown Publishing Group, a division of Random House, Inc., New York, www.crownpublishing.com.

Weir, Allison, ©2003, Mary, Queen of Scots, and the Murder of Lord Darnley. (2004 Random House Trade Paperback Edition, imprint of the Random House Publishing Group, a division of Random House, Inc., New York).

Printed in the United States
By Bookmasters